A Legacy of Death

Banbury Cross Murder Mystery Series Book Four

Ben Westerham

I0654203

Also by Ben Westerham

Harry Minch
Memory of Murder
Lesson for a Thief
Collector of Crimes (anthology)
Shattered Dreams (anthology)

50FOR30 SERIES OF MICRO SHORT STORIES
50for30 Series One
50for30 Series Two

MULTI-AUTHOR ANTHOLOGIES
Breakneck

Published by Close9 Publishing
ISBN 978-1-911085-86-7

For Sylvia Bones.
A bright light that now shines in the midnight sky.

It's all English to me

A WORD ON THE LANGUAGE that's used in this book, so you know what to expect. The version of English that is used here is British. This ought not to present much in the way of a problem for non-British readers. If you do find the occasional word or phrase a little odd, then I hope you still understand the essence of what is being said.

Ride a cock-horse to Banbury Cross

Ride a cock-horse to Banbury Cross,
To see a fine lady upon a white horse;
With rings on her fingers and bells on her toes,
She shall have music wherever she goes.

THIS IS A TYPICAL MODERN version of the popular
nursery rhyme. There are numerous earlier recorded versions
that start with the same opening line.

Chapter One

ASHVIEW LODGE HAD, for many years, acted as something of a second home for Emma Greene. But while the fine old Georgian house had an appeal of its own, the real attraction for her lay in the large, well-tended gardens and the open countryside that lay beyond these. Since she had been a very young girl, Emma had loved to wander the footpaths that criss-crossed the patchwork of fields, some given over to rich carpets of grazing pasture, others filled with ripening heads of golden wheat across which the wind blew in heavy gusts, giving the appearance of an inland sea being swept by an endless succession of rolling waves. But she had not always felt this way about the house and all that lay beyond it.

The first visit she could remember had taken place on a wet, cold, overcast September afternoon, when she was three or four years old. The location of the house, away from the nearby village of Brayfield, had made it feel as though she was a long way from civilisation and its attendant comforts. In addition to the sense of isolation, she had felt intimidated by the relative grandness of the house and, even more so, by its residents, the Glass family. They seemed to live in a world completely different to her own in the small market town of

Evesham, in the nearby county of Worcestershire. Still, she reminded herself, that was a long time ago. She had grown since then, in every way imaginable and there was no longer any need for her to feel intimidated or out of place, whatever other people might think.

It was the first day of August 1960 and it seemed like summer would never end as she sat on the wooden bench under the arbour that occupied a central spot in the main part of the garden. The musky scent of the roses that were in full bloom was delightful and the bees, busy feasting on their nectar, filled the air with a pleasantly comforting buzz. High over the field behind the garden a hawk was hovering, its sharp little eyes searching for a mouse or some other small creature careless enough to present itself as a potential meal.

The glass of water she'd brought from the house now sat empty on the bench, next to her near immaculate copy of Jane Austen's Sense and Sensibility. It wasn't her favourite Austen novel. That was, by far, Pride and Prejudice, but she had read all the others too recently to return to them so soon.

Since her last birthday, in wet and windy April, she had immediately started looking forward to the one that would follow; her twenty-first. Excitement rippled through her at the prospect of officially becoming a woman, though it seemed a little mad that society didn't considered her a woman already. After all, several of her school friends were already married and two of them were pregnant with their first children.

But the Glasses were of a sort who looked upon twenty-one as the age at which a person achieved adulthood, so the landmark mattered to her too. Her mother didn't take the same view of things, but she often didn't. Apparently, Emma's most important task now, according to her mother, was to find a nice, rich man to marry, before settling down to raise a horde of children. It was the respectable thing to do. But Emma was all too aware the world was changing and other avenues were opening for a bright young woman.

A huge, fluffy white cloud drifted in front of the sun and, for a moment, the world acquired a disappointing dullness. The hawk wasn't impressed and drifted away, across the open fields, to disappear over a ridge to the west. After dawdling too long for Emma's liking, the cloud moved on and the world glowed again.

As the rays of the sun returned to warm her face, Emma's thoughts switched to the extraordinary news she had received a fortnight before. It had been news that promised to change her life almost beyond imagination. In her mind she was back in the solicitor's stuffy office, sitting quietly, not much interested in what he had to say, and wondering why she had been dragged along in the first place. She had been unable to grasp what it was he was babbling on about, apart from the fact that she and the Glass family were there to hear a will being read; a will that had little to do with her. But as the pompous man finally got on with reading the actual contents of the document, her attitude changed entirely.

No longer bored silly, she had sat there stunned, unable to utter a word, as the solicitor first revealed who here father was, something she had never known, then announced she was to inherit a very substantial sum of money on her twenty-first birthday. It was, he assured her after he'd finished reading the will, enough for her to live on in comfort for the rest of her life, so long as she was sensible.

Although she hadn't been able to say anything in response, the double shock having temporarily taken away her power of speech, she had decided pretty soon afterwards that there would have to be at least one major spending spree, in celebration of her good fortune. How could she not? Thoughts of taking her best friend, Vicky Hemmings, into Leamington Spa for a day of obscene extravagance filled her head and she'd been crossing off the days.

"Morning, Emma, sweetheart. Enjoying a bit of sun, are you?"

Emma hadn't noticed the part-time gardener, Frank Barnes, making his way towards her from the outbuildings, his barrow piled high with compost, on top of which sat his favourite spade. She rather liked Frank. He was always pleasant and had taught her much about the plants and animals that lived in the garden and surrounding countryside. She also found his country bumpkin burr quite amusing; it was far stronger than that of anyone else she knew and took some getting used to.

"Hello, Frank. It's such a lovely morning, I couldn't stay hidden away inside the house. Did you see that hawk hovering over the old stables?"

"I did, that I did. He had no joy, though. I reckon he needs to come back later. Mister Mouse will be safely tucked up in bed right now, it being so bright out and all. He's no fool, is he? He knows he'd be an easy meal in these conditions."

"Is that compost for the hydrangeas?"

"It is, that. They don't like it when they get too dry. Need plenty of compost to keep the moisture in the ground, it does." As he spoke, Frank glanced up, past the arbour, to where something had caught his eye. "Ah, here comes the young man of the house."

Emma turned to see the figure of Michael Glass walking across the lawn. An uncomfortable sensation of apprehension flickered briefly through her body, but she batted it away.

Frank Barnes tipped the peak of his tatty flat cap in the direction of the skinny, pale-skinned arrival. "Morning, Mister Michael."

"Hello, Frank," replied the quietly spoken Michael Glass, running the fingers of one hand through his short, curly, red hair.

Michael looked at Emma, struggling to hold her gaze. His obvious awkwardness didn't escape the gardener, who was well aware of the feelings the youngest member of the Glass family held for Emma Greene. He had his suspicions, however, that whilst Miss Greene, a pretty little thing who was barely a year older than her would-be suitor, enjoyed the attention, she would be looking elsewhere for her future husband. Still, that was no matter of his. On the other hand, he did have plants to attend to and, happily, they were far less complicated than people.

"Well, I'd best be getting along," said the gardener, tipping is hat again, before pushing his barrow forward.

As Emma watched Frank Barnes depart, Michael first studied his shoes and scratched the back of his neck, before looking up, hoping to find Emma smiling, or at least looking happy to see him. When he found her still staring in the direction of the gardener, he took the opportunity to study the soft, smooth skin on her neck, where it sloped gently down to her partially-exposed shoulder. He had kissed her there once, at a time, not so very long ago, when she had seemed to always be happy to see him; when she had allowed him to hold her hand as they walked out over the fields on warm, sunny mornings and had no hesitation in wearing the daisy chains he made for her with such painstaking care.

More recently, she had stopped being like that. Something had changed. Now she seemed always to avoid spending time with him and she no longer allowed him to hold her hand or run his fingers through her straw-blonde hair. He knew what had changed her. It had been the reading of Uncle Robert's will and everything that went with it. But he wasn't going to give up; they could still be married and raise a happy family together. He knew they could; he just needed time to persuade Emma to see that was true and he knew he could do that.

"Yes, Michael, was there something you wanted?"

Emma was looking at him now, her face stern and unwelcoming, her words abrupt.

"Hello, Emma." He hesitated, finding it hard to get his words out. "You look beautiful in that dress," he smiled.

Her eyes flicked skywards.

"By which you mean that I don't look beautiful the rest of the time?" she snapped.

Michael scratched his ear and looked away, his face flushing red. He shook his head.

"No, I didn't mean that. I meant..."

"Yes, Michael, I know what you meant. I'm not stupid." Emma stood up and turned towards Michael. "Is there something you want, Michael?"

"Well, I thought, perhaps, if you are free," stumbled the disconcerted young man. "We might go for a walk this morning. Like we used to. We could follow the stream to Little Ashford. If you like."

He tried to put on a show of confidence, but inside he felt his heart racing and the rush of colour still warmed his face.

"Michael, we've spoken about this before, many times," came the unhesitating reply, the words bluntly delivered and the face stern. "I am not your girlfriend and we are not going to be getting married. You really must put these silly ideas out of your mind and leave me alone. Find some poor little thing from the village who likes... sticklebacks and bird spotting. I'm sure there's one out there for you somewhere."

"But..."

"No, Michael. Enough. I am not going for a walk with you this morning or any other morning. Now, go back indoors and play with your stamp collection," she snapped.

He felt a stab of pain in his chest and his breathing grew shallow and erratic. The rejection was worse than any before. So blunt. So certain. He wanted to show her how wrong she was, but his head was a tangled mess of half-completed thoughts and the words simply wouldn't come to him. He turned and forced his reluctant feet to move him in the direction of the house, emotion crashing over him in great waves. By the time he reached the open French doors to the sitting room, his hands were rolled into tight fists, his jaw set solid and his eyes were watery with tears. Some might have thought it sadness, even hopelessness, that filled his veins, but he knew otherwise. It was anger; raw, seething anger coursing in his blood.

Emma sighed and shook her head. She had tried so many times to let Michael know there was no romantic future for them, but the silly young man just wouldn't listen and she was at her wits' end as to what to do next to drive the message home. Men could be such idiots.

SUSAN GLASS STOOD IN front of a chest of drawers, her hands resting on its wooden surface. She was in the bedroom she shared with her husband, James, at the rear of the house. It offered a fine, open view of the gardens and the undulating countryside beyond, which had been one of the reasons she and James had taken the room for themselves when they married. She had been arranging a fresh display of monkshood and dahlia flowers in her favourite glass vase, to replace the previous, decaying arrangement, when she noticed Michael walk out of the house, heading towards the arbour, where she already knew Emma to be ensconced.

She had briefly contemplated opening the window and calling him back to the house, but found herself unable to dream up some worthwhile excuse for such a demand until he was too far away to be within earshot.

The arbour had made it impossible for her to see the eventual exchange between her son and Emma, which she found frustrating, but, there being nothing she could do about it, she laid down her scissors and flowers and waited, her eyes fixed on what she could see of the small wooden structure sitting partially surrounded by shrubs in the middle of the garden.

The exchange didn't last long, which she had thought a blessed relief, but it was quickly clear from watching her son walk back to the house that it had been anything other than a happy one. As he got close to the house, she could see that tears had welled up in his eyes and his face was scarlet. She felt a ripple of anger run through her. Really, this was the final straw. She had made her feelings exceedingly clear to Emma the last time she had upset Michael. Now she was doing the same thing again. This time when they crossed swords, she would make sure that young woman never made the same mistake again.

Her hands shaking a little as she tried, not altogether successfully, to quell the growing anger, Susan picked up her sharp-nosed scissors and chopped the bottoms off several monkshood stalks with such aggression that her knuckles flushed white.

Chapter Two

AS WAS NOW HER CUSTOM, Margaret Glass had risen from bed early, a little before six. She had never been one of life's late risers, something she considered a sign of slovenliness, but as age had crept up on her so the time at which she awoke grew ever earlier. Sometimes she wondered if there was any point at all in going to bed in the first place.

Still, being up and about early had it's advantages, she told herself. For one thing, it meant she could usually enjoy her tea and toast in peace before anyone else showed their face and, for a large part of the year, she could enjoy the sights and sounds of the morning sunrise; an example of nature's beauty that not even the setting of the sun at the end of the day could match. She especially liked those mornings, of which this day had been one, when a little blanket of dew sat gently on the surface of the lawn and she could sit in the lounge watching slender wisps of mist rise tentatively into the air as the rays of the warming sun reached out little by little across the great expanse of grass.

It seemed to her that everyone else in the house had by now managed to drag themselves out of bed, although she had yet to receive a good morning from Stephen, the eldest of her two grandsons, whose preference for late nights and equally late mornings was something his parents really did need to knock out of the boy, before it became so ingrained it would be a life-long habit. Her own parents would never have entertained such a casual attitude; there were certain standards one really ought to consider immutable.

Her daughter-in-law, Susan Glass, had brought her a fresh cup of tea when she made her own breakfast, but the china cup, with its rose decoration, now sat empty on the small, round table next to her. In her lap sat a copy of Thomas Hardy's Far From The Madding Crowd, its etched leather spine looking up at the ceiling. Hardy was one of her favourite authors and it had been quite some time since she had last read the book that brought him fame and, no doubt, no little wealth.

The book had absorbed her attention for almost an hour, but first Emma and then Michael, the youngest of her three grandchildren, had broken her concentration as they stopped to say hello on their way through to the garden. She had then found herself entranced by the view through the window. No matter how long she sat and looked, nature never seemed to leave her bored. There was always so much to be seen and enjoyed. It was a shame not everyone in the house saw things quite the same way.

As she sat there, watching half-a-dozen blue tits vigorously searching for insects amongst the leaves of a large weigela bush that grew outside the nearest window, Margaret caught sight of Michael walking towards the house, his face pointed down to the ground and his hands rolled into tight fists.

"Oh dear, Michael, whatever is the matter?" she asked the empty room.

For a moment, she thought he might bypass the lounge and continue along the back of the house, in the direction of the kitchen. But then he straightened his course and stumbled in through the open French doors.

"Michael, dear," she called out. "What is the matter?"

Her grandson didn't so much as glance up or break his stride.

"Michael," she commanded this time, doing her best to sit forward, despite the protests of her joints.

But he was gone, out into the hallway, without a word or look of acknowledgement.

"Michael, don't ignore me," she snapped. "That's very bad manners."

Her words hung briefly on the empty air. She leaned back into the chair and pulled the book into the centre of her lap. She couldn't make up her mind whether she was more offended or concerned. Michael knew better than to ignore his grandmother, but she had to admit he did look rather upset. It would hardly be the first time, of course. He was overly-sensitive and would have benefited from a spell at a private school; not that his father could afford any such thing, more was the pity. It would have brought him out of his shell, she was certain; given him the confidence to engage in meaningful conversation rather than skulk at the back of rooms, hoping no one would bother him. Quite how the boy expected to get along when he started at Reading University in two months' time it was hard to see.

By the time she looked back through the window, the blue tits had moved on. They always seemed worried that, if they were to sit still for any serious length of time, they might not be able to take to the wing again, their muscles wasted through inaction. She thought of herself and the long periods she spent sitting in that same chair. But she contented herself with the knowledge that, for a seventy-three-year-old, she was still very active and it was rare for more than two consecutive days to pass without her taking a long walk along the footpaths that fanned out in all directions from the village. There were certainly those of her acquaintance who were a similar age and had lost far more of their physical vigour.

"Hello, Mrs Glass."

Margaret had been so deeply in her thoughts that she hadn't notice Emma make her way back up to the house. She stood there now, a beautiful young woman with a smiling face that most other women would give all the tea in China to call their own. It was no wonder so many hopeless young men found themselves entranced to the point where they were perfectly happy to make a public spectacle of themselves in the hope she might succumb to their advances. It was more than a little unfortunate that Michael was just such a young man, especially given recent appalling developments. But that was for another time.

"Hello, Emma, dear. Was Barnes taking that compost to the hydrangeas?"

"He was indeed. Heaps of it."

"Very good. They will need it in such warm weather. If he lets them dry out, they will shed all their blooms and then we won't get to enjoy their spectacular display. It's such a shame they seem to have rather gone out of fashion with modern-day gardeners."

"They're quite... showy, don't you think?"

Margaret wasn't sure whether this was meant as a good thing or a bad one, but she suspected the latter.

"In good taste, I would say." She picked up her book and closed it before returning it to her lap. "Michael seemed to be rather upset. I don't suppose you know why?"

Emma flicked a strand of hair away from her forehead, where it threatened to drop in front of an eye.

"No. He ran off back to the house so suddenly I didn't get an opportunity to ask him what was wrong."

Emma knew better than to say a word to the Glass Dragon, as she secretly referred to Margaret, about her exchange with Michael. It would only see her subjected to yet another lecture on the behaviour expected of the proper young lady she was apparently expected to be. Better to steer well clear of that conversation. Michael would get over things soon enough.

"The silly boy tells one so little, it is all but impossible to know what is going through his head. I will have to ask his mother to speak to him," declared Margaret.

She suspected the cause of her grandson's unhappiness was standing right before her. It was hardly a secret Michael had developed a soft spot for the girl, but she had rather hoped it was something that would wear off, once he realised Emma was very definitely not the girl for him. But he had a stubborn streak, like all members of the Glass family, and it seemed he had determined not to give up without a good deal of fight. She had hoped that, after the recent extraordinary news concerning Emma, Michael would finally have realised his folly, but perhaps that had not been the case.

"I think he is just a little shy," declared Emma, wondering how she could extricate herself from this unwelcome situation without giving offence to a second member of the Glass family, but the grumpy old woman always found something to complain about, however nice you tried to be. "I'm sure he'll grow out of that at university. Has he found any digs yet for his second year, do you know? Philippa said he wasn't sure he'd be able to get into halls."

"Did I hear someone mention my name?"

Philippa Glass almost bounded into the room, bursting with an energy that contrasted starkly with the atmosphere hanging over the room. Her grandmother considered such behaviour as needing to be toned down, a great deal, as it was not sufficiently ladylike and almost certain to put off any man who might otherwise consider her a fine catch. Her remonstrances, however, had made absolutely no difference and the granddaughter continued to take life at full tilt.

"Hello, Pippa," replied Emma, smiling broadly at the sight of her favourite member of the Glass family. "I was about to come looking for you. Hoping we can listen to some Elvis together."

"Wonderful idea. But I'm just about to put a saddle on Eliot and ride him out towards Ashford, so we'll need to get together when I'm back. The poor thing hasn't been ridden since the middle of last week. He'll be thinking I don't love him any more."

The words bubbled out of Pippa, like water through a sparkling brook, her head bobbed in all directions and her hands painted erratic pictures as they swept through the air, first one way then another. Her grandmother sighed.

"Come find me when you're back, will you?" asked Emma.

"Of course." Pippa looked down at the book in her grandmother's lap. "Oh, no, you're not reading Thomas Hardy again, grandmother. His books are all so desperately sad. You'll end up throwing yourself under a bus."

Emma smiled; her thoughts entirely.

"He's a masterful writer and I think we could all learn a lesson or two from this particular book," Margaret replied, tapping a finger on the cover of the offending novel, her gaze directed towards Emma.

"Well, I think you should try something more up-to-date, grandmother. You should try something by Iris Murdoch. Much more in keeping with the times."

"Never heard of the woman and I don't suppose I would enjoy her works, even if I could bring myself to read any of it."

"Right then," announced Pippa. "I'm off to the stables. Should be gone half-an-hour or thereabouts. We can make some noise when I get back, Emma. Bye for now, grandmother."

Emma leapt at her opportunity for escape. "I'll come with you as far as the kitchen, Pippa. I could do with a glass of water."

Margaret watched the two young women depart. They were more alike than she cared for, both in terms of their beauty and their outgoing personalities. She could only hope that was where the similarities ended. But that was, right now, the least of her worries.

She brought her hands together on the cover of the book and looked down at the coal-black sleeves of her mourning dress. The death of her eldest son had brought with it changes that presented an uncertain and worrying future for the Glass family and the resulting tensions appeared to be playing on the nerves of most of its members. Outside the house, the world was bright and cheerful; the same could not be said for inside. The sooner matters were brought to a satisfactory conclusion, the better.

She set aside her thoughts and picked up her book, opening it at the marker. There was indeed much to be learned from the tale of Bathsheba Everdene.

Chapter Three

SUSAN GLASS THREW THE unwanted plant stems into the kitchen bin and slammed the lid back in place with a bang so loud it reverberated off the walls. Anger swam through her veins with an enthusiasm and freedom she found a little disconcerting. She needed to regain control of herself, or she would end up saying or doing something she'd regret. One deep breath. Two deep breaths. As she felt the air drawn in through her nose, then out through her mouth for the third time, she closed her eyes and began to picture the magnolia tree in bloom, its long bare branches heavy with large, deeply-scented white flowers. A degree of calm began to settle over her. But this burgeoning sense of peace was broken by the sound of hurrying footsteps. When she opened her eyes, she saw her husband, James, entering into the kitchen.

"Ah, there you are, darling." He sounded a little harassed. "I'm going into the office for a while. Can't imagine I'll be there all day, as there's not that much to do, but need to show my face and all that. They might forget I exist otherwise."

As he spoke, James Glass stood his brown leather briefcase on the stone-tiled floor, then opened a cupboard and fished out a short, round glass, which he took to the fridge.

"I might take the Triumph out for a spin later. See if I've got the tyre pressures properly set up now." He poured milk into the glass, then gulped it in one go.

Susan noticed that her husband's normal clipped public school tones were not quite as sharp as usual, a slight shortening of the breath suggesting he'd been hurrying. She knew the situation at his office had not been pleasant for him for several weeks and wondered if his decision to travel to Northampton had been a last-minute one. She briefly thought of asking, but decided against since there were more important matters that needed addressing.

"That obnoxious niece of yours has been causing trouble again," she announced, surprised at the way the words quivered on her lips, despite the growing sense of calm she had been feeling. "Something really does need to be done about her."

James didn't answer immediately. He stood the empty glass on the nearest worktop, then picked up a hand-towel and wiped away the milky moustache he could feel clinging to his upper lip.

"Our niece," he corrected. "What has she done this time?"

He wasn't sure he could imagine what else Emma could have done to upset their household and the prospect of yet another incident, to add to the already lengthy list of supposed misdemeanours that had unravelled since the reading of his brother's will, was not a pleasant one.

"I was making up a flower arrangement in our bedroom and could see Michael and her talking by the arbour. Of course, I couldn't hear what was said but when he broke off to come back to the house, I could Michael was close to tears and immensely upset. We've told her before not to take advantage of his infatuation with her, but she's clearly not taken any notice. Honestly, I want to slap her face."

Susan could no longer pretend she had restored her self-control; she could feel her hands shaking and the urge to scream at her husband welled up inside her. Indeed, she would have done precisely that had there been no one else in the house.

"Perhaps that's just what she was doing, telling him to find someone else to lavish his attentions on. Maybe it was that which upset him."

"James."

It was only one word but her husband felt the full weight of it. He sighed.

"Alright, alright. You know I've spoken to her, several times, recently. But she's not much interested in what I have to say, not since the reading of Robert's will. That's left her a changed woman; which I suppose is understandable, given the circumstances. I imagine something like that would change any of us."

He had a good deal of sympathy for Emma, but at the same time there was no getting away from the fact her behaviour these past couple of weeks had, at times, been utterly appalling and he felt as much frustration as anyone else about it. And that didn't take any account of his family's changed circumstances, which had brought on stresses and strains of their own.

Susan changed her angle of attack. "I think we should speak to another firm of solicitors, to see if we can't get your brother's will overturned. Surely someone can help us." She brought her hands together in front of her tummy, in an effort to stop them from shaking.

James poked the point of a shoe against the end of his briefcase, wondering how many times his wife might want to revisit this particular well; one that was, they had been told, totally dry.

"We've already tried two and they were both very clear there's not a cat in Hell's chance of doing that. It's not as if we've shied away from the better practices, either. Spade and Hearts are no tuppenny bit firm. If they say there's no chance of overturning the will, then we really ought to be thinking it isn't going to happen."

"Well, I think we should try someone else. What about a firm in Leamington? There are some highly reputable ones there," prompted Susan, her words vibrating with frustration. "I can't imagine your mother is ready for you to give up."

The last sentence nipped unpleasantly at James's self-confidence. He well knew his mother was far from giving up on the matter. He understood both women's desire to tear his brother's will to pieces. Good God, he had his own reasons, very good reasons indeed, to see that happen too, but all the advice they had been given had been clear: the will was sound and there were no possible grounds for a challenge that stood any chance of being successful. He held back the temptation to snap at his wife and decided to take the easy option, for now.

"I suppose we could try one of the bigger firms in Leamington or maybe Northampton. I can ask round at the office. See if anyone can point us in the direction of a good outfit."

"We need to do something, James," added his wife, almost before he had finished speaking. "We can't just sit here and let things carry on like this. We really can't."

"Indeed," he replied, not at all sure what that 'something' might be. "Maybe I can arrange for her to have an unfortunate accident. A fatal one," he quipped, not altogether certain Susan wouldn't jump at the suggestion.

Susan was about to speak again, but she cut herself off, her attention drawn to the short, slim figure of Beryl Bolant, their part-time cleaner, who chose that moment to enter the kitchen. Beryl paused, looked at James, then his wife.

"Something you wanted to say?" asked Susan.

"Is it alright if I clean the kitchen floor now?"

"Of course. Mr Glass is just off to Northampton and I want to see how Frank Barnes is getting on before he does something Grandmother Glass disapproves of. The kitchen is all yours."

James and Susan paused in the hallway, the kitchen door now closed behind them.

"That was awkward," proffered James, nodding towards the kitchen. "She might have got entirely the wrong idea there."

His wife appeared altogether unconcerned. "I don't see why. Not unless you really were thinking of pushing your niece under a bus."

She smiled, turned on her heels and walked off in the direction of the garden.

Chapter Four

STEPHEN GLASS LAY ON his bed staring up at the ceiling of his room, watching a fly in what appeared to be its last desperate struggles to escape from the web of a spider that no longer seemed to be there. He felt an affinity with the winged one, snared and seemingly with no realistic prospect of escape.

Having woken from his slumbers at seven-thirty to find himself suffering with a mild headache, he had phoned the office a little before nine, feigning a migraine. In reality, he simply didn't feel up to pushing himself through another day of work, forced into engaging in conversations he currently had no appetite for and requiring him to be pleasant to people when he would rather avoid other human beings altogether.

He had been stricken by a deep sense of helplessness, festering inside him like a malignant tumour for months and recent developments threatened to see that now erupt into the open, leaving a gaping wound that would never properly heal.

He rolled on to his side, felt no more comfortable than he had done on his back, so swung his legs around and stood up, cupping the back of his head in hands and closing his eyes. As he stood, momentarily light-headed as his heart raced to pump blood through his upright frame, sunlight lanced in through the tall, multi-paned window and warmed the side of his face. It felt pleasant enough to persuade him that a spell in the garden might not be a bad thing. It ought at least to distract him from the dark, depressing thoughts that were clogging his head.

His bedroom was at the front of the house. In order to reach the stairs, he had to take the landing past both his sister's bedroom and the one used by Emma whenever she was staying with the family. It was as he approached the latter bedroom that the door opened and out stepped Emma. She took a moment to notice him, distracted by some minor irritation with her dress, and he briefly considered turning around and pretending he was on his way to his room, but she looked up before he could act. She smiled in a manner that left him uncertain whether to feel welcome or afraid; it was a skill he felt sure she had spent a good deal of time developing.

"Hello Stephen. You do look poorly," she observed, stepping close enough to him so that she could adjust the collar of his shirt. "I suppose it's the stress... of work, I mean. Perhaps you should consult a doctor. I'm sure there must be some kind of treatment for your affliction."

His father had often commented on the beauty of those deep blue eyes, but right now he felt they were taunting him, perhaps challenging him to respond. There was little to be gained from that; he'd tried, more than once, and there had been no happy-ever-after type ending. He bit back the impulse to push past her, to run away, as he was sure she would notice his discomfort. He didn't want to give her the satisfaction. A sickly taste developed in his mouth and it took quite some effort to bite it back.

"Hello Emma." He wanted to say more, but the words stuck in his throat.

"Were you going to say something else?" she asked, tilting her head a little to one side. "Or has the cat got your tongue?"

He coughed, as much to play for a little more time as to clear his throat. There was indeed more he wanted to say and he was now determined to force the words out, no matter how hard it was.

"What we spoke about the other day... can't we come to some understanding now and not leave it to drag on? I..."

"No, Stephen. I told you, I'm not interested in sorting out your problems right now. I have bigger problems of my own to deal with. You should know that."

Her words were harshly spoken and they left him feeling cold and fearful. He dug his fingernails into his palms and tried again.

"But, won't that be better for both of us if we sort this out now? It will let you..."

"Stephen," she snapped, her eyes suddenly fierce. "I said, no."

He looked down at his feet. A hole was starting to open up in one of the grey socks where the big toe jutted out. He could see no benefit in attempting to prolong the conversation and was about to walk away when Emma spoke again, only this time her voice was altogether different, almost amused, and when he looked up he found her staring back at him with something close to a smirk on her face.

"Anyway," she said, jabbing a finger into his chest. "I've made my mind up. I'm going to share your horrid little secret with the others. After all, they have a right to know about your despicable behaviour and the kind of person they're sharing this house with. It isn't right they're kept in the dark and can you imagine how your mother would react if she heard about it from someone else? The poor woman would be distraught. She'd never forgive you."

Stephen felt the blood drain from his face and his mouth turned dry. She couldn't mean it, surely not. She was taunting him; taking her pleasure from watching him squirm. She couldn't do that, she really couldn't. He couldn't let her do that.

"You look like you've seen a ghost, Stephen. If I was you, I'd crawl back to my room and have a nice rest on my bed. That'll give you time to think about what you will do once the others know what kind of a person you really are. I don't suppose they will be happy about you remaining in this house. But I suppose that's not for me to decide. Now, off you go."

She pushed his chest with the palm of her hand. He stumbled back half a step, paused, his head awash with thoughts, none of which he could properly grasp, then turned and slowly walked back towards his room, struggling to put one foot in front of the other.

Emma watched him go and it was only once the bedroom door clicked shut that she allowed the tension to leave her body, a brief sigh accompanied by a softening of her shoulders where the muscles had set so hard they felt as if they had almost turned to stone.

Once upon a time she would never have been able to face down another person like that, not even one as weak-willed as Stephen. But she was tougher now; she had learned her lessons from all the knock-backs and slights she had suffered over the years. Bit by bit, she'd hardened herself to a world that seemed to offer nothing to those who did not choose to put themselves first. Perhaps, in some ways, she wasn't any longer an entirely likeable person, but what good had it done her, being little miss well-behaved? It had left her vulnerable and others had all too often seemed happy to take advantage of that. Well, not any more they didn't. There was still work to be done, but she was already better equipped to look after herself.

With Stephen gone, she had intended to continue on her way down the stairs, but something now stopped her from doing so and it took her a moment to realise what. It was barely mid-morning, but already she had experienced run-ins with several members of the Glass family. It was a pattern that had become depressingly familiar since the reading of her father's will. It was not only unpleasant, but exhausting fighting them off. They seemed to have decided to gang up on her and make it clear she was no longer a welcome guest, despite the assurances her uncle and aunt had given about taking care of her and there always being a place for her at Ashview Lodge. Hypocrites. Liars. They said one thing and did another.

But those frustrations weren't what was behind her feelings of irritation and hesitation now. No, all these little incidents served only to remind her, as if she really needed reminding, of just how huge had been the change in her life. She knew it was something she was still adapting to and a part of her even went so far as to wonder if she ever would fully adapt.

She had been shocked at being told Robert Glass was her father, rather than the family friend that had been led to believe he was. But this knowledge had come at a cost and she struggled with a mix of grief and anger; grief at losing her father before she knew his real identity and anger that the information had been kept form her all this time. She found it hard, if not impossible, to find an outlet for her grief, but the anger was another matter. At first, she had taken that out on her mother. They had argued. No, they had shouted and screamed, not really listening to each other's words, just letting go in an orgy of emotion.

But why shouldn't she have been angry with her mother? Why shouldn't she still be angry with her? Her mother had no right to hide from her the truth about her father. If she had known all along who he was, she would have been able to have a proper father and daughter relationship. Now it was too late. He was dead and the chance was gone, for ever. Her vision began to blur as tears welled up, but she wasn't going to let that happen, not any more. The time for crying had passed. She had shed so many tears already and she was determined not to shed any more.

She breathed in deeply, drawing the air right down into the bottom of her lungs before she allowed it so seep slowly back out. She needed to get away from the house and its residents for a while. To go somewhere she could properly relax, without fear of yet another unwelcome interruption or confrontation. In truth, her options were, as they always were when staying at Ashview Lodge, very limited. She could go for a walk, but that held little appeal on this occasion. She could go down to the village garage, where she could taunt that idiot John Perch, but his boss would soon put a stop to that.

No, she would take the bus into Banbury, where she could stroll from shop to shop, making a mental list of all the beautiful things she would buy when she was given her father's money. The dresses, the shoes, the handbags, the earrings. It was an activity she had already undertaken in a minor way in her home town of Evesham, but Banbury was bigger and the shops offered a better array of items. Of course, she would find even more on offer in Leamington or Oxford, but they would come later. It was a process to be savoured, not rushed.

She collected her handbag from her room and the little blue jacket that had been the last present her father bought for her, then skipped down the stairs and out of the front door, not the least bit inclined to let the others know where she was going. They could be left to wonder and worry. She would take the track over the hill and down into the centre of the village in plenty of time for the next bus.

As she stepped out through the front gate, she glanced up at the bedroom windows and saw the disconsolate face of Stephen Glass looking down at her. Then, sitting there under the shade of an apple tree at the side of the house, she saw Michael Glass. Although he watched her pass, he said not a word to her and she was happy with that.

Chapter Five

SERGEANT STANLEY SHAPES had been alone in the office he shared with his boss, Inspector Leslie Dykeman, at Banbury police station when the call came through from 'upstairs' with the happy news that he and Dykeman had been assigned a new case.

What's more, it was the kind of case he liked best of all: murder. There was nothing to beat a nice juicy murder investigation. In fact, once upon a time he had looked upon the prospect of watching a convicted killer swing on the end of a rope as being one of the most enticing aspects of his job. Justice in action, as it were.

But then he'd done just that, watched a killer being hung by the neck. He'd been given special permission to be present, on a purely professional basis, as the hangman did his work. The prospect had long held a weird fascination for him, like an itch that he had become desperate to scratch, and eventually Dykeman had managed to pull a few strings so he could be there, at the hanging of a violent thug who'd bludgeoned an old dear to death, just so he could steal her silver cutlery. Very sad affair, that had been.

Unexpectedly, however, the one thing he remembered most clearly of all from that hanging wasn't the sight of the

31

killer dangling on the end of the rope. It was the loud, sharp snap the trap-door made as the hangman pulled back the lever to release it. He hadn't been expecting such a sound and he found it was still ringing in his ears as he left the building a short while later. Even now, that was the first thing that came back to him when he cast his mind back to the occasion. It was fair to say that his itch had been well and truly scratched by the experience and he'd not since felt the slightest inclination to attend another hanging.

As he made his way along the corridor and down the stairs to the staff canteen, he wondered what he was going to find when he got there. Dykeman had shown up for their shift late, again, and he'd been no more chatty than he had been for weeks. His boss had spent more and more time hiding in the canteen, pretending he was reading the newspaper or the racing papers, while his half-drunk cup of tea was left to go stone cold. Even Evil Gladys, who ran the canteen with a rod of iron and had a reputation for having a heart of stone, had asked Shapes what was up with his boss, concerned, apparently, for his well-being.

The cause of this drastic change in Dykeman's behaviour was obvious enough, even if the man himself didn't like to admit it. Everyone at the station knew the score, despite Dykeman's refusal to acknowledge, let alone discuss, it. The poor old sod was suffering from a broken heart. Too late in the day he'd realised that the recently departed pathologist for North Oxfordshire, Dr Sheila Delph, was the woman for him. How on earth he'd not clocked that sooner, Lord only knew, since it had been so bleeding obvious even a blind man would have been able to see it. He had eventually opened his eyes wide enough to see what so many others already could, but his timing stunk worse than gone off milk.

When Dykeman finally woke up to the notion that the love of his life was right there in front of his eyes and began to struggle with how to approach the matter, Delph had been swept off her feet by an old friend who'd shown up out of a clear blue sky, like a large, smelly turd falling from a passing plane. Flash git, he was, with money aplenty and a sports car to ferry her to the kind of restaurants Dykeman wouldn't even have known existed. Shown up with only one purpose, he had, and Delph fell for him hook, line and sinker. They'd married just weeks later, as soon as the banns could be read in her local church, and then Mr and Mrs Hardyman had shipped out to Canada, where he'd set up in business as a wholesaler of domestic goods.

Dykeman had been devastated. It had hit him with the impact of a week-old scone and the bruises were still sensitive. Somehow or other, Dykeman had managed to drag himself along to the wedding, insisting it would have been rude not to go. He'd sat in the church, next to Shapes, not saying a word, before, during or after the marriage ceremony. Shapes had driven him home afterwards in complete silence, worried his boss might burst into tears at any moment. What the hell he would have done if Dykeman had lost control, he'd had no idea and kept his fingers crossed, so to speak, they'd reach the house before any such thing happened. Fortunately, Dykeman had been both silent and dry-eyed when he left the car.

Ever since, Dykeman had lost his spark and all interest in his work. When he wasn't lurking in the canteen, he made excuses to leave the office alone for hours on end and even when he was there he sat at his desk sour-faced and silent, not to be provoked by anything Shapes could say or do. Even a recent case concerning a violent break-in at a Banbury engineering firm, where two members of staff were coshed over the head, hadn't managed to coax more than half-a-dozen words out of him.

Things were so bad even an invitation from Tom Gently, the editor of the Banbury Globe, to join him and some others for a day at the races in Stratford had been turned down flat, despite Gently doing his level best to change Dykeman's mind. His boss turning down a day at the races was practically unheard of; in fact, they often spent their time trying to work out ways to spend more time at the races, usually under the pretence their presence was related to some case or other.

Shapes had pretty much run out of ideas for ways to drag his boss out of the depression he'd sunk into. At times it was like quicksand, the harder he tried to drag Dykeman out the deeper he sank. It was a sad state of affairs. Truth is, it was worse than that, considered Shapes, because it was also messing up his own life. Who wanted to spend their time with a depressed man who'd rather be thousands of miles away warming his toes with a woman he now couldn't have? It was Dykeman's own fault and it was well past the point at which he needed to shake himself out of it and stop making life so bloody depressing for those who had to work with him.

These last thoughts passed through Shapes's head as he stepped into the staff canteen, his nose twitching at the savoury smells to be found there. He stopped and looked across to the far side of the room, to a table Dykeman seemed to have claimed entirely for himself. There he was, slumped in a chair, looking into space, an abandoned newspaper and a, no doubt unfinished, cup of tea in front of him. His eyes were dull pools, devoid of spark, and a grey shadow of stubble covered his slightly chubby cheeks and square chin.

Shapes tried to chivvy himself up, hoping the prospect of a murder case might elicit some sign of interest from his boss. There were posh people involved and Dykeman, like Shapes, didn't much care for that sort of privilege. Those sort of people often got above themselves; thought they were beyond suspicion and perfectly free to tell the police how to do their jobs, which always went down about as well as a bucket of cold sick. Shapes smiled and pushed out his chest, almost able to believe this new case could be the start of the road to recovery for Dykeman.

However, Shapes's newly confident demeanour took a turn for the worse almost at once. Before he could take another step forward, he watched in horror as the vast, rolling hulk of Inspector Harry 'Heffalump' Houghton waddled up to Dykeman. The sickening look of glee on Heffalump's multi-layered face said all that needed saying; the hopeless, disgusting git, who never had liked Dykeman, had seen a chance to enjoy himself at his adversary's expense. Given Dykeman's depressed state, he was hardly likely to put up much of a fight. Shapes broke into as fast a walk as he could manage, conscious that he daren't risk running since, if Evil Gladys saw him doing anything of the sort, she'd be sure to take him down with a well-aimed stale Banbury Cake or maybe an entire Shepherd's Pie, still in its tin.

"Morning, Inspector," said Shapes to Houghton, cutting across whatever it was the man was saying to Dykeman.

Heffalump half-turned, a sour look on his face. Excellent, thought Shapes, I've managed to butt in before any real damage has been done.

"What do you want, Shapes? Me and Dykeman was just having a little chat, weren't we, Leslie?"

Heffalump sneered at Dykeman, who continued to ignore him, now looking vaguely towards the newspaper lying on the table in front of him.

The need for rapid action hadn't left Shapes with any time to come up with some excuse for extricating Dykeman, but there was always a sure-fire fall-back position with Heffalump; that being his infamously gargantuan appetite. Offers of food always worked if you needed to distract the man from other things.

"Gladys says they're down to their last couple of sausages. Was thinking of having them myself but know they're one of your favourites." Shapes let the words linger on the air, confident he'd said all that was needed.

Heffalump glanced at Dykeman, then at the plate of egg and chips he held in his hands, and finally in the direction of the food counter, confusion washing over his face. As the confusion began to be replaced by concern, Shapes knew success was his.

"Well, that's very good of you, Shapes," declared Heffalump, already turning towards the counter. "Think I could manage a sausage or two with this little plate of egg and chips."

Shapes watched Heffalump walk away, with his mountain of egg and chips, before turning back to his boss, who was looking up at him with a sad-eyed face and an upside down smile.

"Good news, sir," announced Shapes in as upbeat a tone as he could manage. "We've got a new case and it's a murder."

SHAPES HAD HOPED FOR a better response than the one he got, but at least Dykeman, after seeming to show no interest at all in their new case, had dragged himself up on to his feet and agreed they'd better help themselves to a car from the station's pool. Better still, since Dykeman had no interest in anything at all, he hadn't put up even a hint of a fight when Shapes suggested he drive. Well, thought Shapes, dark clouds and silver linings and all that.

Shapes had then nearly fallen over himself, when they found sitting there in the car park, all alone and in dire need of driving, a Ford Anglia 105E Deluxe. It was the new model, with the styling and chrome adornments that reminded him of the big, flash American cars he saw in so many Hollywood movies. He stroked the bodywork with tenderness and purred like a contented cat as he slid into the driver's seat. Perhaps he'd get lost on the way to Brayfield, their destination, and they'd end up still on the road in an hour's time. It was hardly likely Dykeman would notice, given his current state. As they pulled out of the car park,

Shapes decided that, whatever the day ahead held for them, the morning was already the best he'd experienced in weeks.

BRAYFIELD LAY SOME eight miles north of Banbury, on the road to Daventry in neighbouring Northamptonshire. It ought to have taken about twenty minutes for them to reach the village, but Shapes decided his modest detour, adding a further seven minutes, was entirely reasonable. He might have argued it gave him and Dykeman time to discuss the basics of the case they had been given, but that wouldn't exactly have been true, since Dykeman maintained his radio silence for the entire journey.

Their destination was close to a residence called Ashview Lodge, on the southern outskirts of the village, and Shapes needed to keep his wits about him not to miss the unsignposted track down which they turned from the main road. They hadn't gone very far before Shapes saw the figure of PC Johnston standing alongside the track, waving in their direction. Why he was waving, Shapes couldn't imagine, since he would have needed to have had his eyes shut not to notice the PC standing out in the open.

Having parked on an open section of land adjacent to a field, they climbed out of the car into bright, warm August sunshine; happy weather that had lingered over the southern Midlands for the previous few days. That was good, thought Shapes, as rain had a nasty habit of washing away many clues when you were working out in the open air.

"Morning, Johnston," said Shapes, cheerily, as he rubbed his hands together.

"Morning, Sarge. We're over there," replied Johnston, pointing towards a patch of grass on a gentle ridge nearby.

They made their way up the slope to the top of the ridge, accompanied by the playful calls of a family of house martins that wheeled and swooped overhead, then turned towards the tall figure of PC 'Lanky' George Bunch, standing in what appeared to be, at first sight, an open space of no discernable interest. However, as they closed, the two new arrivals began to see a wide, deep ditch open in the ground behind where Bunch was standing.

"She's in there, sir," the tall constable informed Dykeman.

Dykeman and Shapes walked unhesitatingly up to the edge of the ditch, stopped and looked down. There, in the bottom of the ditch, lay the figure of a young woman, her straw-blonde hair a tangled mess and the front of her thin summer dress stained a deep, dark claret.

"Stone me, that's a bloody long way down," observed Shapes, leaning over the top of the ditch with great care.

Dykeman looked at his Sergeant for a brief moment before responding, "You have noticed the body of a young woman in the bottom of the ditch, Shapes, haven't you?"

"Of course, I have, sir. Hard to miss."

Dykeman's nose twitched. He looked at Bunch. "Who found her?"

"A couple of farm labourers, sir. They're sitting over by the woodland there, on that fallen tree trunk," replied Bunch, pointing towards a small copse that came to an end about fifty yards from where they stood.

"We'll need to have a word with those two before they can go," said Dykeman as he looked again at the body in the ditch before asking in a rather curt tone, "I take it someone has actually checked that she's dead?"

"Yes, sir," responded Bunch, lifting off his helmet so he could wipe away some of the sweat that had begun to build up on his forehead on this warm morning. "I checked for a pulse myself. None there and she's stone cold. Been dead some time, I'd say."

"Do we know who she is?"

"No, sir. The labourers say they don't recognise her."

"Very good, Bunch," said Dykeman, scratching the back of his neck as he weighed up his options. Either Shapes or himself had to get down into the ditch, so they could take a look at the body. More to the point, he decided, was the small matter of getting back out afterwards. It looked to be about shoulder-height deep and four or five feet wide at the top, narrowing to something like three feet at the bottom. He wondered briefly why the ditch needed to be so deep in the first place, but had not the inclination to continue to speculate on that, so went back to assessing his options for inspecting the body. The answer was obvious.

"Down you go, Shapes. See if you can find some form of identification. And don't trample over the body while you're down there. Our new pathologist won't be happy if you go walking all over his first murder victim."

"Me, sir?" asked Shapes, immediately concerned at the prospect. "That hole's nearly as deep as I am tall. I'll never get out again."

"Nonsense, Shapes. A fine athlete like you will have no trouble getting out of there. Anyway, if you do get stuck, Bunch can wander off to that house over there and see if they've got a ladder, can't you, Bunch?"

"Certainly, sir," grinned the amused constable.

Shapes gave Bunch a look that made clear his disapproval before dropping down on to his haunches and easing himself gingerly over the edge, the toes of his shoes struggling for purchase on the side of the ditch as he reached down to the bottom. Once there, he straightened his jacket and looked up. It felt as though he had descended to the centre of the Earth and was now looking up at a thin strip of sky far, far away. He ignored the amused faces of Dykeman and Bunch, turned towards the corpse and squatted down for a closer inspection.

Of course, he was no pathologist, but all the same he was quickly confident the cause of death was one or more stab wounds to the chest, since that was where blood had stained the woman's dress the most. Her skin was cold as a fish to the touch and as pale as whitewash. Bunch was right, she'd been dead for some time; probably since the previous day. In such a deep ditch, he contemplated, she could have remained there for months before anyone noticed her.

She looked to him to be in her early twenties. Would have been pretty, when she was still breathing. And she had a nice figure, though not quite as curvy as he liked in a woman. Such a waste. Had most of her life in front of her. There didn't appear to be any obvious signs of sexual assault, not that he could make much of a judgement on that; they'd have to wait for the pathologist's report for confirmation.

Looking more closely, Shapes cast his experienced and rather cynical eye over the corpse in search of clues or significant facts. No wedding or engagement ring, nor any sign of there once having been one. A thin chain, possibly silver, hung around the woman's slender neck. Interesting was that, he decided, as it suggested her death had nothing to do with theft. The short, blue jacket she was wearing had a small shallow pocket on either side, but when he poked a finger into each one he found it empty. But, joy of joys, partially covered by her right shoulder was a small leather handbag. He slipped it out without any need to disturb the body and opened it. Cash, a clean handkerchief, two cigarettes and a box of matches, plus a round compact that opened to show a small mirror on one side and, on the other, one of those powder puff things women were always dabbing their faces with. That was it; nothing to tell them who she was.

Shapes stepped around and over the corpse, so he could inspect the ditch on the far side, but there was nothing else to be found, not unless it was too small for his getting-on-a-bit eyes to see in the poor light in this subterranean world.

"Done," he shouted up to Dykeman, having to shield his eyes from the glare of the sky as he looked out of the ditch.

"Out you come then," replied Dykeman, who then disappeared from view.

Very amusing, thought Shapes, as he turned to face the other side of the ditch.

"Bunch," he yelled. Nothing. "Bunch, get your ugly face over here, or else."

The innocent looking face of PC Bunch peered over the top of the ditch.

"Sarge?"

Shapes held his right hand up. "Pull me out of here."

Bunch grinned then reached down and grabbed hold of Shapes's outstretched hand.

"The Inspector said we should leave you to get yourself out, Sarge," chuckled Bunch. "He wanted to run a book on how long it would take."

Shapes wanted to swear, but the effort of scrambling out of the ditch didn't leave breath for any such thing, so he gritted his teeth and kicked harder at the wall of the ditch instead as he clambered upwards.

"Well?" asked Dykeman, as Shapes stood there breathing heavily. "Do we know who she is?"

Shapes shook his head as he started brushing dry soil from his jacket and trousers. There was a lot of it, he noticed. "No. Nothing to identify her. Make-up. Money. Cigarettes. That was all."

"Shame," said Dykeman, puffing out his cheeks.

He looked again at the two farm labourers, who were now sitting on the ground, their backs resting against the fallen tree.

"Bunch."

"Sir."

"Pathologist on his way is he?"

"He is, sir. Station put out the call as soon as we confirmed we had a corpse here."

"Good." Dykeman rubbed the side of his nose. "Johnston."

"Sir."

"Get down into the village and see if you can't find someone who might be able to identify this young lady. The vicar would do, I imagine, if you can track him down. Or maybe the doctor, if there's one in the village."

"Right o', sir," replied the constable, who then took half a turn towards the dirt path that angled away over the crest of the ridge and down towards the eastern edge of the village.

"Oh and Johnston," called Dykeman.

"Sir."

"Be quick about it."

"Will do, sir."

As Johnston marched off, arms swinging, Dykeman turned back to Shapes, still busy brushing dirt off his clothes, to the accompaniment of some barely audible mumbling.

"Come on, Shapes. Let's have a word with those two labourers while we wait for the others to show up."

The conversation with the two labourers turned out to be brief. Indeed, it lasted barely two minutes, in no small part because the two men had no interest in wasting words when talking and, therefore, answered the policemen's questions in what Dykeman could only consider to be a succinct manner. Admirable in its own way, he thought, but hardly conversational. No, they didn't know who the woman was. No, they hadn't touched her or even been down into the ditch, since any fool could see she was stone dead. No, they hadn't seen anyone else in the area at the time they made their gruesome discovery. And, finally, no, they had no idea why the ditch had been dug so deep.

SINCE PC BUNCH HAD already taken formal statements from the two labourers, Dykeman sent them on their way as soon as he and Shapes had finished with them. Best not to have other people hanging around needlessly, decided the Inspector. Now he and his Sergeant were sitting on the same fallen tree trunk the labourers has vacated, speculating who would show up first, Johnston or the pathologist. Both men opted for the former.

Dykeman had taken a shoe off so he could empty it of the small stone that had found its way in there, while Shapes was watching a hare that had appeared in a shallow dip in the field away to their left, where the combine-harvester had already done its job, leaving behind a sea of stubble. PC Bunch was sitting on the edge of the ditch, swinging his legs from side to side, his helmet placed on the ground next to him. If not for the body in the bottom of the ditch, it would have made for a tranquil scene of late summer country life, cogitated Shapes, already bored close to tears.

With time to spare for such things, Shapes had been ruminating on the change the new case already seemed to have brought about in his boss. True, the poor sod still wasn't all that talkative, though he never was one for ten words where one would do, but there had been definite signs of things starting to return to some sort of normal. Suggesting he, Shapes, should be left to scramble his own way out of that bloody ditch was old-style Dykeman, that was for sure, as was the snappy way he'd barked out his orders to Johnston. There was a long way to go until things were back to how they should be, but they did at least seem to be heading in the right direction.

Shapes saw something had caught the hare's attention. The long-eared animal went rigid as a board, directed those ears towards the track that led up from the road, twiddled them so as to get them properly tuned in to whatever noise it was, then casually tootled off over the ridge and out of view. He'd barely gone when the sound of a vehicle approaching along the track reached the smaller ears of Shapes and Dykeman.

"Looks like it's our new pathologist," announced Dykeman, as a big lumbering Humber Hawk came into view. "Heard he's got one of those big things."

"Old man's car," declared Shapes, dismissively.

"Should be right up your street, then," retorted Dykeman. "Come on, let's say hello."

The pathologist's car pulled up directly behind Dykeman and Shapes's Anglia and, for a brief moment, the Inspector relished the anticipation of seeing Dr Sheila Delph step out of the Humber. Instead, as the driver's door swung open, he was greeted by the sight of the altogether different figure of Dr Edward Edwardes clambering out of the car with a lack of dexterity common for a man in his fifties. A little on the short side and plump as a pudding, with his wire-framed glasses and bald pate with its ear-to-ear ring of closely cropped grey hair, the doctor looked to Dykeman like the archetypal boffin; the kind of ministry scientist who would make pronouncements about the benefits of drinking milk or the reasons why a pilot's eyes don't pop out of their sockets when he's flying at the speed of sound.

"Morning, Edward," said Dykeman, extending a hand.

"Leslie. I had a little trouble..."

Edwardes broke off mid-sentence, shaking his head. He turned back to the Humber, opened the driver's door and peered inside. Shaking his head again, he closed that door, opened the rear-passenger door and looked inside. Still not happy, he pushed the door closed, walked round the back of the car, opened the boot and surveyed its contents, resting one hand on a hip while he rubbed his bald head with the other, once more shaking his head.

"I thought it was..." he began, without finishing.

Dykeman and Shapes exchanged glances.

"Lost something, Edward?" asked Dykeman.

"I may have... Just a minute," replied Edwardes, as he leaned into the boot and began to move around a substantial collection of coats, umbrellas, bags and sundry other items he thought might come in useful. "Ah, there it is." He reached in and pulled out a brown leather holdall, typical of the type used by doctors. "Thought for a moment there I'd left the thing behind."

"Well, it's good to see you didn't," proffered Dykeman. "Shall we take a look at the body?" he added, gesturing in the direction of the ditch.

"Yes, before that gets lost too," muttered Shapes as they turned to retrace their steps.

Ignoring his Sergeant's sarcastic comment, Dykeman took a look at his watch. Three minutes after ten. If they could identify the young woman without much more delay there would be plenty of time left in the day to get on with making their enquiries. If death had, as appeared to be the case, occurred on the previous day, Monday, then they were already twelve or more hours after the event and time mattered in these cases; the longer it went without an arrest, the more their chances of success decreased. That was a well-known fact amongst members of the constabulary and he wasn't keen to add another failed case to the always growing pile of evidence that the hypothesis was true.

Mind you, he thought to himself, Shapes wasn't altogether wrong in being less than impressed with Edwardes. This was only the second time they had met him in a professional capacity and the first time hadn't gone any too well. They'd been called to a two-up-two-down terraced house in the centre of Banbury where the body of an elderly woman had been found by one of her relatives. It looked like a simple case of age catching up with the poor old dear, who was lying there in her bed, stiff as a board.

Edwardes had arrived late, having initially called at the house next door by mistake, then he'd started referring to the deceased as 'him' before, most impressively of all, he'd made a failed attempt at scrambling on to the dressing table when the woman's black and white moggy ambled into the room, calling for its breakfast. Apparently, Edwardes had an allergy to cats; made him break out in a rash and get badly short of breath. Shapes had been his usual sympathetic self - he could hardly stop laughing - and Dykeman had been forced to hustle him out of the bedroom, while doing his best not chuckle too.

"Good Lord," declared the startled doctor as they arrived at the ditch and he got his first glimpse of the corpse. "That's jolly deep."

"It is," commented Dykeman, as if it was nothing out of the ordinary.

Edwardes looked up and down the length of the ditch, before asking, "And how does one get down there?" He pointed a stubby finger into the ditch.

"Shapes sat on the edge then lowered himself down," replied Dykeman. "If a man in his condition can manage it, I'm sure you'll be fine, Edward."

Edwardes looked at Shapes, then back at the ditch, carefully studying the edge, which he prodded with one shoe.

"Hold this for me," instructed Edwardes, handing his bag to Shapes.

Edwardes lowered himself on to his bottom with his legs hanging over the edge of the ditch. This entailed a good deal of huffing and puffing, which left Dykeman wondering whether an ambulance might need to be called. Gingerly, Edwardes rolled over, on to his stomach, and, with all the grace of a seal out of water, inched himself over the edge. Happily, as far as Dykeman was concerned, once the doctor had got about halfway down, he lost his grip and dropped the rest of the way, landing in a noisy and indignant heap.

"You want to be careful there, sir," suggested Shapes. "You could get hurt landing like that."

Once Edwardes had clambered back on to his feet and brushed himself down, Shapes handed down his bag and the doctor set about his business, observed from above by the three policemen. If the representatives of Her Majesty's Constabulary had been expecting a quick and straightforward outcome to Edwardes's deliberations, they were to be sadly disappointed. After ten minutes had elapsed and the doctor had insisted there remained much to be done, Dykeman and Shapes had wandered back to the fallen tree to sit down and contemplate matters. Time passed further until, just as Shapes was beginning to wonder if he could grab a short nap, Blunt called across to say the pathologist was finished.

"These are, of course, only my preliminary observations", began Edwardes, still standing in the ditch, his hands on his hips. "You should not take them as gospel and I will need to get the body transferred to the hospital before I can carry out a full investigation."

"Understood, Edward," answered Dykeman, by now wondering if they would ever get a verdict from their new pathologist.

"I would say that death was the result of cardiac arrest, brought about by two or more stab wounds to the heart. I cannot be certain about the number of wounds until I carry out my full investigation, but I am content to say there was more than one. I can see no signs of other injuries, aside from some bruising that looks commensurate with the woman having been dumped into this ditch. Again, a full investigation will be able to confirm that, as I'm not sure about post-mortem bruising."

He looked up at Dykeman, apparently expecting questions.

"Any idea as to the time of death?" asked the Inspector.

"Just an initial view, you understand, but I would say death occurred approximately twenty-four hours ago."

The pathologist took a small white cloth out of his bag and wiped his hands on it with considerable care, before returning it to the bag, which he then closed.

"I was hoping it wasn't quite so long ago," said Dykeman to Shapes, scratching the back of his head. "Don't like it when we've got so much catching up to do."

"Er, is there any chance of some assistance in getting out of this blessed ditch," came the pleading request from the depths of the ditch.

"Do we have to?" mouthed Shapes to Dykeman.

Dykeman hesitated, before answering, "You and Blunt had better give him a hand. The Chief Inspector will be getting a complaint otherwise."

Quite how the pathologist didn't break a limb as he was pulled unceremoniously out of the ditch was a minor miracle, thought Dykeman, who merely stood and observed the operation. Shapes clearly found the exercise highly amusing, but the pathologist's grumbles made it clear he didn't see it the same way at all. He was still cleaning himself down when Dykeman noticed PC Johnston making his way back along the track from the village. He was accompanied by a short, podgy man with a bulbous nose that seemed to hide half his face.

"Looks like he's got the vicar," observed Shapes, who had also noticed the returning Johnston.

"He has indeed. Let's hope our victim was one of his sheep."

"Eh? Sheep? Don't you mean flock?"

"If you insist, Shapes."

"Sir, this is the Reverend Charles Beech," announced Johnston, breathing a little heavily. "He's vicar at the village church, St John's."

"Hello vicar. Very good of you to join us," said Dykeman, extending a hand of welcome.

"I am always here to help in any way I can," came the softly spoken reply.

"Has Johnston said anything about why we've asked you here?"

"He has indeed, Inspector. It is quite a terrible thing to hear, of course, but the Lord brings us many challenges in life, each one designed to provide us with the opportunity to show the level of our commitment to His word and I will willingly undertake this one in the same manner in which I approach any other."

Dykeman wasn't quite sure he caught all of the vicar's reply properly, it being a bit of a garbled mouthful, but he got the gist of it, which was all that mattered. "Have you been vicar here for long?" he asked.

"Oh, quite so. Quite so. I believe it is..." he thought for a moment, bringing his fingers together in front of his chest as if he might be about to pray. "Yes, it is a little over seventeen years now. How the years fly by when you are engaged in the joyous business of spreading the good word of the Lord. Do you attend church yourself, Inspector?"

Dykeman coughed, not sure when he had last set foot in a church for something other than a baptism, marriage or death. "Occasionally. When police work allows me the time," he said, without conviction.

"Are you forced to work on the Lord's Day?" asked the Reverend Beech, his voice and his face suggesting he was shocked at the thought.

"I'm afraid the wicked don't respect the Sabbath Day, vicar, so we too are often required to keep up our investigations on Sundays, shame though that is."

Shapes stifled a laugh and he could swear there was more colour than normal in Dykeman's cheeks.

"Ah, but of course," said an apparently relieved Reverend Beech. "It wouldn't do to allow the evil and wicked of this world the benefit of an additional day to make good their escape from justice."

As Beech paused for breath, Dykeman stepped in, keen to get things back on track. "The body is over here," he said, gesturing towards the ditch. "It's very deep, I'm afraid. We'll have to ask you to attempt an identification from the safety of ground level."

"I quite understand. I can assure you my eyesight remains excellent. None of the usual afflictions someone of my age can expect to experience have as yet befallen me, though, of course, we cannot take these things for granted. The years cannot be held back for ever... "

"Here we go," said Dykeman, leading the talkative vicar to the edge of the ditch.

The Reverend Beech looked down at the body of the young woman. He studied her for a moment in complete and unmoving silence, no flicker of emotion on his face. Dykeman wondered if Beech's eyesight was, in fact, anywhere near as good as he had claimed; perhaps, in reality, he was struggling to make out anything more than the vague outline of the body in the ditch.

"So sad," whispered Beech, just at the moment Dykeman thought he might ask him if he was alright. "The poor dear young thing. She wasn't yet twenty-one, you know."

"Do you have a name, Reverend?" enquired Dykeman, realising he too was now talking quietly.

"Oh, yes," came the soft, sad reply. "Her name is Emma Greene. She stays with the Glass family when she is here in Brayfield." He shook his head before closing his eyes and whispering a prayer.

As he waited for the vicar to say his words, Dykeman felt a sense of loss wash over him. He wasn't sure he altogether welcomed it since the intervention of emotion in a case, especially a murder case, could cloud the mind and lead to mistakes being made. All the same, he couldn't help but feel there was a certain rightness in taking a moment to feel the emotion and acknowledge the loss of a life, just so long as it didn't linger.

The vicar having completed his prayer, Dykeman pressed on with his questions, keen to learn as much as he could.

"You mentioned a Glass family. Do you know where they live?"

"Oh, yes, in that large house over there."

All four policemen turned in the direction the Reverend Beech was pointing, to see, about a quarter of a mile away to the south, partially hidden by trees, a large Georgian house.

"Was she a frequent visitor?" asked Dykeman.

"Rather so," answered the vicar. "Perhaps every second or third weekend. Sometimes, in the summer months, she would stay for a week or two at a time. There are so many glorious walks around here that one can enjoy when the weather is as fine as it is today."

"Did you know Miss Greene, yourself? Was she a member of your congregation?"

"Oh, yes, she attended church when she was staying here. The Glasses are regular church-goers, I'm pleased to say, and I can't imagine they would be so welcoming of any guest if they felt disinclined to join them at church. She was a sweet and lovely girl, Inspector. I don't believe I ever heard her say a bad word about another human being and certainly she never used any of that awful language young people like to use these days. I blame the Americans who stayed here during the war. They left behind many things, including their peculiar version of English."

"Was she at church this Sunday just gone?"

"She was. All the family were there. I do believe she had a rather fine singing voice too. That will be such a loss to our church."

"Was that the last time you saw her, at church on Sunday?"

The vicar thought for a moment before replying, "Yes. I'm quite sure I didn't see the sweet little thing again after that, until now. I wonder if the family will choose to bury her here?"

The Reverend Beech seemed then to be lost in his thoughts and Dykeman, sensing he'd extracted from Beech as much as he was going to get, for now at least, decided to wrap things up and instructed Shapes to drive Beech back to the vicarage. Edward Edwardes, meanwhile, now seemed rather keen to get back to the hospital so he could begin preparations for the arrival of the body of Emma Greene. And where was the ambulance, Dykeman wondered? It ought to have arrived by now.

It was as he watched Edwardes struggling to turn his big car around on the dirt track, so he could make for the main road, that Dykeman found his thoughts again returning to Sheila Delph, despite his best efforts to steer them elsewhere. More specifically, his mind returned to the day of her wedding to James Hardyman, that flash harry from her youthful past. He had forced himself to attend, so as not to offend Sheila, and he hadn't enjoyed a moment of it. It hurt to see her, looking so bloody beautiful, walk up the aisle and stand there, eyes staring intently into her beloved's while the vicar wittered on about the joys of matrimony and what a lovely thing it was. Everyone else there seemed as happy as could be, some of them weeping tears of joy, whereas the only tears he wanted to shed were ones of despair.

When the whole horrible thing was over, Shapes had driven him home in silence and he had stood in the middle of his vegetable patch at the back of the house knowing that life would never be the same again. His one chance at love had been and gone and he'd mucked it up. What an idiot.

Just to make matters worse, he now found himself working with the apparently inept and certainly boring Edward Edwardes, just about as far removed from the talented and beautiful Sheila as could possibly be. What on earth had he done to deserve this? He kicked at a large stone, but missed it and nearly fell over in the process. The irony wasn't lost on him.

Chapter Six

AS SHAPES DROVE THEM the short distance to Ashview Lodge, Dykeman ran an eye over the place. Although it wasn't so enormous as to be considered a mansion, it was still a pretty sizeable house, built from what he knew was the local ironstone, topped off with a slate roof. It was typical of the Georgian houses built right across the area, probably the best known feature being the three-by-four glass-panelled windows. This one, though, showed off its more upmarket credentials by having a portico at the front that was supported by a pair of matching pillars. At a guess, Dykeman would say it had half-a-dozen bedrooms and, if form was anything to go by, there would be a well-stocked library and a sitting room as big as the entire downstairs in his own house. How the other half lived.

The house faced west and, having climbed out of the Anglia, Dykeman found it was possible to see, in the middle-distance, the church spires and other taller buildings of Banbury, with the first hills of the Cotswolds rising up behind the town. In between and off to the west could be seen the clustered dwellings of other villages, with farms dotted here and there among the fields. Picturesque, thought Dykeman, if you liked that sort of thing, which was not what could be said about the stench of animal excrement that wafted in on the breeze from a nearby farm.

"Big house," commented Shapes, as he pushed the driver's door shut. "What is it with these toffs? They always seem to want to go around killing each other. Maybe it's having all that money. It leaves them with nothing else to do." He wrinkled his nose as he stood looking contemptuously at the large house.

"You could be quite right there, Shapes. Come on, let's see who's home."

The front door was opened by a slim, plain, though not unattractive, woman with shoulder-length light brown hair, whom Dykeman estimated to be in her mid-forties. She had a small face with an equally small pointy nose that, to the Inspector's mind, made her look distinctly Danish. He wondered if her ancestors might have made an unwelcome arrival in England on a long boat many centuries before.

The woman looked straight past Dykeman and, as her eyes alighted on his Sergeant, her face registered mild concern. It was the sort of look that appeared on the face of many people when meeting Shapes for the first time. Dykeman wondered if his Sergeant ever noticed this reaction and, if he did, whether he was by now immune to it.

"Yes?" she asked, in a matter-of-fact way, holding the door only slightly ajar, as if she feared they might attempt to force their way in.

"Good morning, madam. I'm Inspector Leslie Dykeman from Banbury police station and this is my Sergeant, Stanley Shapes. Are you the lady of the house?"

"I am. There's been an unfortunate incident up by the copse and we believe it may involve a member of this household." He looked past the woman into a large entrance hall. He could see no one else there. "May we come in?" he asked, before adding, "You might want to sit down."

The woman straightened at once, her eyes widening. Dykeman suspected she was doing a mental roll call, trying to account for the various members of the household, in an attempt to identify which one was most likely to be the subject of this unwelcome news.

"Oh," she said, hesitating. "Are you sure?"

"We are," replied Dykeman.

"I see." She looked from one policeman to the other and drew a deep breath before adding, "You had better come inside, in that case."

She led them through a pleasantly cool, double-height entrance hall, the walls of which were decorated with a number of paintings, all of them landscapes or clusters of flowers, and on into a sitting room at the back of the house. Dykeman's judgement had not been wrong. The room was big enough to accommodate four large settees, a matching number of armchairs and various other items of furniture. There were more paintings and an open fireplace with a typically Georgian surround, the highlight of which was a pair of matching columns sporting elongated, curved leaves, of a sort Dykeman had seen at many other houses of a similar age and style. An enormous vase of pink roses stood on a table near the doorway, their musk-like scent tickling the noses of the policemen as they entered the room. To Shapes the place reeked of luxury and the sort of well-to-do life-style that got his back up good and proper.

"Please do sit down," said the woman, gesturing towards a dark green settee to one side of them, before she sat in a matching armchair opposite.

"Could you tell me who you are," prompted Dykeman, keen to find out who they were talking to before he said anything else.

"My name is Susan Glass," she replied, bringing her hands together in her lap.

She was sitting on the edge of the chair, looking pensive and uncomfortable, and Dykeman was all too aware he had news that was unlikely to make her feel any better.

"This is your family home?" he asked.

"Yes, my husband and I live here with our children and my mother-in-law. The house has been in the family for three generations, though we no longer have the farmland that once went with it."

"We understand you have a regular visitor to the house. A young lady. Blonde hair. Pretty."

"Yes, we do. Most weekends," replied Susan, fidgeting on the edge of the chair.

"Can you confirm her name for me?"

"It's Emma. Emma Greene. She's..." Susan looked down at her hands and breathed in heavily before adding, "She's related to my husband, or so we're led to believe."

A peculiar thing to say, thought Dykeman, glancing at Shapes to confirm he was already taking notes of their conversation.

"Was Emma staying with you this weekend just gone?"

"She was, yes. She went home yesterday. She does rather come and go as she pleases."

"Yesterday, you say. What time would that have been?"

"I'm not certain. I saw her in the morning, some time before ten, then heard she had left for home. My husband usually drives her back and forth between here and her home in Evesham, but she sometimes prefers to use the bus. There's a service that runs between Banbury and Evesham once a day, I'm told."

Dykeman scratched the side of his nose. Having confirmed they were dealing with the right family, it was time for the part in such proceedings that he always hated: delivering the bad news. He steeled himself before pressing on.

"I must tell you, Mrs Glass, that the body of a young woman has been found in a ditch up by the copse at the top of the ridge and the vicar has identified the deceased as being Miss Greene. He could be wrong, of course, but he seemed quite certain."

Susan stared at Dykeman for a moment, as if she hadn't properly heard what he'd said.

"Mrs Glass?" prompted the Inspector, fully expecting tears to follow; from Susan Glass, not him.

She slumped back in her chair and held a hand up to her forehead, pressing it against the skin.

"Mr Beech won't be wrong, Inspector. He knows us all too well to make a mistake like that." The words came quietly.

"Would you like Shapes to get you a drink, Mrs Glass. Water, perhaps? Or some brandy?"

Her head moved side-to-side barely perceptibly. "No, thank you."

"Is your husband home?"

"No. He's at work." She had turned her head to one side, towards the nearest window, and her gaze focused, for a moment, on something outside. After a short while she brought her attention back to Dykeman, and asked, "What happened to her? I suppose she was doing something silly, if the accident resulted in her death."

"Well," Dykeman hesitated. "I have to say, Mrs Glass, that it doesn't appear to have been an accident."

She looked at him, her eyes wide. "Pardon?"

"I'm afraid we suspect Miss Greene was the victim of a violent attack."

Silence ensued. Susan Glass looked shell-shocked and Shapes was duly instructed to fetch a brandy for her. Having mumbled a barely audible thank you to Shapes, Susan continued to sit quietly, dabbing at her eyes with a hanky she had seemed to produce out of thin air. Even Dykeman's repeated encouragement that she take a good slug could not induce her to do anything more than take such a small sip she did little more than sniff the drink, which, to Shapes's mind, was a criminal waste. However, in response to yet another prompt from Dykeman, she finally regained some degree of composure.

"I must call my husband," she declared. "He'll want to come straight back. Is that alright?"

"Of course, Mrs Glass. Could I also ask you to instruct any other family members in the house to join us here. It would be helpful to be able to let everyone else know what has happened at the same time. We'll need to ask everyone a few questions as well. Standard procedure, in these situations."

"Yes, I understand." She wiped away a last tear and stood the drink on an ornate wooden table next to her chair. "You might as well use this room, if it's suitable for your needs."

"That's very good of you, Mrs Glass. It will do very nicely."

"In that case, I'll call my husband then ask everyone else to join us here."

As the door closed behind Susan, Dykeman turned to Shapes.

"Well, at least we're in the right place, Shapes. We ought to ask one of the family to confirm our victim's identity, just to be sure. Could wait for the husband to get back, I suppose, just so long as it's before the ambulance shows up."

"Odd thing to say about Emma Greene supposedly being related to her husband," prompted Shapes, tapping his pencil on his notepad.

"You noticed that too. Yes, we'll need to follow up on that."

"Why do people with money like such ugly things?" asked Shapes, making a face as he looked at one of the paintings on the wall opposite.

Dykeman looked at the painting. "I think they call that the Impressionist style. It used to be all the rage at one time, I believe."

"Style? There's a lot of words I could use to describe it, but style isn't one of them."

"Rich people buy things like that because they reckon the likes of you and me can't understand or appreciate it. Gives them a feeling of superiority."

"The same go for this carpet? It looks like someone has been sick all over it," added Shapes, looking over the side of his chair at the thick-pile wool carpet, which sported an intricate pattern of flowers and leaves that had been woven in a dozen different colours.

"I bet it's original Edwardian," suggested Dykeman, poking a foot at the carpet. "Top quality, which is why they've not had to replace it."

The door to the room swung open before Shapes could continue his derogatory assessment of the Glass's tastes in furnishings and décor. This irked him somewhat, as he felt he was just getting into his stride.

"That's all done," announced Susan, in a more confident tone than she had used prior to leaving the room. "James will set off from the office shortly and the rest of the family, those who are here, are on their way down."

"Excellent," replied Dykeman.

Susan stood by the open door, fiddling with the silver bracelet on her right wrist. Almost at once, other family members began to arrive.

A rather tall, slim young woman Dykeman took to be in her early twenties entered the room, hesitant at first, looking to Susan for some indication as to what to do.

"This is my daughter, Philippa," announced Susan.

The younger woman exchanged a welcome with the two policemen, then sat down on a settee, tucking her blue knee-length skirt under her as she did so. Dykeman couldn't fail to notice the look of expectation on her face and guessed that her mother had not told the others why he and Shapes were there.

"In we come, Michael," prompted Susan to a hesitant young man who seemed most reluctant to enter the room. "My youngest son, Michael. Do take a seat next to Philippa, darling," she added, steering him towards his sister with a gentle hand on the shoulder.

Dykeman suspected Michael Glass was not yet of age and he appeared to be a timid little thing, taking a wide arc around him and Shapes as he walked the short way across the room to where his sister was seated.

"There's just my mother-in-law to come," said Susan, stepping into the hallway, still fiddling with her bracelet, noticed Dykeman.

As they waited, Shapes smiled at Philippa. She smiled back. He then tried to engage Michael in the same manner, but the boy simply looked down at his feet.

"Here she comes now," declared Susan as she re-entered the room.

A short elderly woman, who immediately struck Dykeman as being of the stern sort, walked into the room without any hesitation. She fixed a piercing gaze on Dykeman as she did so, causing him to revise his initial assessment of the woman from stern to scary, not least because she reminded him both of a domineering teacher he'd encountered in his earliest school years and an elderly aunt, long since dead, who had made it her life's work to find fault in everything he did.

"Are these the men, Susan?" she in a voice that had all the command and certainty of an expensive Victorian schooling.

"They are, mother. Inspector Dykeman and Sergeant Shapes."

The two policemen felt an immediate urge to stand up, which they duly did.

"I trust they know what they are doing." She directed her comment at her daughter-in-law, but it was clear to Dykeman and Shapes that it was intended mainly for their ears. Dykeman fiddled with his tie. It was an old one, blue with thick black stripes. He had never much cared for it, but somehow hadn't got round to throwing it out.

"I'm sure they do," said Susan turning back to the two policemen. "This is my mother-in-law, Margaret Glass. She and my late father-in-law, Thomas, used to own this house before James and I took it on. It's ideal for raising a family."

Margaret sat down in the chair her daughter-in-law had been using, leaving Susan to stand alongside her.

Dykeman, thinking it best to remain on his feet, stepped a little away from the middle of the room, so he could better address the new arrivals. He clasped his hands behind his back and rocked once on his heels, so as to set himself to begin his piece.

"I am afraid," he began, in a voice that sounded more official than he would have liked, "that I have to inform you of a very unpleasant incident that has happened not very far from this house. It's one that involves a member of the household." He paused for a second, before continuing, "Approximately one hour ago, the body of a young woman was found in a ditch by the copse on the top of the ridge over there." He reached out with his right hand, the index finger pointing in what he hoped was more or less the right direction. "An initial identification has been made and we believe the woman to be Emma Greene. It seems likely that her death occurred some time yesterday and I must make it clear that her death was not a natural one."

He would have paused again at this point, to let the news sink in, but as it happened he had little choice other than to stop because Philippa promptly fainted.

"Oh, Philippa," called Susan, rushing towards her daughter.

"I think, Shapes," said Dykeman. "that another glass of brandy will be in order."

"I think you're right, sir. I'll bring the bottle."

Chapter Seven

AFTER A PERIOD OF MOTHERLY attention, Philippa Glass came to. Following the administration of a shot of brandy by her insistent grandmother, she was helped upstairs to her room by her mother and younger brother. With order restored and both Michael and Margaret Glass shipped off to the study, Dykeman and Shapes found themselves once more alone with Susan Glass. The Inspector thought she appeared to be holding up rather well, under the circumstances.

"Perhaps I should have let Philippa know beforehand that your news concerned Emma," suggested Susan. "The two of them were rather close friends and, as you saw, it's been a terrible shock to her."

"It's never a pleasant part of my job, having to inform friends and relatives of the death of someone they cared for," said Dykeman in a sombre tone, saddened by the distress his news had brought to Philippa.

"I can imagine. I'm not sure I could do it."

Dykeman rapped his fingers on the arms of the chair, allowing for a brief pause, before getting back down to business. "There are one or two other questions I'd like to ask you, Mrs Glass, if you don't mind. It would help us considerably if we can learn a little more about Miss Greene and her movements yesterday."

"Of course. I'm sure we all want to do whatever we can to help you find Emma's killer." Susan Glass looked down at her fingers as she wove them together. "It seems so strange saying those words. They don't sound as though they're coming from my own mouth. Silly thing to say, I suppose. But it's not as if you ever really consider the possibility of something like this happening to someone you know."

"That's a common reaction, Mrs Glass, and you're quite right, of course, it's not the kind of experience anyone ever expects to go through. It's one thing to read about murder in the pages of a crime novel or in the newspaper, but something else altogether when it happens to one of your nearest and dearest." Dykeman paused, looking closely at the woman sitting opposite him. "Are you sure you're alright to go on, Mrs Glass. We can wait until your husband gets home, if you prefer."

Susan shook her head and brought her attention back to the two policemen, unbinding her fingers and letting her hands sit softly in her lap. "No, please do go, Inspector. I think it might even help to settle things in my mind."

"Very good." Dykeman glanced at Shapes to confirm he was ready with his notepad and pencil. "To begin with, then, can you confirm what you know of Miss Greene's movements yesterday morning."

"I would have seen her first at breakfast, in the dining room. We normally all have breakfast together before those who work set off for the day."

"What time would that have been?"

"Seven-thirty start. Things are usually over by eight, occasionally eight-fifteen. I think it was a little closer to eight-fifteen yesterday, though Emma was one of the first to finish."

"And do you know where she went after that?"

"Up to her room, I think. We don't keep too tight a rein on her while she's staying with us, just so long as we know where she is. It wouldn't do to have to admit to her mother know we've no idea where she spends her time."

The mention of Emma's mother brought Dykeman's attention back to Susan's earlier remark about the status of the dead woman in relation to the Glass family. It seemed a good moment to return to it.

"You mentioned your relationship with Emma earlier and you seemed a bit uncertain or, perhaps, surprised about it. What exactly was the nature of her relationship with this family?"

"She was the daughter of my late brother-in-law, Robert. I suppose that makes her my niece." Susan feel silent and Dykeman sensed she was holding something back. She was certainly reluctant to say any more, that was obvious, and it wouldn't do, he decided.

"But you seem uncertain about your relationship with her."

Susan pursed her lips and, as she looked Dykeman in the eye, he thought he saw just the merest hint of something there; perhaps anger. "We only very recently found out she is Robert's daughter. Until then, we had believed her to be his ward. James will be able to give you the full story when he arrives. It came as quite a shock to all of us when we heard the truth and, to be quite honest, I still haven't quite taken it in properly. And now the situation has changed again. It's getting quite hard to keep up."

"I'm sure it is," said Dykeman, thinking it was nothing of the sort. But, there again, the woman was probably in shock. "As you suggest, we'll ask your husband for the details. Now then, you had just completed breakfast..."

"That's right. I passed Emma in the hallway at some time after that. Between eight-thirty and nine probably. I'm afraid I can't be more precise. Then I next saw her talking to Michael and our part-time gardener, Frank Barnes, a little after nine-thirty. I was upstairs in our bedroom, putting together a new flower arrangement, and I could see them in the garden, over there," she said, tilting her head just a little towards the garden.

"And did you see her again after that?"

"I don't believe so." Susan hesitated, her eyes looking towards the ceiling. "No, that's not right. I spoke to her, very briefly, in the kitchen. I can't imagine that was very long before she must have left the house."

"Left the house, you say?" Getting some idea of when it was that Emma departed was a crucial piece of information and Dykeman leaned forward a little as he asked, "Do you know what time that was?"

"No, I'm afraid not. Well, not exactly. It must have been somewhere close to ten, I would imagine. I didn't see her go out myself. It was my mother-in-law who mentioned Emma had left to catch the bus to Banbury. Apparently, she was thinking of making her way back home."

"And home would be where?"

"Evesham. She lives with her mother. James usually drives over to collect her and then drives her back, but occasionally she prefers to make her own way."

"I see. And did she seem upset or concerned in any way yesterday? Anything unusual about her behaviour?"

"Unusual behaviour? No, Inspector. She can be a little demanding at times, like all girls her age. Philippa's been no different. But I do think the news about Robert being her father came as even more of a shock to her than it did to the rest of us, which I suppose is hardly surprising, and I'm certain she was still coming to terms with it."

"I would be surprised if it hadn't knocked her sideways," responded Dykeman before changing tack. "Had you noticed any strangers in the area recently? Or heard about any in the village?"

"No, there's been no one here that you wouldn't ordinarily see at the house and, as far as I'm aware, there's been no reports of any odd-looking people hanging around the village. Why? Do you think someone might have been watching her?"

"At the moment, anything is possible. It's best that we don't write off any options, not until we've built up a fuller picture of what happened." Dykeman glanced at his watch. "Just one more thing for now, if you don't mind. I'd like to take a look at Emma's room before we leave, if that's alright with you."

"Of course. I'll show you up to the room whenever you're ready."

"Thank you, Mrs Glass. We'll do that when we've spoken to the rest of the family."

As Susan departed, Dykeman pondered on what they had been told and there was one thing in particular that already nagged at him. The changed nature of Emma's relationship with the Glass family must have had quite an impact on them all and it was clear that it was still something that unsettled Susan. Whether or not this change in circumstances had anything at all to do with the murder was anyone's guess, but he had a feeling it was something they would need to dig into a good deal before their job was done.

MARGARET GLASS SAT opposite the two policemen, both of whom felt an even greater sense of intimidating authority had now settled over the room. Her shoulder-length grey hair was thinning, but it was meticulously neat and tidy, not a strand out of place. The clothes she wore were all black, a sign she was still mourning her recently departed elder son.

Dykeman had been wondering how best to approach this interview. He had an overwhelming feeling that, should he put so much as one toe out of place, Margaret would show no mercy in putting him right. He always considered it odd, if not downright ridiculous, that he had no problem facing down the nastiest criminals but put him face-to-face with a woman like Margaret Glass and he lost his self-confidence in a jiffy.

"Well?" demanded the elderly matriarch. "Are we going to sit here all day without exchanging a word or do you have questions for me to answer?"

Shapes flinched, glad he wasn't the one asking the questions.

Dykeman snapped out of his musings, embarrassed that he had allowed himself to drift off like that. Not a good start.

"Yes, questions," he stuttered. "Well, then, let's see. Can you tell me when and where you first saw Emma Greene yesterday morning."

"I don't keep notes of that sort of thing, you know," she declared, in a manner designed to brook no questioning. "However, I saw her first at breakfast. We breakfast together in this household. There's none of this modern nonsense, with people popping downstairs whenever they feel like it. My grandchildren have been brought up correctly, for the most part, I am pleased to say. Though there are, of course, areas for improvement."

Shapes, in between scribbling notes, found himself rather impressed with the way the woman could sit up so straight. How anyone could do that for more than a few seconds at a stretch he found simply amazing. He preferred a more relaxed posture, though he realised he was in fact sitting up straighter than usual in her company.

"And after that, when did you see her again?" asked Dykeman.

"That would have been in this very room, Inspector. I often like to read a book for a while after breakfast and I prefer the view one gets from this here, as opposed to the one from the study. Emma had been in the garden and returned to the house. She came in through the French doors there. I believe she had been talking to Barnes, our gardener. She often takes an interest in his work. On this occasion, I believe they were talking about the hydrangeas we have in the walled garden."

Dykeman's own interest was piqued at the mention of gardening, his favourite pastime. "Fine plants are hydrangeas," he commented, with enthusiasm. "Do you have many here?"

"We do. I'm told, often, by the grandchildren they are old-fashioned and fussy, but I don't agree. There are few plants from which one can obtain a more impressive and sustained display of flowers."

Dykeman nodded his head in agreement. "That's true enough. I've one myself. In the front garden. Been there for years, it has." When no further horticultural comment was forthcoming from Margaret, he cleared his throat and returned to the matter at hand. "Did she seem in any way concerned or upset at any point?"

"Not especially. You should understand, Inspector, that Emma was a complicated little thing. I often felt that she had somewhat lost her way in life. I suppose that's not to be entirely unexpected, given the less than ideal upbringing she had, but she did not always make the effort she could have done to help address those deficiencies. She could sometimes be a rather challenging young woman to deal with." The words had a rather dismissive tone to them that wasn't lost on Dykeman, although he didn't allow himself to be influenced by them.

"Yes, I understand she recently found out that your elder son, Robert, was her father. That must have been a bit of a shock for her."

"I remain to be convinced as to the veracity of that claim." There was an unmissable undercurrent of irritation in the way Margaret spoke and her expression darkened markedly. "I fully expect we will find he was tricked into believing he was the father of the girl."

Dykeman found her response to the idea Emma was her son's illegitimate daughter an interesting one. Although it was easy enough to imagine that someone of her generation would have the kind of moral attitudes and ridiculously high standards that dominated in Victorian and Edwardian times, there was the not insignificant matter of the young woman having been brutally murdered. What's more, it had happened while she'd been staying in this very house. He wondered if perhaps Margaret considered Emma's death a blessing in disguise; a convenient way to put an end to a major social embarrassment. He had, of course, only just met the woman, and ought not to be too judgemental, but he'd already got the impression she was cold-hearted enough to see things in just such a light.

Ignoring, for now, the elderly woman's thoughts about the disputed father-daughter relationship, Dykeman returned to the movements of the previous day. "I believe at some point during the day Emma told you she was intending to catch the bus home, to Evesham. Is that correct?"

"It is. She informed me that she wished to return home and was not willing to wait for James to get back so he could drive her there in his motor car. Personally, I would have preferred her to wait rather than take public transport. You can never be sure who you might encounter when taking a bus."

Dykeman had a deeply ingrained dislike of what Shapes liked to refer to as toffs. Some people seemed to think they were a cut above the rest of humanity, whom they had a habit of looking down on from a lofty perch. Whenever the chance presented itself, he rather liked knocking such people off that perch. Did them some good to realise they weren't any better than anyone else, despite their money and their big houses. The Glasses were hardly aristocrats, but he got the distinct impression that Margaret had aspirations in that direction. He bit back the impulse to put her in her place, content there would be opportunities for that later, even if he had to engineer them.

"Why did she want to return home so quickly, do you know?"

"I've no idea. She didn't offer such information and I didn't ask. Though, of course, I do rather wish now that I might have made a discreet enquiry as to what was on her mind. I suppose it might have been possible I could have persuaded her to wait for James to return and then she wouldn't have set off on her own. And you, of course, Inspector, wouldn't be here now, asking me all these questions."

"Indeed," mused Dykeman. Well, at least the woman had finally shown some sort of a heart. "What time did she leave, did you notice?"

"It was perhaps a little before ten. I'm certain it was no later than ten o'clock."

A short, squat brass-bodied clock, sitting on the mantelpiece over the fire, chimed eleven o'clock. Dykeman rummaged in his mind to see if there were any further questions he could usefully ask the woman and decided there were not.

"Well, I think that will be all for now, Mrs Glass. I appreciate your assistance."

Margaret's demeanour softened somewhat, noticed Dykeman, and when she spoke again her tone was distinctly less abrasive. "I may not have looked entirely favourably upon Emma, Inspector, but I am not an unfeeling old has-been. To die at the hands of another human being is a terrible thing to happen to anyone. She must have been appalling afraid, on that hill all alone with her killer and unable to defend herself. I hope whoever was responsible for her death, you will find them so the courts can deal with them in the only way acceptable."

Dykeman got to his feet and straightened his jacket. "Shapes and I will be doing our level best, Mrs Glass, I can assure you of that."

Chapter Eight

"WHAT AN OLD BATTLEAXE," chirped Shapes, once Margaret Glass had departed the room and the door was safely closed.

"I've met warmer corpses in the hospital morgue," replied Dykeman, stretching his arms out in front of him. "Give the woman her due though, she showed some concern for Emma Greene at the end there."

"Wouldn't fancy having her as my granny. Can you imagine it?" scowled Shapes.

Dykeman yawned.

"I'm betting she's a big softy under that tough exterior," quipped Dykeman, grinning as soon as he'd spoken.

"Mind you, she did confirm that Emma left to catch the bus home. That's useful information, I'd say," observed Shapes.

"It is. We'll need to speak to the bus company. See whether or not the driver on the Banbury route can remember seeing Emma. Doesn't look like she made it to the bus stop, but we shouldn't go making assumptions."

Assumptions, Dykeman knew from experience, were dangerous things and best avoided at all times. They had a nasty habit of biting you on the bum.

"Who we got left?" asked Dykeman.

Shapes consulted his notes before replying. "There's Michael, the young lad, and Philippa Glass."

"I'd like to speak to Philippa next, if she's recovered. If she and Emma were as close as her mum says, then we might get some useful information out of her about Emma's relationships. Wouldn't mind knowing if she had any romantic attachments, for one thing."

"Want me to see if she's up to it?"

"Go on then. Bring the lad back if she isn't."

Shapes returned in less than a minute, accompanied by Michael Glass, who entered the room as reluctantly as before. Dykeman thought he looked a quiet lad, who most likely felt awkward in the company of strangers, let alone policemen. He'd have to approach the interview accordingly if they were to get anything out of it.

Michael perched on the edge of an armchair, his head angled away from the policemen and his gaze focused on the carpet. He was a thin, pale-skinned individual with the same pointy little nose his mother and sister possessed, noticed Dykeman. The red, curly hair wasn't something other family members possessed though, unless his father and brother turned out to be carrot-tops as well.

Dykeman planted what he hoped was a reassuring smile on his face before speaking. "A nasty business, this. Must have been a shock to you all."

Michael looked at him briefly, then away again, before he nodded weakly.

"Seems to have particularly upset your sister. Was she close to Emma?"

"Yes," came the softly spoken reply, the single word barely making it to Dykeman's ears. "They always got on well."

"They liked to do the same things, I suppose? Same interests and hobbies?"

"Mostly. Music. Horse riding. Clothes."

"Would I be right in thinking you're studying at university?" It was a hunch on Dykeman's part, but the young man appeared to be beyond his school years and there had been no reference to him working. It was worth a guess, if only to get Michael on to some safer ground and ease him into answering more questions.

"Yes. I started at Reading University last September, studying economics and philosophy. I'm due back next month."

"Enjoying it?"

"Mostly." Michael nodded, his gaze now transferred to Dykeman, which the latter took to be a positive sign.

"Shapes here insists he turned down a place at Oxford University so he could take up the life of a policeman, though I reckon he's lying through his teeth."

Shapes shook his head, his eyes raised to the ceiling. Michael smiled.

"Now, we're trying to piece together Emma's movements yesterday morning so we can begin building up a picture of her day. Anything you can tell us will be a big help. Can you help us with that?"

"I'll tell you as much as I can."

"Excellent. Now then, I understand the family always have breakfast together. Was that the case yesterday?"

"Yes. Grandmother has a flying fit if anyone fails to show up for meals on time, so we all make sure we do. Emma was there."

"And when did you next see her?"

Michael went quiet again, his shoulders sagging.

"We spoke in the garden. Briefly. She wanted to come back into the house."

"Did you see the gardener, Frank Barnes, when you were outside?"

"Yes," he nodded. "He stopped to say hello."

"We believe Emma left to catch the bus to Banbury, but so far no one knows what time that was. Did you happen to see her leave?"

"I was in my room, looking out the window, when she left. It was just before ten o'clock."

"Was she on her own? You didn't see her meet anyone outside the house?"

Michael shook his head.

Dykeman was relieved to get confirmation of the time Emma had left. If they were able to confirm that she never made it as far as the bus then it would go a long way to homing in on the time of death. He considered what other useful information he might be able to tease out of the quiet young man in front of him. The Glass family were already proving to be reticent about offering additional information.

"Would you say Emma's behaviour yesterday was in any way out of the ordinary? Anything on her mind, perhaps?"

"No, she seemed the same as normal. You'd be better off asking Philippa that question. If there was anything wrong, she would be the one to know." The words were again spoken quietly, as much to the floor as they were to Dykeman, and the young man wore a sad little look that suggested he would rather be holed up somewhere out of the way, all on his own.

"If she's up to it, we'll be speaking to your sister next. How did you get along with Emma? Was she the friendly sort?"

"I suppose so. We got along well enough."

Chatty sort, mused Dykeman.

"Did she have any friends in the village?"

Michael shrugged; not that his shoulders moved all that much.

"Some. No one close, not like Philippa."

Dykeman glanced at Shapes, who was busy jotting his version of their conversation in his notepad. The old adage about blood and stone came to mind where Michael was concerned and part of him wanted to reach out, grab the young man by the ear and pull on it until he was yelling with pain. That would soon get some life into him. But that was also likely to lead to trouble, back at the station, more's the pity. With just a little hesitation, Dykeman decided this wasn't the time to speak at any length with the fella; either he was normally sullen and uncommunicative or, perhaps more likely, was suffering the effects of shock. They'd try again some other time.

"Well, we'll leave it there for now, thank you. You've been very helpful, especially confirming the time Emma left the house, which will go a long way towards helping us work out when she died. If anything else comes back to you that you think we should know, you will contact us, won't you?"

Michael nodded. He left the room as timidly as he'd arrived, his movements almost silent, as if he was worried he might disturb someone.

"Odd fella," observed Shapes. "Think he's alright in the head?"

"I should imagine he wouldn't have got a place at university unless he's alright in the head, Shapes. He's probably just a quiet young man who's been shocked to the core by a murder. And it can't be easy for someone like him growing up in the same house as that granny of his. I bet she bosses him around something rotten."

Shapes grinned. "No wonder he's run off to university. I'd stay there all year round if I was him."

"Right then, time to see what we can get out of his sister. Seems to me she's our best chance of getting to know Emma. You wait here while I go and see if I can work my charm and get her down here for a few questions."

"Charm? You, sir?"

PHILIPPA GLASS WAS, Dykeman realised, a very different character to her younger brother. Despite the shock and pain it was clear she was feeling, she couldn't completely keep a lid on her outgoing personality. It showed through in a half-formed smile of welcome and in lively eyes, despite the tears that still lingered. Dykeman felt instantly hopeful they would get a good deal more helpful information about her good friend than they had from her brother. All the same, he told himself, best not to get too far ahead of things, just in case she crumpled into a heap when asked the first question.

"Good of you to join us so soon after the traumatic news," said Dykeman, easing Philippa into the interview. She was quite tall for a woman, maybe five and a half feet, he thought. And with her slim figure, long legs and straight blonde hair, hanging down to the middle of her back, she made quite an impact. He was a bit surprised not to see her wearing an engagement ring. Maybe, he thought, she'd had offers but hadn't considered them up to scratch. And why not? As far as he was concerned, she had every right to be choosy.

"It's quite alright, Inspector. It's such terrible news, of course, but I want to do everything I can to help you catch the awful person who took Emma from us." There was more than a hint of determination in Philippa's voice.

"I understand the family normally have breakfast together. Something your gran insists on, we were told. Did you have breakfast with the others yesterday morning?"

"I did. And you're absolutely right, Grandmother is very particular about such things. She's a lovely old thing, but some of her views are rather old fashioned. Mother and father prefer to take the easy way out and avoid arguing with her about such things, although I suppose I would do the same in their position. She can be a bit of a dragon."

"And was breakfast the first time you saw Emma yesterday?"

"No, I spoke to her briefly outside the bathroom a little earlier. She was on the way out as I was on the way in."

"And after breakfast?"

"I saw her here, in the living room. She was talking to grandmother. I think Emma had just come in from the garden. I was about to take my horse out for a ride, as the poor thing hadn't been out for a day or two. Emma and I agreed we'd meet in my room when I got back and listen to some records on my gramophone. We've very similar tastes. The sort of thing grandmother doesn't approve of," she added, smiling.

"What time was that, when you were listening to your records together?"

"Oh, we didn't in the end. When I got back from my ride, mother told me Emma had decided to take the bus back to Evesham. I was a little surprised, to be honest, but she was quite a strong-willed person and if she made her mind up about something there was little chance of changing it."

"So that was a sudden decision, Emma deciding to go home?"

"It was, as far as I was concerned. But, there again, as I wasn't here at the time it's difficult to know what made her decide to go home." Tears began to well in Philippa's eyes again and she dabbed at them with a hanky Dykeman could see was already very damp. She added, in a hesitant voice, "I wonder... if I hadn't left the house when I did, perhaps we would have listened to our records together and then she wouldn't be dead..." she tailed off into silence, lifting a stray hair away from the front of her face.

Dykeman felt a pang of sympathy for Philippa. Guilt. It was a common problem. There was usually someone or other in a murder case who decided that if they'd only done something differently, then their relative or friend would still be with them, living and breathing. He supposed it might be true every once in a blue moon but, mostly, it was wishful thinking. At best, all it would most likely do would be delay the inevitable; a determined killer would usually be happy enough to bide their time until an opportunity presented itself. The trouble was, the sense of 'what-if' hung heavily over some people, like the smell of one of those mouldy French cheeses.

"Have you any idea at all what might have made her change her mind like that? Seems a bit sudden, as far as we can tell."

"No, none, I'm afraid. She seemed quite happy when I spoke to her."

Dykeman tapped his fingers on a knee and glanced up at one of the unimpressive paintings before bringing his focus back to Philippa.

"We've been told Emma received some surprising news recently. That your Uncle Robert was her father. How did she react to that?"

"I think we were all astonished, Inspector. I know I was." Philippa tucked the damp hankie into one of the sleeves of her blouse. "Emma didn't want to talk about it at all at first. I know she was as surprised as the rest of us, but I think she also found it hard to believe that all these years Uncle Robert had kept quiet about it. There he was, taking care of her and her mother, supposedly at the request of a dead friend, when really he was her father. She tried not to show it, but I suspect she was also very angry at not having the chance to enjoy a proper father and daughter relationship."

"Did that news change anything else in her life? Was she, for example, romantically involved with anyone?"

It had occurred to Dykeman, given what they'd heard so far, that one possible motive for Emma's murder was love or, more specifically, a lover rejected after her change of circumstances. Love and lust, he well knew, were right up there with greed and revenge when it came to motives for murder.

Philippa grimaced and rubbed the palms of her hands on her thighs. "He won't thank me for telling you this, but Michael has always had a soft spot for Emma."

"Ah," interrupted Dykeman, before he could stop himself. "That would account for his being so subdued at the news."

"Yes," Philippa nodded. "He's taken it really hard. I think she was his first crush and, like they say, those are always the deepest."

"Did Emma respond in kind, or wasn't Michael her cup of tea?"

"Michael tried very hard, maybe too hard, to persuade Emma to be more than a friend, but he never was her type, unfortunately, and, well, she was sort of seeing someone else." There was an unmissable note of hesitation in her voice as Philippa spoke the last few words.

Dykeman's eyes lit up. "You say 'sort of'. Bit of an on-off relationship, was it?"

"Well, I think it was nothing more than a bit of fun for Emma. She liked the attention. I suppose all women like a little attention from a man every once in a while."

Although he kept his thoughts to himself, Dykeman found it impossible to imagine that Philippa had any trouble getting more than a little attention from members of the opposite sex.

"And how did the young man in question see things?" he asked.

"I never saw the two of them actually together, but, well, from what I've heard I think he saw more to the relationship than Emma did." Philippa bit her bottom lip and Dykeman got the impression she felt a little guilty at having shared such thoughts with him.

"The course of true love never did run smooth," chirped up a voice from alongside the Inspector, before he could get his next words out.

Dykeman turned slowly to his right. "Thank you for those words of wisdom, Shapes," he said, his voice thick with sarcasm.

Dykeman turned back to Philippa. "And would you happen to know the name of the young man in question?"

"I do. It's John Perch. He works at the garage in the village."

"Excellent," declared Dykeman, pleased to have a lead of sorts to follow up. "And what kind of a fellow would you say he is? The friendly, well-behaved sort you'd be happy to bring home to meet your parents, or the bad sort you'd prefer your parents never got to hear about?"

"Well... he'd probably be somewhere in-between. He's been nice enough to me, but he does have something of a temper. I suppose Emma would have found it amusing to bring him back here for grandmother to meet, but I'm sure she would have been hoping to marry someone with better prospects."

"The rest of the family wouldn't have been too pleased with this young man getting a toe in the door, then?"

Philippa shook her head. "No. I shouldn't imagine grandmother would have allowed it. If Emma had done something silly and married John, she wouldn't ever have been able to bring him back here. But she never was going to marry him."

Dykeman was about to ask another question when a loud thud resounded off one of the large windows looking out on to the garden. He looked up but found nothing to indicate what had made the noise.

"Pigeon, sir," observed Shapes, in a casual tone, as if seeing a bird flying plumb into a window was a daily occurrence for him. "Flew straight into the glass. I reckon he's still on the ground now, concussed. Stupid bird."

"I see," replied Dykeman watching for signs of a stunned pigeon clambering up on to a branch or taking to wing. There was nothing to be seen of the bird. Dykeman scratched his neck, then turned back to Philippa. "Well, that will be all for now, Miss Glass. I appreciate you talking to us now, when I'm sure you'd rather have been left alone, and I can assure you that you've been a big help."

"You will get whoever killed Emma, won't you, Inspector? I can't bear the thought of the killer getting away with it." Tears began to well up in her eyes again and her words tailed off as she struggled to hold back the crying.

"We'll be doing our level best, Miss, I can promise you that."

As he closed the door behind the departing Philippa, Dykeman turned to his Sergeant and announced with gusto, "A lead, Shapes. A real, solid lead for us to follow up."

"You think this Perch fella might have got the old heave-ho and lost his rag?" asked Shapes, tucking his notepad and pencil back into his jacket pocket.

"It's possible," replied Dykeman, rolling gently back and forward on his heels and toes. "Plenty of other murders have been committed by a jilted lover. Anyway, prime suspect or not, at least we've got something to work with now. We've got a name on our list. It's also someone from outside the family who can give us their perspective on Emma."

"List, sir? Not much of a list with only one name on it." Shapes wrinkled his nose.

"Every list has to start somewhere, Shapes. Now then, after all that work, I wouldn't mind a nice cup of tea and some biscuits."

He was about to send Shapes off in search of Susan Glass when the sound of agitated voices reached them from the hallway. It seemed, from what Dykeman could make out, there was a new arrival.

Dykeman had only just manoeuvred himself to one side when, following a short, sharp rap, the door swept open. Into the room stepped a tall, slim man wearing a navy blue suit and matching waistcoat. From the look on his face, it was clear to the policemen that he was racked with anxiety and apprehension. He stopped almost at once and turned to Dykeman.

"Inspector Dykeman?" The voice betrayed the man's nervous state.

"I am he."

"James Glass. My wife, Susan, called me at work to give me the terrible news. I got here as soon as I could."

Chapter Nine

JAMES GLASS DROPPED himself into the same chair that had been used by the other members of the family who had already been interviewed. He brought his hands together on his belly, stretched out his legs, crossed, then re-crossed his feet, and finally decided to pull his legs up against the front of the chair. Little beads of sweet glistened at his temples and he began to rub his thumbs together as he spoke. "I can't believe this," he said, with the slightest tremble in his voice. "Are you sure it's Emma?"

"We believe so, yes. The Reverend Beech was good enough to make an identification and he was very certain it's Emma. All the same, we'd like you to confirm that before we leave, if you don't mind."

James closed his eyes for a moment and gently nodded.

"On the way here, I was praying it was all some horrendous mistake and I'd get back home to find it was some other poor young woman lying in the bottom of that ditch." He shook his head. "Christ knows how her mother's going to take it. Emma was her only child."

"We can arrange for our colleagues on the Worcestershire Constabulary to inform Mrs Greene. They'll need to speak to her anyway. Have you got an address for her?"

"Of course."

Shapes scribbled in his notepad as James gave him an address in Evesham.

"Is Mrs Greene married?" Dykeman asked.

"She's divorced. It was just the two of them. Her and Emma."

"We'd best let the Worcestershire force know that, Shapes."

"Sir."

Dykeman turned back to James Glass. "We've started piecing together a picture of Emma's movements yesterday, but it would be a great help to know more about Emma herself, including the relationship with your brother, if you don't mind."

James puffed out his cheeks. "Where to begin? Well, I suppose we might as well start at the beginning. My brother, Robert, had always led us to believe Emma was the illegitimate daughter of a close friend of his and Jane Greene. Supposedly, shortly after this friend died from his wounds in the war, Robert received a sealed letter from a firm of solicitors. The letter was from this friend and it asked Robert to take care of Emma until she came of age. It seemed the chap didn't have a great deal of money to leave and he couldn't face the thought of Emma and her mother being left to struggle through life, should he not see out the fighting safely. Well, Robert always was the sort of man you could rely on in such a situation, so it never came as a surprise to any of us that he accepted his friend's request. He provided Emma and her mother with a modest allowance each month and took care of any unavoidable one-off bills that cropped up."

"Was your brother married?"

"He was. To Patricia. She was a wonderful woman, but she was unable to have children; ironically, as it turned out. She took a long time to get over that diagnosis but, while Robert was disappointed, he seemed to just take it on the chin and move on. Patricia died in a terrible accident in Egypt several years ago, when the hotel they were staying at partially collapsed. It was only blind luck that Robert was elsewhere at the time."

"Whereabouts did your brother live?"

"Middle Claydon in Buckinghamshire. It's a few miles south of Buckingham. It's where Patricia grew up and where they were married. And it was also convenient for Robert's work. He ran the Aylesbury branch of a transport business."

"I suppose you would have seen quite a lot of your brother, then?"

"Yes. We're a pretty tight-knit family and I can't imagine any of us would ever want to move very far away."

"Did your brother bring Miss Greene here with him when he visited?"

"Often, yes, especially if he came to stay for the weekend. I think he saw it as helpful for Emma to be able to be with people close to her own age, rather than being forced to spend the time alone with him after Patricia died."

"Did Emma's mother ever join them here?"

"Very occasionally. She has a job in Evesham that can require her to work on Saturdays and, to be honest, I don't think she was all that comfortable here. It's not the sort of environment she's used to."

Dykeman understood well enough what was meant by the last comment; Emma's mother obviously hadn't been brought up posh. He wondered if the Glass household had looked down their noses at her, leaving her feeling so uncomfortable she'd decided to stay away from them.

"Would you say that Miss Greene was happy when she stayed here?"

James's left eyebrow danced upwards and his eyes briefly widened.

"Of course." There was a hint of surprise in his voice. "I can't imagine Robert would have continued to bring her if she hadn't want to come along. It's been quite a few years now, Inspector, and Emma isn't the timid sort, so I'm sure she would have spoken up if she'd ever had any reason to feel she didn't want to spend time here. We certainly enjoyed having her around. Especially Philippa, who loved having another girl to spend time with."

"What about outside this house? Did Miss Greene spend time with anyone else? Friends from the village, perhaps?"

"She certainly went down into the village on many occasions. It's a safe..." he rubbed the fingers of one hand against his forehead and puffed out his cheeks, realising how the words he had been about to utter were now inappropriate. Things had been changed forever by the tragedy. "It was always a safe place here," he said, the sadness he felt audible in his tone. "We never had any problems letting the children roam free over the countryside when they were growing up. That went for Emma as much as it did our own children. We told them not to do anything stupid, of course, or anything that would upset the farmers. But they would often head off out on a morning with food and water and not come back for hours."

"Sounds wonderful," commented Dykeman, not believing it for a moment, he being a man who much preferred to spend his time in the welcoming embrace of urban life rather than the smelly, empty and frequently dangerous countryside. Anyone who thought sheep were cuddly things hadn't seen one of 'em close up. "What about friends in the village? Anyone Miss Greene got on with particularly well?"

"I suppose there were a few children from the school that our own offspring grew up with that Emma would have known pretty well, but no especially close friends that I'm aware of."

"We hear she had developed a relationship of sorts with a young man from the village garage. John Perch. Do you know much about that?"

James shifted in his seat and thin lines appeared on his forehead as his eyes narrowed.

"It's something I'm aware of, but Susan or Philippa would be able to tell you more about it than me. To be blunt, I got the impression Emma was stringing the poor lad along. Not the most commendable behaviour, I suppose, but you know how women can be sometimes, especially when they're young. I imagine she rather liked the attention."

"Did Perch ever spend any time with her here?"

"He's been to the house occasionally but that never had anything to do with Emma. I have a small collection of classic motorbikes and sometimes use the village garage to carry out work I can't do myself. Perch has collected or returned one of the bikes on at least two occasions since he started working at the garage." James's brow furrowed a little more deeply and he looked intently at Dykeman. "You don't think he might be responsible for what happened to Emma?"

"I wouldn't like to say right now, Mr Glass. Until we've gathered more evidence, we have to keep an open mind to all possibilities."

"Of course. It's just that, well, it's hard to imagine anyone here in Brayfield doing anything like that."

"Well, let's not get ahead of ourselves. It might turn out to be someone with no connection to the village at all, other than they happened to be passing through when they bumped into Miss Greene. It's also possible our killer knew her in Evesham and for some reason or other decided to kill her here, maybe hoping to put us off their track." Dykeman turned to his colleague and gestured towards the notepad, "How we doing, Shapes? Keeping up with us, are you?"

"All ship-shape here, sir," came the mildly offended reply.

Dykeman turned back to James. "You have some part-time staff here, I understand."

"That's right. There's a gardener and a cleaner. Susan also occasionally brings in a cook to help out when we hold a dinner party, if there are more than half a dozen of us eating."

"They all local, are they?"

"Yes. From the village. We've used the gardener and cleaner for a few years now and they're both absolutely reliable, if that's what you're interested in knowing."

"Thank you, Mr Glass." Dykeman rapped his fingers on the arms of the chair as he weighed up his next question. It was time to shift things on to more sensitive ground.

"I understand it was only recently that Miss Greene discovered your bother was, in fact, her father. That must have been quite a shock to her. How did she seem to take the news?"

James's shoulders softened and the corners of his mouth turned down. He was silent for a short while before answering. "Just like the rest of us, Inspector, I should imagine. Absolutely stunned." The tone of his voice betrayed the surprise James still felt.

"You had no idea at all that your brother was Miss Greene's father?"

James shook his head. "None. I couldn't believe what we were being told by the solicitor. We all just sat there in stunned silence. I thought perhaps my mother might have known, or at least guessed, but she was just as ignorant of the truth as the rest of us." He paused, then asked, "How do you manage to keep something like that hidden from your own family for so long?"

Dykeman didn't reply right away, conscious of the emotion coursing through the other man's veins. He tried to imagine how he might react to finding out he had a niece he'd not known about before, even though he'd spent a good deal of time with her for most of her life.

"What about the terms of the will, Mr Glass? Did Miss Greene stand to benefit to any great extent?"

James's demeanour changed in an instant, noted Dykeman. The man opposite him visibly stiffened and his face took on a sour look.

"She was due to become quite a wealthy young woman," his replied, his words spoken somewhat coldly. "My brother was moderately well off. There's the house, of course, and a sizeable holding of shares and Government stock, along with some significant cash deposits. He also had a stake in a bakery firm in Banbury, which has been estimated to be worth around fifty thousand pounds, though I suspect it's worth more than that. Assuming Emma chose to take sound professional advice, I can't imagine she would ever have had to work another day in her life."

The significance of this news was not lost on Dykeman. With such a large amount of money at stake it immediately brought into play the possibility that Emma was murdered for her inheritance. That, in turn, rather changed his view of the people he had spent a good part of the morning interviewing. Who, he wondered, stood to benefit from Emma Greene's death? Would it be her mother, the Glass family or perhaps someone else they had yet to identify? Things were now looking very interesting indeed, he mused contentedly.

"You say 'she was due to become' a wealthy woman, Mr Glass. Hadn't she inherited her bequest yet?"

"No. Robert had decided she should inherit on her twenty-first birthday. He didn't say why. Maybe he didn't want her to come into the money until she was mature enough not to waste it all on frivolities or be conned out of it. You can imagine the sort of men who would have started sniffing around once she got her hands on all that money."

"And when would she have turned twenty-one?" Dykeman asked, fully expecting the date of Emma's coming of age was not very far away.

"Next April."

Not as soon as Dykeman had expected, which he found a little odd, though not overly perplexing. Maybe the killer was the sort who liked to get things done in plenty of time.

"Do you know who gets the money now?"

"I know you might be surprised to hear me say it, but no, I don't. With Patricia already dead and now Emma, I don't know if the money goes to her mother or to us, or perhaps it's shared between us all. There aren't any other immediate family members. I suppose I will have to speak to the solicitor."

Dykeman did, indeed, find it somewhat hard to believe James, but he ought not to get ahead of himself. For now, however, they were almost done. There remained a couple more things to clear up.

"Indeed. I think we'll also be needing to speak to this solicitor. What's his name?"

"It's Rich & Cueillettes. Their Banbury office. The family has used the firm for all its legal dealings since my parents were married. Always very capable and professional."

"Er, sir," came an embarrassed plea from Shapes.

"Yes, Shapes?"

"How do you spell that? Cruelettes?"

Dykeman was tempted to have a laugh at his Sergeant's expense, but the truth was he didn't himself have a clue how to spell the name, or pronounce it, for that matter. He turned to James, who put Shapes out of his misery by spelling it out, twice over.

"One more thing before we're done here, Mr Glass. Can you tell me your whereabout yesterday morning?"

"Of course. I had breakfast with the rest of the family. You've probably heard already that my mother insists we breakfast together. I went into the office around ten and was back home about three. I sometimes prefer to bring paperwork home with me when there's nothing else to keep me in the office."

"There are people at your office who can confirm that?"

"Indeed. The office was busy, so there will be plenty of people who saw me come and go."

"Very good." Dykeman turned back to Shapes. "Anything I've missed, Shapes?"

"No, sir. Nothing else I can think of."

"Which just leaves the formal identification, I'm afraid, Mr Glass."

James closed his eyes for a moment and breathed out heavily. "I'm ready."

Chapter Ten

THERE HAD BEEN NO UNEXPECTED drama when it came to the moment when which James Glass looked down at the dead woman lying in the bottom of the ditch. He spoke briefly, to confirm it was his niece, then turned away and stood in silence, looking up at the sky. Dykeman thanked him and, the purpose of their visit completed, he led them immediately back to the house, where Susan Glass was waiting for them. She had made sandwiches and tea, which the policemen consumed with gusto. James, Dykeman noticed, slipped away without another word.

Having been refreshed with a seemingly endless supply of tea and the mountain of cheese sandwiches, Dykeman and Shapes decided to move on from Ashview Lodge. There was, in fact, one further member of the family to be interviewed, the eldest son, Stephen. He was, though, out and about on business and, there being no clear idea as to when he would return to the house, Dykeman decided to take their enquiries elsewhere. They would speak to Stephen Glass some other time.

As their car reached the top of the ridge near to the scene of the crime, the two policemen saw an ambulance had arrived to ferry the body of Emma Greene to Banbury

Hospital, where Edward Edwardes would carry out his full appraisal. Shapes chuckled at the sight of the two ambulancemen, aided by a couple of constables, struggling to lift the corpse up and out of the ditch in which he'd found himself trapped. However, he lost his sense of humour in an instant when, failing to watch the track ahead properly, he steered the car over a particularly nasty pothole, subjecting himself and his boss to a bone-jarring shaking that brought forth some colourful language from the embarrassed Sergeant.

James Glass had told them the garage John Perch worked at was at the far end of the High Street, which meant all they had to do was follow the main road into the centre of the village. As they trundled down the said road, Dykeman looked around him and concluded it was a pleasant enough looking place, if you liked that sort of thing.

The High Street passed down the right-hand side of a large rectangular green, sparsely populated with a handful of oak and ash trees. The war memorial, a base of ironstone blocks topped off with a large stone cross, sat in more or less the middle of the green. Most of the houses appeared to have been built between the seventeenth and early nineteenth century, some of them still sporting thatched roofs, though most had been upgraded to slate. A smattering of people were going about their business and a lorry making a delivery to the general store was parked at the roadside.

As promised, to their right, opposite the green, was a row of shops, the Red Lion pub and, at the far end, the Brayfield Motor Garage. From the road it looked a modest affair, a small wooden building at the front with a narrow entranceway to one side. Shapes opted not to tackle the entrance, concerned he might find himself having to either reverse out on to the road or else turn the car in a narrow space, neither of which he much fancied.

"Nice little place," remarked Shapes as they stepped out of the car. "We could get a pint at that pub back there after we've spoken to this Perch fella." He rubbed his backside as he spoke, his bottom having started to feel the numbing effects of his having been sat down for too long.

"You can have your drink later, when we're done for the day. We've got to get over to Evesham next, then all the way back to the station, and I don't want you nodding off at the wheel," grumped Dykeman, trying to work out how best to gain access to the garage. "Looks like you have to go in through that side entrance," he announced, pointing at the wooden building in front of them. "Come on."

The two policemen found the owner of the garage, Arthur Lanes, sitting at a battered desk in a dimly lit office hardly big enough to accommodate a couple of thin people standing up. A short, wiry man with dark, thinning hair and grease-coated hands and forearms sticking out from rolled-up shirt sleeves, he looked up at Dykeman, in the doorway.

"Can I help?"

To Dykeman's trained ear, the garage owner sounded hopeful some new business was about to be dropped in his lap. It was a look that evaporated in an instant once Dykeman introduced himself and Shapes, then asked to speak to John Perch.

Lanes pushed back his chair and climbed to his feet. "He's out back, working on old Hocking's tractor. Wrecked the clutch on the top field, he did, trying to pull a fallen tree out of his barley." Lanes's voice was thick with the sort of countryside accent Dykeman always found hard to understand.

As the Inspector stepped aside, Lanes walked out into the yard and directed his attention at a small, black van, its rear end propped up on axle stands. "John, my boy. Some men to see thee." He turned back to Dykeman, "He in trouble again, is he? What's he done this time?" There was a note of irritation in the garage owner's voice.

Dykeman responded with a diplomatic answer that gave little away, "We've no reason to think he's done anything wrong, Mr Lanes. We're hoping he can help us with our enquiries about a friend of his."

"Some of his friends ain't the sort to be seen with, if you ask me, but I suppose that's his business not mine. So long as he shows up here on time and does his job right, I'm alright with the lad." He turned back towards the van and called again, this time with more urgency in his voice, "John, boy. There be some men here to speak to you. Where's you gone?"

Almost at once, a tall, well-built young man, Dykeman guessed was in his early twenties, stepped out from another doorway, this one set into the wall of the larger, brick-built building that sat behind the wooden structure. His short, brown hair was a mess and his face, along with pretty much every other part of his exposed skin and his clothes, was streaked with grease. He was trying, without much joy, to wipe the worst of the mess from his hands using a dirty scrap of material.

"Who's that looking for me?" he asked, his countryside twang laced with a hint of annoyance, noticed Shapes.

"These two policemen asking for you, they are," replied Lanes. "Come on, get yourself over here. They don't have all day, do they now?" Lanes turned to Dykeman. "I'll leave you to it. Don't suppose you want me hanging around."

Not waiting for a response, Lanes walked off towards the rear of the premises, saying something to Perch as they crossed. Whatever it was, neither policeman could make it out.

"John Perch?" asked Dykeman.

"That's me," answered the younger man, eyeing the new arrivals with suspicion. "What you lot going to blame me for now?"

"We're not here to blame you for anything," answered Dykeman, tempted to take an immediate dislike to the grumpy mechanic. Why did people always assume the police were there to accuse them of things? "We're hoping you might be able to help us with our enquiries. There's been an unfortunate incident up at Ashview Lodge."

"Ashview? What sort of incident?" Perch's brown eyes bore into Dykeman.

"It concerns a young lady we understand was friendly towards you."

Perch looked from Dykeman to Shapes, then back again, the skin at the top of his nose wrinkling. "Do you mean Emma?"

There was, noticed Dykeman, a very definite note of uncertainty in Perch's voice. Whether that indicated concern for himself or his would-be lover it wasn't possible to tell, more was the pity.

"It does indeed involve Emma," he replied, as he continued to watch Perch closely.

"What's happened?" asked Perch, a hint of uncertainty in his voice as he rubbed the greasy cloth absently-mindedly across the back of one hand.

"I'm afraid to say Miss Greene has died." Dykeman delivered the words without hesitation, keen to see what sort of response they elicited. When none was forthcoming, Perch just standing there in silence, the policeman landed a second blow, "Or, to be more accurate, she's been murdered."

Perch appeared to freeze, even his eyes stopped blinking. When his mouth did open again, the words he wanted to speak seemed to have trouble forming and it took quite some effort to force them out. Once he did, Dykeman hardly found them informative. "You what?"

"Murdered," repeated Dykeman to the wide-eyed mechanic.

"Emma? Killed?"

Dykeman could see from the contortions on Perch's face that he was struggling to comprehend what he'd just been told. Either that or he was a damn good actor. Best not jump to any conclusions, the Inspector reminded himself.

"Do you need to sit down, Mr Perch?" Dykeman asked, not sure there was anything to hand that would pass for a half-decent seat.

"No, I'll be fine," stammered Perch. He shook his head and looked down at the ground. "Why?" he asked, his words barely audible to Dykeman.

"Well, if we knew that, we'd have arrested the killer right away," answered Dykeman, at the risk of stating the obvious.

From behind the policemen came the deep, throbbing rumble of a passing tractor, the vibrations from which gave a quiver to them both; an odd sensation that neither was in a hurry to experience again. The noise was sufficient to bring a temporary pause to proceedings. By the time the sound had died away, Perch appeared to have recovered some of his composure.

"What happened?" asked Perch.

"Someone stabbed her," said Dykeman. "As far as we can tell, the murder happened yesterday, but we're waiting on the pathologist's full report on that. For now, we're trying to piece together her movements yesterday and we understand you and her were, what you might say, good friends."

There was a deliberate edge to Dykeman's words, one he hoped might elicit a strong response from Perch and thereby give them a clearer idea as to just how much he thought of Emma Greene.

"We was friends," offered Perch, his tone rather cold, thought Dykeman.

"Friends," repeated the Inspector, a slightly tilted eyebrow the only visible suggestion he thought otherwise. "Did you see anything of your friend yesterday?"

Perch scratched the back of his neck and seemed to find a sudden interest in the brickwork of the main garage building.

"Didn't see her yesterday, no," he replied, after some thought.

"You didn't perhaps so much as pass her in the street, maybe down here in the village?"

Perch shook his head. "No," he said, definitely.

Dykeman rubbed his chin. "How long had you and Miss Greene been friends?"

"Years. I used to see her around the village when she first started coming here. Good looking girl she was, even then. After a bit, we started playing together as kids. Usual stuff."

"So, you've known her a long time?"

"Suppose so."

"What if I told you we'd been led to believe that you and Miss Greene had become more than just friends recently?"

Shapes, busy writing in his notepad, found himself growing increasingly irritated with his boss's line of questioning. Perch was clearly being careful with his answers, which suggested there was more to things than he was owning up to, and once upon a time Dykeman would have gone in for the kill without any pussy-footing around. Now, though, he seemed to be letting Perch off the hook, just when it seemed he needed a bit of forceful handling. It had to be another sign that Dykeman had gone soft since he'd had to sit and watch Sheila Delph being swept off her feet by another man. These were worrying times, indeed, and the sooner they came to an end the better."

Perch sniffed and wiped the back of one hand across his chin, looking briefly at the notepad Shapes held in his hand.

"Might have," he volunteered.

"Might or were?" prompted Dykeman, a little more forcefully.

Perch shifted on his feet.

"I reckon she might have been expecting me to propose to her," added Perch, sounding as though he was expecting a challenge on the matter.

"Marry you, eh?" queried Dykeman. "And what makes you say that?"

"Well, she had a thing for me, she did. Said so herself. It's why I'm so shocked," he added, without a great deal of sincerity, as far as Dykeman was concerned.

"Had the two of you been courting, then?

"Yeah, you could say we'd been courting, sort of."

"Common knowledge, was it?"

"People roundabouts might have known, not that I went around boasting about it. Big catch she was."

There was more than a hint of youthful boasting in Perch's words and body posture. Dykeman couldn't yet decide if that was the result of heartless arrogance or worry; worry that he and Shapes might not be willing to believe a garage mechanic could win the hand of a beautiful, soon to be well off, young woman.

"You sure it's her?" asked Perch. "I mean, has someone from here had a look at her?"

The unexpected change in tack caught Dykeman off guard. They were back to the stunned and concerned Perch of a minute or so ago.

"It's her, I'm afraid. We've had a confirmed identification."

Perch blew out his cheeks and shook his head again. "I can't believe it. I really can't believe it. Who'd want to do that? And what for?"

DYKEMAN AND SHAPES left John Perch sitting on the small, battered wooden stool they had found in his boss's pokey office. He was still shaking his head in disbelief as they walked back to the car.

"What do you reckon, then, sir?" asked Shapes, across the roof of the Anglia. "Changed his tune a few times there."

"I don't think he's telling us the full truth, Shapes. But could he have done it? Hard to say. If Emma Greene really did have a thing for him, then why would he want to bump her off. On the other hand, if Philippa Glass is right and Emma was simply stringing him along, then who knows."

"Sounds like he's been in trouble before. Want me to see if there's anything on record?"

"Yes. Best see if there's any history of violence." Dykeman looked at his watch. "We're meeting Inspector Cranfield at Evesham nick at half-one. That ought to leave us plenty of time to get over there. You can drive. Give me chance for a nap."

"That's alright by me. I can put this little beauty through its paces," said Shapes, patting the car roof with affection.

Chapter Eleven

ALL IN ALL, SHAPES considered the journey to Evesham to have been a highly successful one. Just the two wrong turns on such a lengthy drive wasn't worth bothering about, especially since his navigator had been asleep for much of the time, only conveniently waking up as they approached the outskirts of the small Worcestershire town.

"Did you see those monkeys the Russians sent into space came back safe and sound?" asked Shapes, as he pulled out to pass a slow-moving van.

"What?" Dykeman wasn't sure he'd heard right. "Monkeys? Oh, the Russians. Yes, I did." He straightened up in his seat, loosening stiff joints, then rubbed his bleary eyes. "Why does anyone want to go putting monkeys in a spaceship?"

"I reckon we ought to volunteer some of the crooks we get down the station to go on the next trip. Tell them if they make it back in one piece they can have an early release for good behaviour."

Dykeman looked sideways at his Sergeant. It was, he thought, probably a good thing that Shapes had absolutely nothing to do with the Russian space programme.

"Grand idea, Shapes. I'm sure the Russians will be only too happy to take you up on the offer." Dykeman stared out of the car, trying to work out where they were. "We there yet?" he asked, not even certain they had reached Evesham, let alone the town's police station.

"Almost," replied Shapes, in a deeply satisfied tone. "The station should be somewhere on this road. On my side."

They were, by this time, driving along the High Street, flanked on either side by rows of shops, a smattering of traffic passing in either direction and a goodly number of the local population going about their business. To Shapes's observant eye, the place didn't look much different to Banbury, though it did seem to be a bit on the smaller side.

They had just passed a single-decker bus, picking up passengers from a stop outside a tobacconists, when Dykeman waved a hand in front of Shapes's face and called out, "There it is. Next to the library."

Barely managing to avoid having an eye taken out by one of Dykeman's fingers, Shapes looked hard at the buildings on his right, picking out the small, two-storey police station that sat back a short way from the road. The brick building looked a lot like an ordinary detached house and, without the big sign out front, it would have been easy to miss it. He pushed at the car's indicator stalk before turning into the small car park at the rear of the building.

"Right then," declared Dykeman, full of enthusiasm. "Let's see what this Inspector Cranfield has for us. I've never met him, but Sergeant Blunt has and he reckons he knows what he's doing, so we should be alright."

A LEGACY OF DEATH

Inspector Henry Cranfield was a tall, plain man with rather well-tanned skin and dark brown hair, plus a close-cropped moustache that decorated the skin above his top lip. Dykeman thought it made him look seedy, but there again he was no great fan of moustaches, so perhaps he was biased. Cranfield greeted the Banbury policeman with a firm handshake that, thought Shapes as he struggled to hold back a grimace, bordered on the excessive.

"How did you get on with the family?" asked Cranfield, as soon as the introductions were out of the way. He spoke with the last, clinging remnants of a Liverpudlian accent that he had done his level best to maintain since he had moved south with his wife nearly fifteen years before. It irked him grievously that both their boys had long since lost their own accents, having been mere toddlers when they'd moved.

"I'm not too sure about that," replied Dykeman, rubbing the fingers of his right hand. "It's a complicated relationship they have with the dead woman. Mind you, we did find out she was due to inherit a tidy little sum next year, on her twenty-first birthday."

"Ah." Cranfield's face lit up. "Now there's a thing. Does it look like one of them might have done it?"

"Too early to say. They don't seem like the sort to go around stabbing folk, but that, of course, means absolutely nothing. We've still got one member of the family to speak to and there's a young fella with a temper who the deceased seems to have been stringing along. And that's even before we think about suspects outside of the family and close friends."

"Got to say, I'm jealous," smiled Cranfield. "We've not had a murder on this patch since 1958 when a farmer's wife shot him dead with his own shotgun. We didn't even have to do much work on that one because the old woman handed herself in. She'd had enough of the grumpy git after fifty-four years of an unhappy marriage. Suppose it did away with the cost of a divorce."

"True," chuckled Dykeman. "A bit drastic though."

"Right, then," said Cranfield, "Down to business. I've got the mother, Jane Greene, in one of the interview rooms. I drove over to the family home earlier to give her the bad news and thought it better to bring her back here rather than have a bunch of police cars parked up outside the house. As you'd expect, she's taken it very badly. Calmed down a tad in the last half hour or so, but you'll need to go carefully if you're going to get much out of her at the moment."

"Fair enough," replied Dykeman, glancing at his Sergeant, who had a nasty habit of upsetting a good many people merely by showing his face on such occasions. "For now we're mainly trying to piece together a general picture of the daughter and her movements yesterday. We can always come back for a second conversation tomorrow, if she's not up to much today."

"Sounds like a plan. I suppose we might as well get on with it, in that case. This way gents."

Cranfield took them down a short, brightly-lit corridor. At the far end were two doors, one of which was marked 'interview room one'. Without pausing, Cranfield pushed the door open and led the two Banbury officers inside. A young, grim-faced WPC stood with her back to the wall to their left, hands clasped in front of her. Cranfield introduced Constable Simms to the two arrivals and a round of nodding heads followed. Sitting on a metal-framed chair on the other side of a small plain desk was a short, plump, auburn-haired woman, her head hanging down towards her chest and her hands gripping a sodden handkerchief. She looked up as they entered the room, her eyes red and her face streaked with tears. Dykeman thought she must be in her mid-forties, though it was hard to be sure, given the mess her face was in.

"Mrs Greene," spoke Cranfield in the softest of tones. "This is Inspector Dykeman and Sergeant Shapes from Banbury police station. As we discussed earlier, it would be most helpful if you could answer a few questions. Just a few things to help them with their enquiries. They are happy to come back tomorrow with any additional questions if you find it too upsetting to continue today."

Jane Greene responded with a silent nod of the head, at which Cranfield turned to Dykeman and Shapes and gestured towards the pair of chairs in front of the table. As they tried to get themselves comfortable, Cranfield took up station next to his WPC.

"It's very good of you, Mrs Greene, to talk to us at this time," started Dykeman, in a sombre tone. "I appreciate things must have come as a terrible shock to you."

She looked at him through her tears before asking, in a voice Dykeman found surprisingly assertive and focused, "Was it one of those bloody Glass people who did it?"

Caught off balance, Dykeman shifted awkwardly in his chair, attempting to eek out a little more thinking time. He wasn't sure what he'd been expecting her opening words to be, but it sure as heck wasn't what she'd just asked. Although it was framed as a question, he got the impression it was more like an accusation. That was interesting in itself and had already told him much about the nature of the relationship between Jane Greene and the Glass family.

"Very early days in our investigation at the moment, Mrs Greene. Certainly too early to start reaching any conclusions, even tentative ones," he replied, trying to sound like the voice of authority. "We will, though, be looking into every possible..."

"Did they cut her up badly?" Jane Greene demanded, her face all at once turned hard as stone and her eyes boring into Dykeman, who began to feel distinctly uncomfortable.

Shapes scribbled away energetically in his notepad, glad he wasn't the one asking the questions. He'd expected they would find Jane Greene in such a bad way they'd have trouble getting much out of her, but here she was, coming out of the stalls fighting. And she already looked to him like the sort of woman you didn't want to go messing around, not if you wanted to keep the use of both legs and everything in-between. He took care to avoid making eye contact with her, paying more attention to the quality of his note-taking than he usually would.

"The wounds," answered Dykeman, with a little hesitation. "are not, er, as bad as some I've seen. It appears she was stabbed two or three times, in the heart or thereabouts. Apart from that, your daughter had some bruises and cuts, I assume from having been pushed into the ditch where her body was found." He stopped himself from going further, not sure just how much information Jane Greene was content to receive and thinking he might already have said too much.

"Well, you bloody well don't need to look any further than Ashview Lodge for her killer," she snapped. "They never wanted her to get her father's money. That's why they did it, so they get all the money. And it's not as if they don't have enough already."

Dykeman was nothing short of astonished at the transformation in the woman sitting opposite him to the one he'd seen when he entered the room. He began to consider how best to amend his approach to what was a key interview. Apart from anything else, it seemed very likely he had an opportunity to ask more questions than he had been anticipating, without any likelihood of the bereaved mother breaking down, since her mind had clearly already moved on from thoughts of bereavement to ones of revenge. He wondered, briefly, what sort of revenge she might be prepared to consider acceptable recompense and then decided he really ought to focus on making the most of the opening he'd been presented with.

"We understand your daughter received some surprising information about her father recently, is that correct?"

Jane Greene looked away and stared blankly at the empty white wall to her left. After a moment, her gaze returned to the waiting Inspector. "Yes, she did," she said in a matter-of-fact manner.

"So, it's true that her father was Robert Glass?"

"Yes."

It occurred to Dykeman there had been another rapid change in Jane Greene's emotional state, but he couldn't decide whether she now seemed more confused or conflicted. Either way, it appeared she couldn't make up her mind how best to respond.

"That seems to have come as a surprise to the other members of the Glass family," he prompted, trying to prod at a soft spot.

Jane Greene shrugged her shoulders, as if to suggest she didn't care. Dykeman felt disappointed; he had been hoping for more of a reaction.

"Were you and Robert Glass the only two people who knew the truth?"

"Yes. Robert said that was best. I wanted Emma to know, but he insisted it was too soon."

"I see. We know he was married at one time, but why did he want to keep Emma in the dark for so long after his wife died? Seems a bit odd."

"Robert worried Emma wasn't grown up enough to cope with knowing. Said she could be told once she'd turned twenty-one and had become an adult."

Dykeman rubbed the stubble below his bottom lip. "And how did Emma respond when she was told the truth?"

"She went mad. Swore at me and called me terrible names for keeping it from her all these years and her only finding out after her father had died. She wouldn't listen when I told her it was her father who wouldn't let me tell her. She was going to move away from here. Told me she never wanted to see me again, she did. And after all I'd done for her, struggling to bring her up on my own."

The tears they'd seen when they'd arrived were long gone now, noted Dykeman. Jane Greene was hard as nails, if he wasn't mistaken. Like mother like daughter, he wondered? It was often the case and Emma's declaration that she wanted to leave seemed to indicate it.

"When did you and Robert first meet?"

Jane's hazel-green eyes fixed on him and he could tell from the small movements of her jaw that she was grinding her teeth. For a moment he thought she wasn't going to answer.

"During the war. I lived in Portsmouth then and he got posted down there for a while with his work. We met in a pub and took a fancy to each other. That sort of thing happened during the war, of course." She looked across briefly at Shapes, before adding, "To a lot of us, anyway. I fell pregnant but I knew he was married, so I'd have to bring the kid up on my own and I wasn't, you know, going to have it ended. Not right, that sort of thing. He moved me and Emma up here to Evesham after a bit, so he could be closer to her. I told people I was a war widow, if people asked about Emma's dad. Robert gave us a few quid every month to help pay the bills. Can't complain too much about that, I suppose."

"Did you ever think Robert's wife might have suspected the truth?"

"Don't reckon so. If she did, she never said anything. Or, at least, not so far as I know."

"Emma's father, I understand, started taking her to Ashview Lodge from a young age. Did you ever go with them?"

"A few times. But I could tell that stuck-up lot didn't really want me there. Probably thought I should have been working in the kitchen or scrubbing the floors." Fire danced in her eyes as she spoke.

No love lost there, thought Dykeman. Perhaps they did need to look more closely at the possibility one of the Glass family had killed Emma Greene. However, it also occurred to him that what he was hearing was only one person's point of view; what he could really do with next was speaking to someone who knew Emma well, but wasn't a member of either the Glass or Greene families.

"Did Emma have any especially good friends here in Evesham? Someone she might confide in."

"She could always confide in me," replied Jane, in a voice that suggested she'd just been offended. "There's one girl, Vicky Hemmings. They've been friends since primary school. Suppose she might be able to help you."

Excellent, thought Dykeman, that sounded like just the sort of person they needed to speak to. All in all, things had gone considerably better than he had expected. In fact, they'd gone very well indeed. They'd got some straightforward answers to their questions, a fair idea of the bad-tempered relationship between the two families, or some members of them, and now they had someone to speak to without any blood ties. An excellent little interview.

"Well, you've been very helpful, thank you, Mrs Greene. I shall contact Inspector Cranfield if anything crops up later and I need to speak to you again. I, er, imagine you will be wanting to see your daughter's body," he added in a tone he hoped sounded sensitive. "She will have been taken to Banbury hospital by now, but either myself or perhaps

Inspector Cranfield can help you with access, when you're ready, of course."

Anger subsided and fresh tears began to fill Jane's eyes. She started dabbing at them again with the sodden hankie. She went to say something, then broke down altogether, her body shaking as she sobbed uncontrollably. Cranfield directed WPC Simms towards the grieving mother before escaping from the interview room along with Dykeman and Shapes, neither of whom considered themselves the ideal person to comfort the bereaved.

With the interview room door closed, Cranfield turned to the two visiting policemen. "That went better than I was expecting," he said, his moustache dancing up and down on his top lip as he spoke. "What do you think?"

"I agree," replied Dykeman, trying his best not to stare at the amusingly wriggling 'tash. "I thought we'd not get much out of her and have to come back tomorrow, but once she got going she didn't seem to mind sharing her thoughts with us one little bit."

"Clear enough she doesn't get along with the Glass family. Did they feel the same way about her?"

"Didn't get much out of them about the mother, although I got the impression they won't be too upset if they don't ever see her again. They're a very different sort of people to her. Helpful, too, to find out a little of the daughter's background, though I'm not sure we can take everything the mother said at face value."

"No, I'd say not," agreed Cranfield, glancing at his watch, an expensive-looking gold affair, noticed Shapes. "Listen, if you've not got to rush back, there's someone else I'd like you to meet. I think she might be able to help you get a better picture of the daughter. If you'd like to speak to her now, while you're doing that I can see about tracking down this Vicky Hemmings. You might get chance to speak to her too before you head back to Banbury."

"If it helps us get a better understanding of what sort of person Emma Greene was, then we've got time. Thanks Henry."

Chapter Twelve

STANLEY SHAPES WAS less than impressed as he followed Cranfield and Dykeman out of the station and on to the High Street on foot. To his mind, exercise was definitely something best taken in moderation and reserved for those occasions when it was otherwise unavoidable. Fortunately, it turned out their walk was not a long one. Bergen and Bergen, a ladies clothes shop, was only some hundred and fifty yards or so away. All the same, by the time they arrived at their destination, Shapes was sure he could feel the beginnings of a strain developing in his left calf, leading him to the entirely reasonable conclusion that once they were inside the shop he would need to make it a priority to find somewhere to sit down and rest his aching leg.

Bergen and Bergen occupied one of the smaller premises on the High Street. It looked like it has been knocked around a bit over the years and Shapes found it hard to work out just how old the building might be. He was, though, quite impressed by the matching pair of floor to ceiling windows that flanked the glass-panelled front door. A small brass bell, connected to the top of the door-frame, rattled loudly as Cranfield pushed open the door.

Dykeman never felt safe, let alone comfortable, in a ladies clothes shop. They were far too feminine for his liking, especially the ones that sold embarrassing things like underwear. As they stepped into this particular shop, he looked with concern from side to side and front to back, relieved to find there were no bras or knickers on display. He allowed himself to relax, just a tad.

Before the door had clicked shut, a tall, elegant woman with long, burnished brown hair and a pair of brown-framed glasses perched on the end of her nose appeared from behind a rack of floral summer dresses. She smiled warmly.

"Hello Henry. Are these the two gentlemen you mentioned on the phone?" Dykeman couldn't help noticing that her voice seemed to manage the impressive feat of being simultaneously soft and welcoming, whilst also assertive and assured.

"Hello Denise. They are indeed. Inspector Leslie Dykeman and Sergeant Stanley Shapes." Cranfield half-turned to the two Banbury policemen and added, "This is Denise Bergen, owner of this fine shop and employer of Emma Greene."

Denise Bergen extended to Dykeman a slender, immaculately-manicured hand. As he shook it, he noticed she was wearing a perfume with a soft floral hint that he found rather appealing.

"Henry told me the shocking news about Emma, Inspector," said Denise Bergen. "It's hard to believe such things really do happen. Poor Emma. I do hope it was over quickly. It must have been awful for her."

"From the look of things, I would say she died pretty quickly," replied Dykeman. "Small mercy, I suppose."

"Indeed. Henry thinks I may be able to help you with your enquiries. I've known both Emma and her mother, Jane, for quite some time. What would you like to know?"

"I understand Emma worked here?"

"That's right. For the past eighteen months or so she's worked here part-time, three or four days a week, as need dictates. I have a small staff and we all do pretty much anything that is needed. Setting up displays, re-stocking, attending to customers. Whatever arises. In actual fact, Jane worked here for a few months several years ago. It wasn't really her sort of thing, though, so she found something else."

"How would you describe Emma?" asked Dykeman, keen to get an alternative, hopefully unbiased, view of the murdered woman. "What sort of person was she?"

"Well, most of the time she was a confident, out-going young lady who could be a good deal of fun to be around. Several of our regular customers had developed quite a preference for being served by Emma; they always found her so helpful and pleasant."

There was a little hesitation towards the end of the last sentence and Dykeman didn't miss it. "It sounds to me like there's a 'but' coming next," he prompted.

"I'm afraid there is. I wouldn't wish to overstate things, but Emma could be rather difficult at times. A little selfish and thoughtless towards others. I did come close to dispensing with her services on once occasion when she upset one of my long-standing members of staff, but I was always willing to show Emma more understanding than I would others. Life must have been difficult for her, growing up with no father around and a mother who, I'm afraid to say, sometimes seemed to show little interest in her daughter."

Dykeman's own interest was very definitely piqued by the last comment. "What makes you think Jane Greene had little time for her daughter?"

Denise carefully and precisely re-set her glasses, placing them a little higher up her nose. "Although Jane worked here for only a short time, she nonetheless felt free to make comments about her daughter's attitude and behaviour. I got the clear impression the mother was rather jealous of the attention her daughter got from Robert Glass."

Interesting, thought Dykeman. They'd heard very little so far about Robert Glass and his relationship with the mother and his daughter.

"Did you ever meet Robert?"

"Yes, on several occasions. He would sometimes bring Emma here to buy a new item of clothing. I couldn't claim to have developed much of a relationship with him, but he was always a pleasant and friendly individual and he certainly seemed to care a good deal about Emma. In fact, I was entirely convinced at first that he must be Emma's father, popping back now and then to see his daughter, and I only knew better when Jane informed me I was mistaken."

Dykeman and Shapes exchanged a look, but the Inspector was keen to get what he could from Denise Bergen before telling her the truth of things.

"Did he ever bring Jane here?"

The shop owner thought for a moment, her deep brown eyes looking into the space between her and Dykeman.

"Yes, I believe he did. Just the once. Several years ago. If I remember correctly, he bought Mrs Greene a skirt and a blouse. That's right, I can remember because she appeared to be rather ungrateful, which struck me as odd, especially bearing in mind the items were quite expensive."

"Anything else you noticed about Robert?"

She shook her head.

"As I said, although I knew him to say hello to, that was all our relationship amounted to. It did, though, upset Emma a great deal when he died. They had clearly become very attached to one another and I had to send her home on one occasion because she was too upset to continue working."

"Did Emma say anything to you about the terms of Robert's will?"

"No. Why, did he leave her a small gift?"

"Quite a large one, as it happens."

"Oh."

"So, she didn't tell you that he really was her father?"

Denise's eyes flickered and the fingers on both hands opened out into a fan.

"Good Lord. No, she never said a thing. Had she always known?"

"No. It was announced as part of the will."

"The poor girl. All these years and she never knew the man who kept showing up to help look after her and her mother was in fact her father. What a shock that must have been. But what," she hesitated, before continuing, "what about Jane? How very odd. Maybe that was why she and Robert didn't appear to be getting along too well when I saw them here."

"Very likely indeed," said Dykeman. "Well, you've been a great help, Mrs Bergen. It's the first description of Emma we've had from someone outside of the Glass family and her mother. It's certainly helped give us a clearer picture of what sort of young woman Emma was and her relationship with her parents. I appreciate you taking the time to speak to us."

"It wasn't a problem at all, Inspector. I'm glad I was able to help you."

As they walked back out on to the street, bright sunshine warming their faces, it seemed to Dykeman they were unravelling an increasingly complex web of relationships. One that would need to be carefully unpicked if they were to get to the bottom of this case. While there was a possibility the killer could turn out to be someone from outside the family, his gut was increasingly nudging him towards the idea that the more likely suspects were to be found amongst the members of the Glass family and, just possibly, even Emma's own mother. It was a teasing little challenge that he realised he was finding more and more interesting with each little step they took towards unearthing a solution.

Chapter Thirteen

BY THE TIME THEY ARRIVED back at Evesham police station, the three policemen had already debated the significance of the information they had just acquired from Denise Bergen and had agreed on two follow-up actions. For his part, Cranfield would extend his enquiries to include the local bus company in an effort to find out whether there had been any sightings of Emma Greene on the route to and from Banbury in recent days. Meanwhile, Dykeman and Shapes would make arrangements to speak to the Glass family's solicitors the next day, in the expectation they would be able to get more detail on the terms of Robert Glass's will.

As it happened, they had barely set foot back inside the station when Cranfield was informed by the desk sergeant that one of the constables had an address for Vicky Hemmings, Emma's closest friend. Said address duly retrieved, Cranfield led Dykeman and Shapes out to the station car park, batting away Shapes's offer to drive them to their next destination in their shiny new Ford Anglia. The rather elderly Morris Minor they were obliged to climb into did not impress the disappointed Sergeant one jot.

Number fifteen Gloucester Close was one of two dozen semi-detached houses that had been built in the early 1930s on a greenfield site on what was at the time the western outskirts of Evesham. Since then, the town had continued to creep further westwards in little steps. Even now, it was just possible for the policemen to make out a new building site beyond the houses that backed on to Gloucester Close.

As with its neighbour at number seventeen, number fifteen had, noticed Dykeman with a good deal of satisfaction, a lawn maintained to such an impressive standard it would have been near impossible to find fault with it, even had he got down on his hands and knees to carry out a close inspection. The same could not be said of all of the other nearby properties, some of which were rather neglected. The sound of young children playing spilled over from the rear garden of one house and the smell of cooked fish tickled at their noses, a development which inevitably left Shapes feel hungry.

The front door to number fifteen was opened by a woman Dykeman took to be in her very early twenties. Her long brown hair was tied back in a ponytail, exposing a pair of ears so tiny Dykeman wasn't sure he'd ever seen a smaller pair. The rolled-up sleeves of her blouse and the knee-length pinny that hid most of her blue skirt made it clear she had been busy doing housework prior to their interruption. Her blue-grey eyes sized them up, one after the other.

"Yes?" she asked in a voice that betrayed a definite degree of suspicion.

"Inspector Cranfield, from Evesham police station," replied the taller man, holding up his warrant card. "Would you be Vicky Hemmings?"

There was a brief pause before the woman answered. "That's me. Why?" She kept a firm hand on the door, which remained only partially open.

"We understand you are a good friend of Emma Greene. Is that correct?"

"That's right. We've known each other since we were little ones." She eyed Cranfield closely.

"I'm afraid I have to tell you that Miss Greene has been involved in an unpleasant incident and these two gentlemen, who are from the North Oxfordshire police force, are trying to work out what happened. You may be able to help them with their enquiries. They're trying to get a better understanding of Miss Greene and her family relationships."

"Oh," came the startled response, as Vicky Hemmings's hand dropped away from the door and down to her side.

"Can we come in?" asked Cranfield, anxious not to continue their conversation on the doorstep where those with big ears might overhear.

"Yes, of course. This way."

She led them through to the front room where the four of them took up all the seating on offer. The room was stuffy and a heavy wood-framed clock ticked loudly on the tiled mantelpiece. The smell of laundry soap was heavy on the air in the room, as it had been in the hallway.

Although Cranfield did his level best to break the bad news about her friend to Vicky Hemmings in as sensitive a manner as possible, the three officers were nonetheless obliged to wait several minutes for the distraught young woman to overcome her shock and for her tears to abate to a point where she was capable of answering their questions.

However, it soon became clear that she was determined to help them in any way she could to track down her friend's murderer; indeed, Dykeman found her determination so overwhelming that it left him wondering what might happen to the killer should they ever find themselves alone in a room with Vicky.

It was Dykeman who asked the first question, one he hoped it would be a simple matter for Vicky to answer. "What sort of a person would say Emma was?"

"She was lovely. So friendly and caring. She would speak to anyone. Outgoing, you'd say. She was the best friend I ever had."

"What about her relationship with her mother? How did they get on?"

"Alright, I suppose. Most of the time." She blew her nose into a tissue and dropped it into the bin.

"Most of the time?" prompted Dykeman.

"Well, her mum could be a grumpy so-and-so sometimes. I think she was jealous of all the things Robert Glass bought for Emma. Clothes, shoes, a nice watch he bought her from some posh jewellers in Stratford. They argued sometimes. Emma didn't always like her mum, not when she was in one of her moods."

"I see. Was it ever anything more than arguing?"

"What, like fighting, you mean?"

"That or anything else you can think of."

"No. They didn't fight. Not hitting each other type of thing."

"And what about Emma's father? Did she tell you she'd found out who he was?"

"Yes. Robert Glass. I was amazed. Why didn't he tell her before he died? What was that all about? I just didn't get it; why he made her wait all that time."

"I imagine he had his reasons," replied Dykeman, not willing to volunteer information unless he needed to. "What about Emma? How did she take the revelation?"

Vicky was silent for a moment, running a slim finger along the silver necklace that hung across her collarbone.

"Sometimes she was really angry. With her dad, I mean. She said he'd cheated her out of a proper father and daughter relationship. I think she would have wanted to live with him and not her mum if she'd known sooner. Other times, though, she was happy. She even laughed about it all one time."

"Laughed?"

"Yeah. It was the money her dad left her. She knew she was going to be rich. Said she'd be able to do whatever she liked, not what her mum or anyone else made her do. She couldn't wait for her next birthday. That's when she was to get her dad's money, did you know that?"

"We did. What about her relationships with men? Did the news about inheriting her father's money change any of those relationships? We know she'd been seeing something of a garage mechanic in Brayfield."

Vicky smiled. "Poor lad. He reckoned Emma was going to marry him. That's what she told me. But she said she was just having a bit of fun. Nothing nasty, just teasing him a bit. She wanted to marry a film star or a rock and roll star, like Elvis, not a garage mechanic. She said she told Perch to leave her alone, because he started getting too clingy."

Excellent, mused Dykeman. Here was confirmation he'd been hoping for. "When did she tell him that, do you know?"

"Weekend before last. She said he wasn't very happy. Called her nasty names."

"Did that bother her?"

"Didn't seem to, no. She had a thick skin when she needed to."

The discussion was, felt Dykeman, going rather well. True, he'd only just met Vicky and he ought not to fall into the trap of taking whatever she said as the Gospel truth, but she seemed to be a level-headed young woman, observant and willing to share her thoughts and observations. Her answers to his questions were starting to fill out their understanding of Emma and the world she had lived in very nicely. There was one further avenue to explore.

"What about the Glass family? How did she get on with them?"

"She liked Philippa. They got on very well. I think Emma would have been happy to spend all her time at their house with Philippa, because they liked the same things and she always said Philippa was nice to her from the start. Most of the others were alright, I think. The old woman always bosses people around, she said, and the parents were sort of alright."

Dykeman noticed how the look on Vicky's tear-stained face altered and the tone in her voice changed as she spoke about the Glass parents. "Sort of alright doesn't sound like it was altogether OK," he prompted.

She angled her head away and seemed to be mulling something over before she turned back to the waiting Inspector. "Well, I suppose there's no reason I can't tell you now." She glanced at Cranfield then back at Dykeman. Neither man said anything. "She didn't like the mother very much. You see, Emma quite liked the youngest boy, Michael, but the mum threw a right strop when Emma started spending more time with him. Emma got angry to begin with and kept saying how she'd like to push the mum out of one of the bedroom windows. But one day, when we met up, she was smiling her head off and said she had reached a new understanding with the mum."

Vicky paused and looked down at her hands, seemingly reluctant to say anything more.

"Did she say what this new understanding was?" asked Dykeman.

As silence enveloped the room, Vicky began a close inspection of the fingernails on one of her hands.

"Miss Hemmings," prompted Dykeman, his voice distinctly more assertive than before. Emma Greene was dead, for God's sake, so what did it matter now what her friend told them about her.

She looked back up at Dykeman, finding it hard to maintain eye contact. "Well... Emma said the mum offered her things if she would leave Michael alone."

"Things?" asked Dykeman, now starting to get a little exasperated. "What sort of things?" he pressed.

"Presents, I suppose you could say. Trips to the cinema, a new pair of shoes, that sort of thing."

Dykeman exchanged a look with Shapes. This was new, mused the Inspector. He wondered how far this arrangement went.

"Sounds like this wasn't a one-off," he prodded, eager to know more.

She shook her head before replying. "No. Emma was so happy when she told me, because she'd already made up her mind to get everything she could out of the mum. She said she'd ask for more and more things, or else threaten to start teasing Michael again."

As far as Dykeman was concerned, what he had just been told sounded very much like blackmail. It may have been on a smaller scale than the sort of thing you read about in the newspapers and saw in films, but it still came down to the same thing. He scratched the side of his nose.

"How long had this been going on?"

"A couple of months, more or less."

"And what did she mean by teasing Michael?"

"Perch wasn't the only man Emma liked to string along. She liked the attention. She wasn't a nasty person," added Vicky, in something of a hurry. She just liked men to pay her attention. We all do. I think I'd have done the same thing if I was as beautiful as her."

Dykeman couldn't help thinking there was a hint of desperation in the last comment. Vicky didn't want her best friend to sound like she'd been a nasty piece of work.

"Was it only ever little things that she demanded or was there ever a lot of money involved?"

"Only little things," answered Vicky quietly. "She really was a good person, Inspector. They should have been nicer to her, then she wouldn't have done that sort of thing, I'm sure about that."

Vicky had started to both sound and look a rather sad individual, thought Dykeman, as if the fight had started to seep out of her. He was glad, very glad, she'd told them about her friend's less than creditable behaviour towards Susan Glass, but it had clearly taken a toll on her and he couldn't help feeling sorry for the young woman. Given how helpful she'd already been, perhaps it was time to wrap things up for now with one final question.

"Were there any other men in Emma's life? Especially anyone she was seriously involved with."

"No. No one else." The words came very quietly now and Vicky had returned to gazing at her hands, which sat cupped in her lap.

Ah, well, decided Dykeman, they'd got plenty from her already and there was no reason to put the grieving young woman to any more trouble when all it was likely to do was upset her even more. For now they were done. He thanked Vicky for her time and understanding, making it as clear as he could that she had truly helped them in their pursuit of her friend's killer. His assertion didn't appear to do anything to lift the burden of guilt she was now clearly weighed down by, but time, he told himself, would come to her aid there.

As Vicky watched the three policemen return to their car and drive off, tears began to well up in her eyes once more and she noticed her hands were trembling a little. It occurred to her that after the initial shock at being told her friend had been murdered, the simple process of talking to the policemen had diverted her thoughts, re-directing them towards doing what she could to help catch the killer. Now she was alone, there was nothing to distract her any more and, as she shut the door to the outside world, she began to sob uncontrollably.

AS HE DROPPED THEM off in the station car park, Henry Cranfield promised to get back to Dykeman and Shapes as soon as possible with whatever information he obtained from the bus company. He was in an upbeat mood, not hesitating to let the two Banbury detectives know just how much spending a few hours working on a murder case had brightened up his day and, if there was anything else he could do to help, they shouldn't hesitate to get in touch. Dykeman was grateful to receive such an offer, since he fully expected there would be a need to revisit Evesham before the case was solved.

"He was a happy chappy," commented Shapes as Dykeman steered the Anglia out of the car park and on to the High Street.

"Fortunately for us. I don't like it when we have to get another force involved. Too many toes to avoid treading on and egos that get in the way. Not everyone's as easy going and understanding as we are, Shapes."

Shapes looked sideways at his boss. "Whose ego would that be?"

Dykeman ignored his Sergeant's attempt at a wind-up. "What do you reckon, then?" he asked, as he slowed the Anglia at a junction, taking care to read the signpost correctly. Didn't want to go making any silly navigational errors this soon on their drive back to Banbury.

"You mean, who do I think did it?"

"If you like."

"That garage mechanic, Perch. He didn't look the least bit happy she'd dumped him after stringing him along all that time."

"A jilted lover's revenge?"

"Sounds good to me."

"A definite possibility." Dykeman eased the Anglia through a right-hand turn before fumbling the gear change as he reached for second. "Bloody gearbox." He made a second attempt at second gear, pleased not to muck it up again. "You'd better get someone to take a look and see if Perch has got a record. In fact, they might as well do that for everyone we've interviewed today. Can't do any harm to build ourselves as complete a picture as possible. The whole lot 'em could be a bunch of crooks and gaol birds for all we know."

"Will do. Tell you what, though, I can't wait to speak to the Glass's solicitor, so we can find out how much loot this lot are fighting over."

"That, Shapes, is a very valid observation. Our meeting with them tomorrow should be most interesting."

Shapes sneezed, once, twice, three times. From the depths of a trouser pocket he produced a tatty hanky and blew his nose.

"What about the questionable arrangements our murder victim had agreed with Susan Glass?" resumed Dykeman. "Doesn't sound to me like this is a case of happy families."

Shapes stuffed the hanky back into his pocket and sniffed. "Yeah, that was a turn up for the books, alright. Emma can't have been the sweet little thing that vicar reckoned she was."

"Indeed not. You know, it seems to me, Shapes, we're dealing with a complicated young woman here; one who was badly scarred by her difficult upbringing. No dad around, or so she thinks. A so-called friend of her dad's, who looks like he spoiled her rotten. A jealous mum. And on top of all that, the family of this so-called friend, who resented having her around the place. Not much of a surprise, I reckon, if all that lot messed her up."

"She must have been nice some of the time. The vicar and her friend thought she was wonderful."

"I'm sure she was perfectly capable of being a pleasant young woman, when she wanted to be. We've met a few like her over the years, after all. Yes, I think she buttered up those she didn't have any need to dislike, but was perfectly capable of being a selfish, nasty piece of works when the mood took her."

"True enough, I suppose. Mind you, there's a lot of women like that, in my experience."

Dykeman was temporarily at a loss for words, wondering just what experience with women it was that Shapes had been referencing, since his attempts at getting close to any member of the opposite sex invariably saw them turn a nasty shade of green before running for the hills just as fast as their legs would carry them. Maybe it was something he had dredged up from his youth.

"I know we can't write off the possibility of her having been done in for some other reason, maybe an attempted theft or rape, but I'm coming round to the idea that it's this dark side to her character that's behind her murder. Somewhere along the way, she's upset someone so badly it's tipped them over the edge."

Coming off a sharp left-hand bend, they found themselves closing rapidly on a cyclist. Much to Shapes's disgust, Dykeman slowed heavily and gave the cyclist, a young bloke with short red hair, a very wide berth indeed as they passed him.

"Must have been something pretty bad to make them want to kill her. Anyway, like I said, my money's on Perch," said Shapes, before yawning.

"Well I'm keeping my powder dry until we've spoken to the solicitor," replied Dykeman, unwilling to commit himself just yet.

As they began to motor along a stretch of straight, open road, Shapes leaned back in his seat, resting his head against the body of the car, and looked out of the window. Fields everywhere. Boring, empty grassy fields. Why had Dykeman insisted on driving when he'd been having such a good time racing along the country roads? Dykeman never liked driving, not if he could avoid it. The grumpy old sod had done it on purpose, just to put an end to his fun. More fields went past. Shapes closed his eyes and his head began to fill with images of himself hurling a car round Silverstone race circuit, hot on the heels of Formula One champion, Jack Brabham. Another couple of bends and he'd have him. Then it would be a straight run to the finish line and the glory of victory. He fell asleep just as he pulled out to make a passing move on the great racing driver.

Chapter Fourteen

WEDNESDAY MORNING FOUND the world covered in a wet sheen that glistened in the warming sun. A steady drizzle had fallen for an hour or so overnight, leaving behind it a cool freshness that Dykeman had found especially pleasing when he'd carried out an inspection of the vegetables in his garden before heading into the station. The carrots were looking as good as they'd ever done. So were the runner beans and the beetroot. But the cabbages were still looking badly frayed at the edges, the result of his having failed to get them netted before the cabbage white butterflies started depositing their eggs; the caterpillars were greedy little so-and-so's and they'd done their worst before he'd noticed them. He'd have to be more careful next year.

He would, in fact, have liked to linger for longer, the postman having delivered the latest edition of the quarterly journal of the Banbury Vegetable Growers Association, an organisation of which he'd been a happy and active member for many years. On such occasions, if the weather was good enough, he liked to carry a chair into the garden and sit there, with a cup of tea, slowly working his way through the pages of the journal, with a particular eye for opportunities to improve the size and quality of his crop ahead of the annual Association show. Unfortunately, taking time out of a morning for such a pleasant activity didn't really sit well with him when he was in the middle of a murder case. It would just have to wait until later.

During his walk to the station he gave some more thought to life without Sheila Delph. He felt as if he'd finally come to terms with the truth of the situation, that he was unlikely to ever see her again and, even if by some miracle he did, it would still be in the knowledge that she was now some other fella's wife. That last bit still stung, a bit like he imagined it would do if he was to roll around naked in a field of stinging nettles. But that was just tough, he'd told himself, for the umpteenth time. She was gone and that was that. He reminded himself he had his work and his garden to occupy him and there was always Shapes to wind up and laugh at. Given time the pain of loss would slowly seep away and, who knows, one fine day he might find another woman he could admire from a distance and never do anything about.

He pushed open the door to the little office he shared with Shapes to find himself presented with the kind of sight that re-affirmed his belief in Shapes's ability to take his mind off the pain of losing Sheila. His Sergeant was sitting in his chair, his sock-less feet resting on the edge of his desk. In his right hand he held a small pair of scissors which he was using to dig out dirt from under his toe-nails.

"You're disgusting sometimes, Shapes, do you know that?"

"Morning, sir," replied Shapes, cheerily. "Have to make the most of quiet times like this to get these things done. Don't want to get trench foot."

He put down the scissors and rubbed the toes of his left foot, a satisfied look on his face, before starting to pull on a short black sock.

"Trench foot?" Dykeman shook his head and made his way to his own desk.

"Soldiers in the First World War used to suffer from that because they didn't take proper care of their feet. Nasty stuff it is."

Shapes dropped the scissors in the top drawer of his desk and began to pull on the other sock.

"They got trench foot from standing in two feet of rank water for days on end. It rotted their feet," pointed out Dykeman, as he scanned his desk for any newly-delivered paperwork.

"Can't be too careful about these things. Remember when Heffalump got that nasty rash on his backside?"

"That was a bee sting. An allergic reaction." Dykeman's attention was drawn to a short, typed note he could see was from the Chief Inspector. He picked it up. "Bloody Nora, what's he on about this time?"

"Economies. Says we're to drive the patrol cars more slowly so we use less petrol," sniggered Shapes. "Fat chance."

"Economies? He should spend less time and money entertaining anyone he thinks can help him get his OBE, or whatever it is he's after," grumped Dykeman, screwing up the memo and dropping it in the bin.

"Where we starting today, then? Back to the Glass family?" asked Shapes, as he swung his feet off the desk and slipped them into his shoes.

"No, it's the solicitors first thing."

"So it is. I'd forgotten about them."

Shapes thought about bending down to tie up his laces then decided to swing his feet back up on to his desk. It would be easier that way.

"Don't tell me you've finally learned how to tie your own laces?" grinned Dykeman.

Shapes glanced at his boss. Seemed his sense of humour was making a definite return. He picked up a hand-written note from of his desk and held it out for Dykeman. "This just came in from Bunch. He picked it out of the notes from yesterday's door-to-door sweep across Brayfield."

Dykeman stepped across the room and took the proffered note. He smiled as he read it. It transpired that a woman working at one of the shops on the High Street had seen Emma Greene getting on the five-past-ten bus to Banbury.

"Well, well, well, Shapes. Looks like Brayfield will be our second port of call this morning."

RICH & CUEILLETTES Solicitors were not a firm that either Dykeman or Shapes had needed to have any dealings with in the past. However, as seemed to be mandatory for all solicitors with premises in Banbury, they occupied a two-storey premises built of the local sandstone some time during the seventeenth century. The immaculately maintained lawn at the front of the building and the heavy oak door pointed towards the usual extravagances found at such places, mused Dykeman, as they walked up the short path from the Oxford Road. It was the sort of thing that got right up his nose, but he made his customary effort not to let that show; at least, not to let it show too readily.

It was nine-fifteen on the dot as Dykeman swung open the front door and the two policemen found the tall, imposing figure of Peter Rich waiting for them in the reception area. He whisked them off without delay to his office at the rear of the property. Large oak desk, plush carpet, shelves full of legal texts and journals, and the kind of comfy chair the likes of Dykeman and Shapes could never hope to have for their own homes, let alone their place of work. In other words, everything Dykeman would expect of a solicitor's office. A ripple of irritation ran up his spine.

"I don't believe we've meet before," said Rich, his voice a deep gravely affair that escaped from under a largely ginger moustache, so bushy it hid most of his mouth. His short curly hair was similarly coloured, as were the bushy eyebrows. It reminded Dykeman of a fictional character he'd read about during his school days, but he couldn't put his finger on who that was.

"We haven't," replied Dykeman, easing himself further into one of the exceedingly comfy high-backed chairs in front of Rich's desk. "I thought we'd paid at least one visit to every firm of solicitors in the town over the years, but seems I was wrong about that."

"My partner, Antoine Cueillettes, and I set up the firm thirteen years ago. We started out in a poky little building on Britannia Road. Horrid place, not at all suitable for giving clients the right impression, but needs must and all that when you've yet to establish a name for yourselves and money is tight." Rich reached for the phone with a large hand, hair sprouting from the back of every finger, as he added, "But I'm forgetting my manners. Can our receptionist get you a coffee or a cup of tea, Inspector? And you, Sergeant?"

"No, thank you. We polished off a cuppa before we left the station," replied Dykeman before Shapes had an opportunity to take up the offer, as he invariably did. "Didn't we, Shapes?"

"Sir," came the unimpressed confirmation.

"So, down to business are we?" asked Rich, leaning back in his chair, his enormous hands coming to rest on the front of his navy-blue jacket. "I understand you'd like to ask me some questions about Robert Glass's last will and testament. Is that correct?"

"We do," replied Dykeman, pleased they weren't going to waste time on small talk. "But first, I need to ask you if you're aware of the incident that took place at the Glass family home in Brayfield on Monday?"

"Ah, the murder of that poor young girl. Yes, I heard about it yesterday afternoon," said Rich in a sombre tone. "Terrible thing. Terrible. I can never understand what it is that drives someone to take another person's life, not even when they're desperate. But I suppose I'm fortunate enough to have a settled personality, rather than find myself struggling with the demons that plague some individuals."

Demons? It seemed to Dykeman there were a few of those involved in this particular case. Whether or not one of them had anything to do with the murder of Emma Greene was another matter.

"I take it you were aware of the contents of Robert Glass's will before it was read to the family?"

"Indeed. I personally helped him to draft it."

"What about the announcement that he was Emma Greene's father, did you know about that too?"

"I did. I must admit he was at first reluctant to tell me. Not entirely unreasonable, of course, as these sorts of things can be difficult to discuss with a third-party. But I pointed out that, if there was some particular reason he was intending to leave the bulk of his estate to Miss Greene, then informing me at the time we were drawing up the will would allow me to provide him with the most appropriate advice and ensure the chances of a successful challenge from the family were kept to a minimum. This persuaded him to put all his cards on the table. And I must say that, once he'd told me the truth of the situation, I was very glad he'd done so. Forewarned is forearmed and, in this case, we were able to take particular care with the drafting of the will."

"Did Robert anticipate any trouble from the family?"

"I believe he thought it possible, though hoped they would see sense, in time. I concurred, about the possibility of a challenge. It seemed a distinct possibility."

"And were all the members of the family here when you read out the will?"

"I believe so, yes. Old Mrs Glass included."

"How did they react to the news Emma was Robert's daughter and that she was going to get most of his money?"

"Stunned silence at first. I rather suspect they all thought they had misheard me. I must admit there was a part of me that rather enjoyed the drama," he smiled.

"And once they realised they'd heard you right?"

"Indignation. Denial. Frustration. Pretty much the full gamut of emotions you would expect in such a situation."

"And did anyone show a particular hostility?"

"The younger Mrs Glass was pretty outspoken. She was none too pleased with the modest sums left to the other family members." Rich began to tap the ends of his fingers together. "The older Mrs Glass simply refused to believe that her son, Robert, was really the father of Miss Greene. She dismissed it out of hand, like some inconsequential piece of tittle-tattle." He wagged an index-finger in the air, as he added, "I would say, though, the daughter was the most upset. There were tears from her and I think she alone appreciated the significance of the news to Miss Greene. I gathered from James Glass the two young women were rather good friends."

"Mm," was all Dykeman managed at first, as he took on board this fresh information. There was, he soon realised, something more that he would like to know and the carrot-topped solicitor was, he hoped, just the man to help him. "Did Robert Glass already have a will before drawing up the one we've been discussing?"

"He did, yes. It had been drawn up by another firm – it was before our time – shortly after he'd married. The initial reason he gave for drawing up the new one was the need to take into account his wife's death and their lack of children. By which I mean, of course, children they had together. I got the impression this had then prompted him to consider what he ought to do for Miss Greene in the event of his own death."

"Who got all his money under the old will, his wife?"

"That's correct."

"Was there much difference between the two wills when it came to hand outs for the Glass clan? I assume he left them something."

"He did. Small bequests, mainly for the children. But, no, there was very little difference in that respect."

Interesting, mused Dykeman. From what they'd been told, there seemed to be no reason there for one of the Glass family to put an early end to Emma Greene's life. Or was there? Did the solicitor have more to tell them? He leaned forward, his eyes fixed on the other man. "Who gets to benefit from Robert Glass's estate now? Emma Greene's mum, perhaps?"

Peter Rich shook his head. "No. For one thing, I have no idea whether or not Miss Greene left a will of her own. However, that is entirely moot. Since Miss Greene did not come of age, she never got to inherit her father's estate, because he stipulated in his will that she would inherit upon reaching the age of twenty-one. I should add that the money has been held in trust since Robert Glass died and would have passed on to Miss Greene on her twenty-first birthday. Quite a birthday present that would have been."

The solicitor quite deliberately left things there, practically purring as he spoke. He knew full well what Dykeman's next question would be but he was so enjoying himself that he preferred to string things out. Have the fun last a little longer.

Dykeman's eyes lit up and he felt just a hint of excitement spark inside him.

"In which case, who gets the money now?" he asked, already certain he knew the answer.

Rich held back a smile that he thought would look unprofessional but did choose to delay his response just a little, savouring the moment for all it was worth. It was, after all, a murder case the two officers were engaged on and here he was, currently the centre of attention, the possessor of information he well knew was crucial to their investigation. It was also tantalising to consider the possibility that it was a member of the Glass family that had despatched Emma Greene to an early grave and how, just days before, he had shared this very room with that individual.

"Since both Mr and Mrs Robert Greene are deceased and Miss Emma Greene died before she came of age, the estate will go to..." Rich managed to produce a rather feeble cough. "the estate will go to the Glass family, in the main."

"You're sure about that?" demanded Dykeman, fully aware of the significance of this information.

"Indeed, I am. The will clearly stipulates that in the event of Miss Greene's premature death the bulk of the estate passes to Robert Glass and his dependents."

Dykeman was about to ask for further details but brought himself up short. "You said, "the bulk of the estate" passes to the Glass family?"

"I did, indeed."

"So who else gets a payout?"

"There are several charitable bequests. The usual sort of thing for a well-off individual like Robert Glass. There is also money set aside for Mrs Jane Greene."

"Emma's mum?"

"Correct."

Dykeman and Shapes exchanged a glance.

"How much does she get?"

Rich opened a desk drawer and pulled out a light-brown envelope. "I removed Robert Glass's will from our files in anticipation of this sort of question," he said, sliding several sheets of paper out of the envelope. He scanned the final page with a well-practised eye. "Yes, here we are. Mrs Greene will enjoy the benefit of five thousand pounds, paid out in one sum."

He turned the page around for the benefit of Dykeman, who pulled himself forward to the edge of his seat so he could read through the relevant section himself.

"Five thousand pounds. That's quite a pretty sum of money," he commented. "She gets the money regardless of her daughter's death?"

"She does."

Dykeman pondered. It seemed they now had two clear possibilities as far as a potential motive for the murder of Emma Greene was concerned. To the initial motive of love, or more likely lust, they could now add greed; two of the oldest motives for murder there'd ever been.

"Has anyone challenged this will?" he asked, tapping the paper with a rigid finger.

"No one has, as yet, actually gone as far as to initiate proceedings, however there have been two enquiries from other firms of solicitors, both of them having been asked to ascertain the validity of the will" replied Rich, rather disdainfully thought Dykeman, who looked up to see an expression of mild annoyance on the face of the solicitor.

"The Glass family?" asked Dykeman, certain he was right.

"Indeed. Mr James Glass has been acting on behalf of the family; though, I should add, he made no secret of the fact he would be looking to challenge his brother's will. He said as much before they all left here after the will had been read."

"And you're sure it's watertight?"

Rich breathed in slowly, then took great care to angle his head in such a way that he was looking down his nose at Dykeman, as he replied. "As a professional yourself, Inspector, I'm sure you appreciate the care we take to ensure that the service we deliver to our clients is of the very highest standard. As such, you can rest assured that Robert Glass's will is, as you put it, absolutely watertight." He wrinkled his nose, then aimed a raised eyebrow at Dykeman.

The amused Inspector savoured the little show that had been put on for his benefit. He briefly toyed with the idea of encouraging an encore, but decided against, on the basis that, amusing though it might be for him and Shapes, it wouldn't do much good in helping them find their killer. Anyway, if he did persist, there'd no doubt be a complaint fired off to the Chief Inspector, who had a deep dislike of anyone on his payroll upsetting members of the town's legal community, with whom he liked to play golf.

"Nothing from Mrs Greene?"

"Not as yet," answered Rich, who began to subside into a more relaxed posture once more.

"Interesting," observed Dykeman, looking again at the sheets of paper laid out on Rich's desk and asking himself why the mother of the deceased had not made a move to challenge the will, since she stood to become a very wealthy woman if she should be successful. It was a thought that prompted one final question.

"How much is Robert Glass's estate worth?"

"It's not possible to be precise, since a large part of it consists of investments of varying sorts, but I wouldn't be surprised it is amounts to about half-a-million pounds."

"WOULDN'T YOU CHALLENGE this here will if you were Jane Greene?" asked Dykeman of his Sergeant, as they stopped in the reception of Banbury police station. He'd been itching to get that one, out but held off until then, reluctant to discuss the case on the walk back from Rich & Cueillettes.

"Too bloody right I would," replied Shapes, who had already given a great deal of thought to how he would spend half-a-million pounds, if it ever happened to come his way, though with no wealthy relatives there was very little chance of that. "What's she got to lose? Nothing, except spending a few quid on some solicitors and that'll not make much of a dent in the five grand she's going to get."

"That was my thinking too." To betting men like Dykeman and Shapes the odds seemed entirely favourable. "Maybe she's got something lined up and we just don't know it yet."

Shapes's eyes narrowed as he assessed his boss. "Your money's on Jane Greene bumping off her own daughter before moving in to grab all the loot for herself? Bit much, ain't it?"

"Don't be a half-wit, Shapes. She would have been better off letting her daughter inherit then topping her, if that's what she's up to. There doesn't seem to be anyone else Emma would leave her estate to, apart from her mum."

"So, you reckon it's one of the Glass family, out to stop Emma getting her hands on all that money when they probably think it's rightfully theirs?"

Dykeman didn't like to own up to favouring any particular suspect so early in a case, let alone to his Sergeant, who would jump at the chance to insist they had a little wager on the outcome. They both wanted the odds stacked nicely in their favour before making any such agreement and they were a long way from narrowing the odds on anyone. He decided to play for time by being evasive.

"I don't reckon to anyone particular right now, Shapes. Although it has to be said the Glass family do have a good reason for bumping off Emma, we can't write off her mum or the jilted Perch just yet."

Shapes recognised waffle when he heard it, but he knew better than to try to tie down his boss when he was reluctant to stick his neck out. Shame, he thought, still convinced it was Perch who did it.

Sergeant Stanley Blunt had been on front desk duty since seven-thirty that morning and it felt as if it had taken most of his time since then to find a constable to whom he could hand on an elderly couple who wanted to report a hit and run incident they had witnessed, involving a parked car and a water board van. Terrible, they'd said, how the driver of the van failed to stop and leave a note of his details. Typical of people in this day and age, Blunt had offered in sympathy, knowing that nothing else would do. The two old folk had still been muttering away as PC Rob Dartington led them off to take a statement.

This had left Blunt free to pass on a message to Dykeman. It was, he suspected, a rather important one. He picked up the small piece of paper with the note written on it and waved it at Dykeman.

"Inspector," he called.

Dykeman turned. "Morning, Blunt. Is that for me?"

"It is, sir. About your case, sir."

"Well, read it out, man," ordered Dykeman.

Blunt brought his eyes to bear on the hand-written words. "It's from PC Fry. Says he spoke to the woman who saw Emma Greene get on the Banbury bus on Monday morning. Says she's going to be at work in the Brayfield General Store all day."

"Thank you, Blunt. Well, then, Shapes, we ought to be getting along to Brayfield without delay. Another important conversation awaits our attention." He turned towards the exit, then paused, a hint of a smile on his face. "You can drive, Shapes. That trip back from Evesham yesterday gave me a headache."

Well, he couldn't deny his Sergeant the pleasure of driving for two days in a row; he'd be a right grumpy git all week if that happened.

Chapter Fifteen

THE BRAYFIELD GENERAL Store was flanked by a butcher's and a baker's, the latter boasting a front window display of cakes and pies that Shapes positively drooled over before Dykeman dragged him away.

"But couldn't I buy a couple of cakes for later?" asked the near desperate Sergeant, as he was bundled towards the General Store's front door.

"After we've finished in here," barked Dykeman, not sure whether to be embarrassed or annoyed at his Sergeant's pathetic behaviour, although he had to admit some of the cakes did look remarkably good.

The Brayfield General Store seemed to Dykeman to be packed with just about every item that anyone could possibly ever want to buy. In fact, the range of goods on sale was so comprehensive there seemed little reason for any of Brayfield's residents to go anywhere else to do their shopping, other than a desire for a change of scenery. It was busy, too. Women, mostly, and two young children who were doing their level best to escape from the control of an elderly man who had the most enormous eyebrows Dykeman thought he had ever seen. The place had a smell, one that the curious Inspector struggled at first to put a finger on. Then it came to him; it was the pungent, over-scented aroma of soap, being emitted by a hoard of bars that had been used to build a flawless pyramid on the far end of the shop's main counter.

A rather serious looking middle-aged man, wearing a blue and white striped apron and a white shirt, the sleeves rolled up to the elbows, stood behind the counter totalling up the bill for a young woman's shopping. All the while, he engaged her in polite if mundane conversation. Dykeman waited for the woman to say her farewells then stepped up to the counter, flourishing his warrant card.

"Inspector Dykeman from Banbury police station. Would you happen to be the owner of this fine shop?"

The other man peered over his glasses at Dykeman's warrant card, taking his time to assess its photograph, then looked up at the Inspector himself. He seemed to be content that all was in order.

"I am. George Watling. Third generation to own this shop and hopefully I won't be the last. What can I do for you, Inspector?"

"I'm looking for a Miss Ivy Davey. Is she working today, by any chance?"

"Ivy, you say. She's out back, Inspector. I'll fetch her for you."

"If you've somewhere private we could talk to Miss Davey, that would be very helpful," said Dykeman before the shopkeeper could escape.

"Privacy, eh. In that case, you'll be needing to use my office. It's very small but if it's privacy you need it's all I have to offer." He lifted the section of counter top directly in front of him and stepped on to the shop floor. "This way, if you please."

While Dykeman had been busy with the shopkeeper, Shapes's attention had been taken by the sight of one particular member of staff. A young, red-headed woman with a curvaceous figure and a pretty face was busy stacking tins of soup on a nearby shelf. She was, he thought, exactly the kind of tasty morsel he'd like to take away from this or any other shop. She looked over at the two policemen. Shapes grinned at her in what he considered to be an appealing manner. She made a face that reminded him of a sick baboon he'd seen on a school trip to London Zoo many years before, then disappeared into the back of the shop in an unseemly hurry. Once again, Shapes told himself, his chances with a lady had been ruined by the grumpy presence of his boss.

"Shapes," snapped Dykeman. "Come on or you'll get left behind. And what were you looking at, anyway?"

"Nothing. Just thinking about those cakes at the bakers."

The shopkeeper showed them into a room that was as small as he had warned. Dykeman decided it could barely have been larger than a wardrobe. One chair, a tiny wooden desk and some shelves above that, straining under the weight of a full complement of lever-arch files that were full to bursting. The air was thick with the stink of cigarettes, encouraging Dykeman to leave the door open as the shopkeeper left to find Ivy Davey.

If Dykeman had been asked in advance what sort of person he might expect Ivy to be, then, as soon as he set eyes on her for the first time, he knew his answer would have been wrong. As she squeezed into the office, his senses were overwhelmed by a rotund figure with a big smile, a large bundle of curly red hair and an effervescent personality. It was easy to imagine she never arrived in any room without being noticed by everyone there.

"Inspector Dykeman from Banbury police station," declared Dykeman, speaking across Shapes, who had managed to get himself wedged between his boss and their witness.

"How exciting," bubbled Ivy. "And who's your handsome friend?" she asked, her wide, round eyes fixed firmly on Shapes.

Dykeman wasn't sure he'd ever had to put so much effort into holding back a laugh. Shapes, handsome? That was a first. Next she'd be saying she liked his foul breath and unkempt hair, his flatulence and his nose-picking. Dykeman swallowed the mirth and settled for a grin instead.

"This is Sergeant Shapes."

Ivy somehow managed to move yet closer to Shapes, flashing her green eyes and rolling her heavy shoulders.

"We don't get many like you in these parts, Sergeant" she said, in a tone that made it plain she was very pleased to see him.

Shapes swallowed and tried, unsuccessfully, to lean away from Ivy, then fumbled with his notepad as he attempted to retrieve it from his jack pocket. Dykeman dug his fingernails into the palms of his hands and kept on grinning. He was on the precipice now; one more push, no matter how small, and he'd explode with laughter.

"What can I do for you, Sergeant Shapes?" asked Ivy, her considerable bust pressing up against Shapes trembling frame.

Shapes mumbled complete gibberish and went bright red. Before he or Dykeman could say anything meaningful, Ivy made the most of the opportunity this presented to ask a question or two herself. "What's your Christian name?" Her eyes continued to dance and sparkle. "Sergeant Shapes seems so formal in this tight space, don't you think?"

Since Shapes no longer seemed to possess the ability to speak and, instead, stood there mute and wide-eyed, Dykeman answered for him, in a tone that might just have betrayed his considerable amusement. "It's Stanley Shapes, Miss Davey. And he does like to be called Stanley rather than Stan by those he considers close friends."

"Stanley," purred Ivy, her eyes all aglow. "A real man's name is that, Stanley."

Shapes wondered if he was having some sort of out of body experience. The kind of thing he'd read about in The Daily Mirror, his favourite newspaper. All he'd been aware of when Ivy Davey had squeezed herself into the office and pressed right up against him was her considerable cleavage, the mass of curly red hair, large, round, green eyes, that bore into him like laser beams from Buck Rodgers's space ship and the smell of onions that appeared to linger about the woman. It seemed as if all his blood had drained to his feet, leaving him light-headed and glad he was pressed up against the office wall, fearful he'd otherwise fall down. Now, with Ivy's heaving bosoms pinning him against the wall, he felt as if he'd left his body and was looking down on the scene from above. Maybe he'd had a stroke and his spirit was hanging around, waiting to see if anyone had noticed.

"Right then," announced Dykeman, deciding gleefully there was no chance of escape for his Sergeant. "If you don't mind, Miss Davey, we'd like to ask you some questions about the statement you made to one or our constables earlier this morning."

"Of course," replied Ivy, her eyes not leaving Shapes for a moment. She lifted a hand to the Sergeant's jacket lapel, tugged it into place, then gave his shoulder a firm squeeze.

"Apparently," continued Dykeman, "You saw Emma Greene board the Banbury bus on Monday morning. Is that correct?"

"Oh, yes, that's right," answered Ivy, glancing for the briefest moment in Dykeman's direction. "I was out front, rebuilding the display of kitchen utensils we have on the pavement. They'd been knocked over again. And there she was, waiting at the bus stop just down the road. I know her, you see. All the regular staff do. I was just finishing up when the bus shows up and she gets on." Ivy's hand had now moved on to Shapes's tie, which she pushed right up under his chin, a place it had not visited for quite some time.

"What time was this?" asked Dykeman, wondering if his Sergeant would still be able to breathe.

"It was the ten-past-ten bus," she replied. "On time, as usual."

"And you're sure it was her?"

"Oh, yes, it was her alright."

"Did you happen to notice if she was alone when she got on the bus?"

"Oh, she was alone." Ivy fluttered her eyes once more at Shapes before turning her head towards Dykeman. "At least, she was alone when she got on the bus. But she wasn't alone at the bus stop."

The remnants of the grin that had been on Dykeman's face disappeared in an instant.

"A man, by any chance?"

"She was a pretty little thing, was Emma Greene. Had lots of men chasing after her." Ivy Davey turned her attention back to Shapes, tapping the end of his nose with a single plump digit. "She especially had that young 'un, John Perch, following her around like a little lost lamb."

"You're saying it was John Perch she was with at the bus stop?"

"I am, that."

"Did anything stand out to you? Did they look happy? Was he helping her with a bag? Anything at all?"

"Oh, they were arguing," answered Ivy cheerfully. "Or, more like, she was saying things and he was arguing. I couldn't hear what about, but it was easy enough to see he wasn't happy. When she got on the bus, he stormed off towards the garage. Has a nasty temper, does John Perch."

Dykeman rubbed his chin. This had been a more fruitful discussion than he'd been expecting. Perhaps Shapes had been right all along in seeing Perch as the prime suspect. Good job, thought Dykeman, he'd not succumbed to his Sergeant's suggestion they put down a little wager. The odds had just shifted, considerably.

"Was there anything physical? Did he, perhaps, try to stop her getting on the bus?"

"No, nothing like that. Emma got on the bus and he walked off towards the garage in a proper huff."

"And did you see anything of Emma after that?"

"No. That was the last time I saw her."

"Well, you've been incredibly helpful, Miss Davey. Shapes here will take down your formal statement while I have a word with Mr Watling."

Shapes spluttered uncontrollably and his eyes widened with fear. What the hell was Dykeman doing leaving him alone with this scary woman in this tiny little room? He'd never see the light of day again. For God's sake, how was he going to get out of this one? He panned his eyes right then left, but Ivy, it seemed, had already got all the options covered, and there was, in reality, just the one way out. She managed to push him towards the back of the room while simultaneously squeezing to one side, in order to let Dykeman escaped from the tiny office. Dykeman, the git, noticed Shapes, was grinning like a demented hyena as he glanced at Shapes on the threshold of the doorway. He'd get him for this. If it took him weeks to come up with something suitable, he'd get his revenge.

"Come and sit down here, Stanley, next to me," ordered Ivy, as she pushed Shapes on to the single chair in front of the desk. "Now then, where would you like to start?"

"Well, er... Miss Davey..."

Dykeman's shoulders were shaking with silent laughter as he ambled off towards the front of the shop. It was quite possible those were the last words he'd ever hear from Shapes. He'd give things twenty minutes or so, then go back to scrape up whatever was left of his Sergeant. He began to contemplate which of the station's constables he'd prefer to have as his new subordinate, now it looked like there might be a vacancy to fill. Ah, what a day it was turning into.

IN MATTER OF FACT, it was only twelve minutes later when Shapes opened the passenger door of the Anglia and slipped silently and slowly into the seat, his eyes fixed straight ahead. There was, thought Dykeman, a faint tremor about his Sergeant. Whatever could have happened? Ah, the mind boggled.

"Quite the woman, that Ivy Davey, wouldn't you say, Shapes?" asked Dykeman, as he started up the engine.

There was no reply from Shapes, who continued to stare silently into the distance.

"Cat got your tongue, Shapes?" asked Dykeman, feigning a casual demeanour. "Come on, spill the beans. What happened in there?"

"She likes cats," came the quietly spoken reply.

"And policemen," sniggered Dykeman.

Shapes turned his head towards his boss, something of a frown on his face.

"Is she married?"

There was a short silence before Shapes replied. "No. Widowed."

"So..." Dykeman nudged his Sergeant with his elbow.

"So what?"

"Did you ask her out? She looked pretty keen to me. Why do you think I went to so much trouble to make sure the two of you were along in that room?" Dykeman tittered. God, life was good right now.

"No."

"No? I'm disappointed in you, Shapes. The poor woman looked desperate. She'll have a proper complex now she couldn't even get a grumpy old sod like you to ask her out." Feeling rather deflated, Dykeman pushed the car into gear and pulled away behind a passing lorry.

"She asked me," announced Shapes in a matter-of-fact manner, his gaze fixed on the road ahead.

"Do what?" asked the stunned Inspector, fumbling second gear. "She asked you out. And tell me you accepted, Shapes. Please, tell me you accepted.

"I did," smiled his Sergeant.

Dykeman wasn't quite sure how he managed to keep control of the car at that point as he began laughing uncontrollably, his whole body shaking, and his eyes filled with tears of joy.

Chapter Sixteen

"SO, WHERE YOU TAKING her?" asked Dykeman of his Sergeant, as he pulled the car to a halt outside the Brayfield garage, mere seconds after leaving the General Store. He was barely able to get the words out amid the tears and laughter.

"The cinema," came the quietly spoken reply.

Dykeman wasn't quite sure he'd heard right. "You what?" he asked, wiping away some of his tears.

"The Brides of Dracula."

Dykeman's laughter spluttered to a stop. He pulled on the handbrake and took the car out of gear.

"Let's be clear, you really are taking Ivy on a date? A holding hands, gazing into each other's eyes type of date?"

"She didn't give me any choice." Shapes's voice was devoid of emotion, but his face betrayed the shock he had experienced.

"You old Devil, Shapes," boomed Dykeman, slapping his Sergeant on the shoulder. "I didn't know you had it in you. Well, I'll want a full report when you get back from that date. Better send my best suit off to the cleaners so it's ready for the wedding."

Shapes failed to rise to the bait, though Dykeman wondered if that was simply because he was in shock. Ah, well, he'd pick up the thread later. See what more fun he could have from this totally unexpected development. He fair bounded out of the car and then had to wait as his Sergeant emerged at something more akin to a snail's pace.

"Come along, Shapes, there's work to be done."

The garage owner looked both surprised and, thought Dykeman, a little irritated at seeing the two policemen again. He lingered over the cleaning of some mechanical part that the enquiring Inspector didn't recognise before grudgingly directing them to the back of the garage, where Perch was supposedly hard at work.

If the garage owner had been mildly irritated by their arrival then, mused Dykeman, Perch looked downright worried, which induced in the senior policeman the not unreasonable desire to know why that might be.

"There he is, Shapes," declared Dykeman. "I said he'd be hard at it, doing his best to earn an honest crust."

"Sir."

"Hello Perch. You got a minute or two?"

Perch had been leaning over the engine of a tatty and rusty Morris that looked to Dykeman as though its days as a viable mode of transport was surely at an end. Pulling himself fully upright, Perch placed a small spanner on the frame of the engine bay and wiped his hands on his dirty trousers.

"Er, of course, Inspector. Is it about Emma, again?"

"What else could it possibly be?"

"Er, yeah. I guess it would."

Dykeman fixed Perch with a beady eye. "It seems you weren't entirely open and honest with us yesterday, Perch."

The Inspector took a breath, hoping Perch might feel a little unnerved by the pause. "Fancy guessing what I might be referring to?"

Perch looked at Shapes, instantly aware what was being referred to and wondering how best to answer. He felt a knot tighten in his stomach and the taste of bile wash across the back of his tongue. He looked back at Dykeman.

"Er. Well... No, I don't know what you're talking about," he stated, in as confident a tone as he could manage.

"Pull the other one, Perch. It's got bells on it. You were seen with Emma Greene on Monday. We have a witness. A very good witness. And she says the two of you were arguing. Right bad mood you were in, by all accounts."

Perch glanced down at his dirty shoes. Bloody Nora, who had blabbed? He'd been landed right in it. Well, if someone had seen him and Emma arguing, there wasn't any point in trying to pretend it hadn't happened. He looked up, at Dykeman's shoulder.

"Yeah, well, we might have had a bit of a disagreement."

"A disagreement, you say. Sounds to me like it was a lot more than that. And just what would this disagreement have been about?"

Perch sniffed and studied the grease and dirt on his hands. "She dumped me. Reckoned she had better options than a garage mechanic once she got her hands on all that money from the will. Stupid cow didn't know what was good for her. I told her, she'd get taken for a ride by some wide boy out to get his hands on her money, but she just laughed. Said she could look after herself."

That was easier than expected, said Dykeman to himself. Now it was time to press home the attack. See just what Perch would own up to.

"A little bird told us you were expecting to marry Emma Greene. That right, is it?"

Perch looked away, something like a snarl appearing on his face.

"Well?" Demanded Dykeman.

"Might have been," replied Perch, sourly.

"Must have been quite a blow to have her give you the old brush off like that. Bit embarrassing, I'd say, especially when you'd already told half the village she was yours for the taking."

Perch's narrowed eyes looked at Dykeman from under a furrowed brow. Excellent, thought the Inspector to himself; Perch was coming nicely to the boil.

"She led me right up the garden path, she did. Won't be able to show my face down the pub for weeks."

Dykeman couldn't help thinking that here was a man with a possible motive for murder, especially if he was, as they'd been told, someone in possession of a foul temper. But did he do it? Was he even capable of doing it?

"When was the last time you saw Emma?"

"Monday afternoon. I saw her get off the bus from Banbury. I would have gone after her there and then, but I had to finish off the job I was working on, so I took the track up to the house later on. Wanted to have it out with her. If she wouldn't change her mind then at least I could tell her what a selfish bitch she was. But when I got to the house, the old woman told me Emma 'ad gone out horse riding, with

Philippa Glass. Don't know if she was telling me the truth or not, but what else could I do except come back here."

"Monday afternoon, you say," repeated Dykeman, immediately homing in on what he knew was crucial new information about the timing of Emma's murder. Crucial, that is, if they could trust Perch. They'd certainly have to check his story with Margaret Glass.

"Yeah. About quarter past one she got back."

Dykeman swivelled his head in the direction of his Sergeant. "We'll need to check that, Shapes."

"Sir."

"So, you didn't see anything of Emma after she got off the bus? Not then or up at the house later?"

"Nothing. The boss can tell you I didn't leave here 'til about two. And the old woman can back me up."

Dykeman turned things over in his head. Of course, it didn't put Perch in the clear just because there were people who could confirm those timings. He might have bumped into Emma on his way back to the garage, done her in, shoved her in the ditch, then carried on his merry way, although that would have been tricky if she had really been out horse-riding.

"What do you reckon, Shapes, we done with him for now?"

"Reckon so, sir."

Shapes had drawn a large, dark exclamation mark on his notepad right next to the sentence recording Perch's statement that he went after Emma on her return to the village. As far as Shapes was concerned, that was almost as good as an admission of guilt. Never mind all that waffle about what time he reckoned he'd run off up to Ashview Lodge. They'd soon show what a load of old twaddle that all was, once they'd checked up on things with the garage owner and the older Mrs Glass. Yes, as far as he was concerned, there was only one serious runner left in the field and right now they were about to enter the home straight. If only he'd been able to badger Dykeman into putting a couple of bob on things, he'd be looking at a tidy profit right now. Bloody nuisance that was, Dykeman keeping his hands in his pockets for fear he'd be made to look a fool.

Chapter Seventeen

DYKEMAN INSTRUCTED Shapes to park the car on the cobbled area in front of the old stables at Ashview Lodge. He wanted to see if they could approach the house from the rear, in the hope of catching off-guard whatever members of the Glass family happened to be home. Might as well reduce their time for dreaming up clever answers to his questions.

As well as members of the family, Dykeman had two other people on his list; the part-time gardener and the cleaner, both of whom he would make sure they interviewed in private, well away from the potentially intimidating gaze of Mr or Mrs Glass.

As Shapes stepped out of the Anglia, he noticed Philippa Glass leading a horse out of the stable block. It was a fine specimen, its pale brown coat glistening ever so slightly in the late-morning sun. It was keen too, pulling repeatedly at the reins. If it had been about to run in a race, he would have been happy to put a couple of bob on it. Each way, of course.

But it wasn't the horse, impressive sight though it was, that got the bulk of his attention. No, that went to Philippa Glass, whose tall, slim figure looked all the more appealing for being clad in jodhpurs and riding boots. God had made jodhpurs just for the benefit of men like him, as far as he was concerned and he found he couldn't help but stare at this wonderful figure of a woman. The occasional flick of her riding crop only added to her appeal. His day dreaming was brought to an unwelcome end by a sharp pain in his rib cage.

"Stop ogling, Shapes, and wipe away that dribble from the corner of your mouth. You're spoken for now, remember," added Dykeman, with something close to a snigger, as he turned towards the house.

The look of startled surprise on the face of Susan Glass was exactly the kind of thing Dykeman had been hoping for when he rapped on one of the glass pains in the French doors that closed off the sitting room from the outside world. She had been standing by the open doorway that led into the hall, talking to a woman Dykeman took to be the cleaner. That was good too, as he hadn't been sure whether or not the staff would be there. By the time Susan had walked across the room and opened the door, it seemed she had regained her composure. Dykeman was neither fooled nor disappointed by this. He was confident that, under her calm exterior, she was still feeling a good deal off-balance, which was exactly how he wanted things.

"Inspector Dykeman, how unexpected," declared Susan Glass as she held the door open so he and Shapes could enter the house. "Please do come in."

"Thank you," replied Dykeman. "I hope we're not imposing ourselves on you at an inconvenient moment," he added, surprising himself at how sincere he'd managed to sound. They were, he noticed as he looked around the room, the only ones there.

"Well, actually, I was..."

"Only, there have been some important developments," cut in Dykeman. "And we have some more questions to ask, starting with your staff. In private, it goes without saying." This time there was an undeniable firmness in his tone.

He had been as polite as he could be on their first visit, when announcing the death of a family member, but this one was going to be different. People had been holding out on him and Shapes. Some, it seemed likely, had even gone so far as to mislead, maybe even lie to them. That sort of thing annoyed him no end. He'd not go so far as to be downright rude, not unless it was necessary, but he would most certainly be more... what was the right way of putting it... businesslike. Yes, that was it, businesslike.

"Oh." Susan glanced at Shapes then back at Dykeman. "Do you mean you might know who killed Emma?"

"We have our suspicions, but more than that I can't say, for now." He scratched his chin. "Was that the cleaner I saw you talking to just now?"

"Yes. Beryl Bolant. She comes in three days a week. More often when we've been entertaining." There was, noticed Dykeman, the slightest hint of hesitation in Susan's voice, as if she was concerned by the possibility he might want to talk to the cleaner. Which, of course, he most certainly did.

"Excellent. Do you have somewhere me and Shapes can talk to her in private?"

"Well, she'll be in the kitchen now. It has a door, so I suppose you could simply close that. Would you like me to take you there?"

"No, we'll be fine, thank you." He went to move but then stopped. "Is the gardener around as well?"

"He is. Would you like me to send him along to the kitchen?"

Definitely a sliver of annoyance there, decided Dykeman. Good. People with the wealth to employ servants and gardeners never liked it when the police demanded to speak to them in private. It seemed to cross some unspoken line, one that considered them to be significant people in their own right, not that it bothered him in the slightest. What was their problem? Worried the staff might actually tell the truth?

"That would be very helpful," replied the Inspector. "Come on, Shapes, the day is now half gone and there's plenty still to be done. Nearly rhymes does that. Did you notice?"

Shapes merely shook his head and turned his eyes to the ceiling.

Beryl Bolant let out a little gasp of surprise when she turned round to see the two policemen entering the room. She had been washing up the remainder of the breakfast service, her mind on the present she needed to buy for her father's birthday on the coming weekend. She had hoped to get him a new jumper, but the one she had wanted hadn't been available in his size when she'd been into town to buy it the previous Saturday. The other ones she'd looked at just weren't right and that had left her in a bit a tizz. Ruminating on her predicament had ensured she was far too absorbed to hear Dykeman and Shapes approaching across the hallway.

Dykeman smiled, pleasantly, he hoped.

"Sorry to disturb you, Mrs Bolant. I'm Inspector Dykeman and this is Sergeant Shapes. We're investigating the murder of Emma Greene and have one or two questions for you, if you don't mind."

"Oh, I see," she said, not at all sure that she did. She dried her hands on her pinny then fiddled with her hair, as much out of habit as anything else. The mention of that terrible murder was very unsettling. She'd heard things said about it; bad things. Someone had said Emma had been slashed from head to foot, just as if Jack the Ripper had reappeared to launch another sickening campaign of murders. She'd also been told the police were convinced the killer had sacrificed her in some horrible Satanic ritual and were now busy trying to round up all those who had taken part. She'd hardly been able to sleep these past two nights for fear it might be her turn to be attacked next.

"We won't keep you long and it's nothing to be worried about. Just one or two things we're trying to clear up. It will help us narrow things down a little," said Dykeman, hoping to put the concerned-looking cleaner at ease.

"Of course." Beryl brushed a hand repeatedly down the front of her pinny in the hope of straightening it out, not seeming to have noticed that it was already as straight as it was ever likely to be.

"Worked here long, have you?"

"A few years. They took me on when old Mrs Sluice retired. Got so she couldn't manage the walk up here from the village, the poor old dear. Died last year, she did. Her husband, Arthur, hasn't been right since, not that you can blame him, of course. Who wouldn't feel terrible losing their wife after forty-two years of marriage.

The words tumbled from Beryl's mouth in a fashion that suggested to Dykeman she was distinctly uncomfortable. He'd have to make a little extra effort to keep her on track.

"How well did you know Emma?"

"Well as could be expected, I suppose. We'd say hello and talk about the weather, that sort of thing. But I'm just staff here, after all, so it's not like I would talk to her like she was my own daughter. Wouldn't be right, would that."

"I understand. Would you say she was happy when she stayed here?"

Beryl's gaze moved away from Dykeman and settled on a green and white striped tea towel that sat in a heap on the worktop next to her. She picked it up and began to fold it into neat quarters.

"I suppose so." She picked half-heartedly at a corner of the tea towel. "Though it's not for me to say, is it now?"

Dykeman rapped the fingers of one hand on the side of his leg. The woman's hesitant answer seemed to him to be as much a request as it was a reply; a request for his permission to speak her mind. Well, that was easily enough addressed.

"But it is indeed for you to say, Mrs Bolant. This is a murder case and you are entirely at liberty to speak your mind. If there's something we should know then it's your duty to speak up, without fear of recrimination or accusation." Nicely put, he told himself.

Beryl placed the folded tea towel on the work-top and tapped it lightly with one finger. Her eyes fixed once more on Dykeman's.

"Well, it's only my own thinking, you understand, but I don't reckon she was always too happy to be here. Can't have been easy for the poor girl, can it, being passed around like that. She needed a settled, proper family home."

"Were there ever arguments?"

There was no immediate reply from Beryl, who went back to prodding at the tea towel.

Dykeman had the feeling there was something really useful to be dug out here, if only he could hit upon the right spot to dig. He tried again, pushing his spade into the ground in a fresh spot. "Were there any members of the family she didn't get on with?"

Beryl took a deep breath, the roses on the bib of her pinny rising then falling as the air escaped her nostrils with an audible sigh.

"I don't reckon I'm saying anything out of turn to tell you the younger Mrs Glass wasn't too keen on her being here so often. Sometimes she'd say it made things difficult, when she wanted to have just the family here for the weekend. Miss Greene wasn't family to her. But..."

Beryl's cheeks flushed, just enough for Dykeman to notice, and she pursed her lips. When, after a little while, it became clear she wasn't going to pick up where she left off, the short-changed Inspector had no hesitation in giving her a firm prod.

"It really is most important we hear every little bit of information that might be pertinent to our investigations, Mrs Bolant. What might seem irrelevant to you or, dare I say it, even mere speculation, could very well turn out to be the vital clue that makes the difference between our apprehending the killer and their remaining at large."

It still took a moment for Beryl to convince herself she should speak her mind. Even once she did, it seemed to Dykeman that she was addressing his tie the whole time, since that was where her gaze was fixed.

"I don't want to go casting aspersions where they shouldn't be cast," she said, all of a hurry. "But Mr Glass always seemed to pay the girl special attention, maybe more than was proper, or so some people said. It was the circumstances, I'm sure, but people do talk, don't they?"

Dykeman was caught unprepared and found himself temporarily silenced. The possibility there might have been some sort of improper relationship between James Glass and Emma Greene was not one he had, until now, even begun to consider. She had been a beautiful young woman, that much was clear, and, it was true to say, they had already established that she had not been backwards when it came to teasing men. In the case of Perch it seemed pretty clear she had even gone so far as to give the mechanic the impression she was prepared to marry him. Did that really mean she might have ensnared James Glass, her uncle, in some sort of relationship?

Then he thought again about the words Beryl had just used. She had said that Glass paid Greene special attention, not the other way around. He rubbed his chin firmly. This was tricky ground they were stepping on to now. Gossip and tittle-tattle was one thing, accusing a man of having an affair with his niece was another altogether. But there again, he might not have known at the time that Emma was his niece. That had been recent news. And with that thought possibilities raced through Dykeman's mind, not the least of which was how Emma might have sought to benefit from such a discovery, if she had indeed been seduced by James. Yes, this was very tricky ground indeed.

"Did you ever see or hear anything to suggest this might be more than mere gossip?" he asked, more hesitantly than he had intended.

"Well, sometimes he did look at her in an odd way, if you get what I mean."

"But you never saw or heard anything definite? The sort of thing that left you in absolutely no doubt?"

She took her time before answering. "No, I suppose I never did that."

Dykeman now felt a little uncertain how to proceed, not wanting to move on from so important a topic but at the same time clear that he should not begin to put suggestions in Beryl's mind. He'd not got far in weighing things up when she spoke again.

"But that wasn't the only thing," she said with considerable assurance.

Dykeman raised an eyebrow. "Yes?"

"On Monday morning, I had some work needed doing, here in the kitchen, and when I arrived to make a start Mr and Mrs Glass were already here, talking. I say talking, but it was more like they were arguing. It was about Miss Greene and I definitely heard Mr Glass say he wished Miss Greene would have some kind of terrible accident so the whole horrible mess would just go away."

Dykeman tilted his head upwards and scratched at his thick neck. It was a deliberate ploy; one aimed at ensuring he took a moment to consider what he had just been told. It was important not to go jumping to any conclusions, especially if they seemed clear-cut. He could hear Shapes tapping his pencil on his notepad, a sure sign that his Sergeant's interest had been piqued. Dykeman brought his gaze back to Beryl, whose eyes met his own with a steady focus.

"And just what 'horrible mess' would he have been referring to?"

"I don't rightly know," replied Beryl, without hesitation.

Dykeman was about to follow up with a further question, but he'd barely opened his mouth when the cleaner gave a little flick of the head, then picked up where she'd left off, only this time the little sparkle in her eyes and the gossipy tone in her voice made it clear she was warming to her task and, quite possibly, relishing her little moment in the limelight.

"But I suppose it had to do with the dead Mr Robert Glass's will. They weren't happy, you know. The whole family were upset Miss Greene was going to get all the money. Very angry was Mrs Glass. Not that I go sticking my nose into other people's business, but I'd have to be deaf to not hear them all talking about it."

"Is that the older Mrs Glass or the younger one?" asked Dykeman.

"They both wasn't happy about it. Old Mrs Glass said her dead husband would have sorted out things straight away. He never left things to settle themselves. But it was mostly young Mrs Glass. I heard her tell her husband he had to do something before it was too late. Very bad tempered, she was."

Well, thought Dykeman, someone had certainly sorted things out. For now, however, he needed to tread cautiously. There seemed every possibility the murder was related to this trouble with the will. But it wasn't the only option they had to consider. Shapes could be right, it might be that a humiliated John Perch lost his temper and took the ultimate revenge.

"Did Robert and James get on well, as far as you could tell?"

"I think so. I never saw them argue," answered Beryl after a moment's consideration.

"And how did Robert get on with the other family members?"

"They all seemed pleased enough to see him when he came to stay. If there was any falling out I didn't see it. He was always nice enough to me."

Dykeman glanced at Shapes, who shook his head. There were no questions from him.

"One last thing, Mrs Bolant. Were there any visitors to the house on Monday morning?"

She gave the matter some thought. "None that I know of. But I was busy with my work, so someone could have been and gone without me seeing them."

Indeed they could, thought Dykeman, though he very much suspected that whenever there were visitors to the house when the cleaner was working she would soon know all about it. She didn't strike him as the sort of woman to miss much.

"You've been most helpful, Mrs Bolant," smiled Dykeman. "It's always useful to get an unbiased view of things from a third party, and especially from someone who knows the set-up, as it were."

"I'm glad you think so, Inspector. I always try to do my best, whatever it is I'm asked to do."

"Would Mr James Glass happen to be at home today?"

"He is, that. In the study last I knew. It's at the front of the house, on the left," replied Beryl, waving a hand in the general direction of the study. "I can show you, if you like," she added, eagerly.

"No, no, that will be fine," responded Dykeman, quickly. "We noticed it on our previous visit."

As they walked out into the hallway, Shapes leaned in close to his boss and whispered, "Unbiased, eh? How comes you were buttering her up like that?"

Dykeman gave his Sergeant the old raised eyebrow treatment, before replying, "Like I've said many times before, Shapes, the staff in houses like this often know more about what goes on in the place than any of the family members do. It's always best to keep them on your side, especially the nosey ones."

"Mm. So, you don't think she might have done it then, murdered Emma Greene?"

Dykeman stopped in the middle of the hallway and turned to face Shapes, his brow furrowed. "Why the hell would she have wanted to do that?"

"I don't know," answered Shapes, with a shrug of the shoulders. "But she might have done it. Maybe Emma upset her."

"Upset her, Shapes? It would have needed to be some serious upsetting to cause the woman to stick a knife in Emma's midriff."

"Maybe. Just saying, that's all."

As they continued towards to the study, Dykeman found himself suddenly irritated by his Sergeant's comments. Not because they were as daft as he'd suggested they were, rather, they were annoyingly sensible and he realised he'd made a bit of a bloomer proceeding on the assumption the cleaner couldn't possibly be on their list of suspects. However, acknowledging the mistake to himself was one thing, what he absolutely wasn't going to do was give Shapes the satisfaction of knowing he was right. He'd not hear the last of it.

Chapter Eighteen

DYKEMAN AND SHAPES found themselves presented with a silent and unoccupied room when they entered the study and were pushed to call upon the help of Michael Glass in locating his father. James was, in fact, in one of the converted stables, tinkering with one of his motorbikes. As the policemen walked into the narrow wooden building, their eyes temporarily dazzled by the bright overhead lights, James looked up and over the petrol tank of a gleaming Triumph.

"Oh, Inspector, you're back. I didn't know," he said, straightening up. He glanced at his hands, both thick with grease and grime. "Apologies, we'd best not shake hands. You'd not be able to get the stuff off for days."

"That's no problem, Mr Glass," said Dykeman. "Nice looking Triumph you've got there."

"It certainly is. A Tiger T110, though some people prefer to call it the Ton-10. I bought it from the former owner in St Albans a few years ago. Had been after one for ages, but couldn't really justify spending the money. When I saw this one up for sale at a very attractive price, I couldn't resist. Lovely to ride, but does get the occasional oil leak."

"You had a motorcycle once, didn't you, Shapes?"

"I did," replied Shapes, stepping a little closer to the Triumph. "Nothing as nice as this one, though. Pre-war was mine. Bloody thing kept breaking down, so I sold it to a Teddy Boy for his first bike." Shapes cast an appreciative eye over the Triumph.

James picked up a dirty cloth from the handlebars of the motorbike, wondering why the police were back. The whole situation with the murder and the questions they'd all had to answer just the previous day had put quite a strain on all of the family, especially his wife, who had even gone so far as to suggest they leave Brayfield for a few days. Find a nice hotel, somewhere in the Cotswolds, perhaps. He'd rather liked the idea, but he couldn't afford to spend any more time away from the office and, well, it might not have looked any too good if they were seen clearing off at such a time. Unfeeling, some might say. All the same, he felt a flutter of unease in his belly at the reappearance of the policemen. There were questions he would rather not have to answer and it seemed highly unlikely they had shown up just to admire his motorcycle collection.

"So, how can I help you?"

"When we spoke yesterday, you owned up to the family being surprised at the news your brother was Emma Greene's dad and said there was some unease at the terms of his will. You mentioned not everyone was happy with it, if I remember correctly."

"That's right," replied James. "Heck of a surprise it was, to discover Robert was Emma's father. I think anyone would have been shocked, under the circumstances."

There was, thought Dykeman, the tiniest hint of irritation in the other man's voice. "And the terms of the will?" he prompted.

"Well, it was Robert's money, of course, so he was perfectly at liberty to do with it as he saw fit. Only reasonable to want to make sure his daughter was properly taken care of, wouldn't you say?"

Definitely a sliver of annoyance there now, mused Dykeman. "But not everyone saw it quite like that, did they?"

A furrow appeared on James's forehead and his eyes narrowed a touch. "I'm not sure what you're getting at, Inspector."

"Let me help you, then. We had a word with Robert's solicitor earlier this morning, didn't we, Shapes?"

"Certainly did, sir. Very helpful man, he was," replied Shapes, confidence ringing in his voice.

"He was very clear in his recollection," said Dykeman, picking up the thread from where he'd left off, "that several members of the family, yourself included, were very far from happy with the terms of the will. In fact, he told us that since then he's been contacted by two other firms of solicitors, both instructed by yourself, to see if there isn't some way of overturning the will."

Dykeman left his words hanging in the air, well aware of the power that came with a moment's silence. It had a habit of intimidating a suspect and he was perfectly willing to accept that James was a potential suspect.

James looked from one policeman to the other, then rubbed the fingers of one hand across the back of the other.

The furrowed brow disappeared and there was hesitancy in his voice when he spoke again. "Well, of course, as I said yesterday, there was some, er, disappointment with the terms of the will." He cleared his throat in an unconvincing manner. "It's only reasonable that we take steps to make sure the will is, er, a sound one."

Dykeman could see the man's discomfort as clearly as he could the hair on his head. It seemed he'd touched a sore point, just as he'd hoped, and he wasn't about to let the man off the hook. It was time to prod again.

"Did you have any reason to suspect your brother's will wasn't sound?"

James rubbed again at the back of his hand and a little colour crept into his cheeks, noticed the Inspector.

"Well, it's not so much... how can I put this?"

James directed a feeble smile at Dykeman as he struggled for the right words. This was precisely the topic he had hoped the policemen wouldn't want to ask questions about and he could feel himself getting warm and uncomfortable. Why had he been placed in such an awkward situation when it had been others who had hounded him into hiring those firms of solicitors to see if they couldn't get the will over-turned? Now he was going to have to come up with some way of limiting the damage this conversation risked doing to his reputation. God only knows what the police would think if they wheedled all the details out of him.

"Mr Glass, you were saying," prompted Dykeman, leaning forward.

"Er, sorry. Yes. I was just thinking what an extraordinary and terrible few weeks it's been. Robert and I were very close, you see. It hit me hard when he died. And then, what happened to Emma... Terrible. Terrible."

Dykeman wasn't entirely convinced by this display. For one thing, it seemed to be steering them away from the challenge he'd put to Glass. Time to shove the man back on track.

"I'm sure it's been a very upsetting time, Mr Glass, but right now we need to keep our focus on the murder of your niece and Shapes and I are only going to solve that if we get to know all the facts." He paused for a brief moment. "That's all of the facts, Mr Glass, even the awkward ones."

"Yes, I quite understand, Inspector."

"Now then, what made you think it might be possible to challenge your brother's will and why did you even want to try doing so?"

James placed his hands on the fuel tank of the motorbike and looked the policeman straight in the eye. When he spoke he did so clearly and without hesitation.

"As was the case for my brother, we only have Jane Greene's word that Robert was Emma's father. That's all. There's no other way to verify the claim and, from what my brother told me, there was quite a gap between the time he left Portsmouth, where he had his affair with Jane, and when she approached him with the news he had a daughter. I'd always been aware that when it became clear my sister-in-law couldn't bear Robert any children, he took it very hard. It did, without doubt, leave a big gap in his life and it didn't take a lot to imagine he would be susceptible to the kind of claim Jane made. Under the circumstances, it seemed entirely right and proper to challenge the veracity of the will."

That was more like it, thought Dykeman. At last they seemed to be getting to the truth of the matter. Did it help them move the case forward? Well, that might only become clear later on.

"Will you carry on trying to overturn the will?"

"I'm not sure. The advice to date hasn't been promising, but that doesn't mean we're prepared to give up. Not just yet."

Dykeman noticed the little beads of sweat that had appeared on James's forehead and his face now had a soft sheen that hadn't been there when they'd arrived. He wondered how James was going to respond to his next question.

"I appreciate your openness, Mr Glass. Now then, there's one other thing I need to ask you. We have a witness who heard you say to your wife that you wished Emma Greene would have some sort of nasty and preferably fatal accident. Something about hoping the whole horrible mess would just go away. Doesn't sound too good, does it, not in light of what happened shortly afterwards?"

James felt a sickening cold flush wash through his body. He was glad he was still leaning on the motorcycle, otherwise he might well have struggled to keep himself properly upright. Who the hell had heard that remark? Then it came to him; Beryl Bolant, of course. That damned woman never missed a thing. What was he to say now? He could hardly deny it, not without calling Bolant a plain-faced liar. Perhaps he could suggest she misheard, but the Inspector didn't seem like the sort to believe such a thing. A trickle of sweat ran down his back.

"Some people have very large ears, Inspector," he found himself saying, not sure where the words had come from.

"Seems so, Mr Glass."

The two men looked at each other. Shapes watched them, well aware that his boss had the upper hand. He'd seen him in action far too often to think Dykeman would muck up such a fine opportunity and wondered how Glass might try to escape from his predicament. He didn't strike Shapes as being the inventive kind.

"Well, Mr Glass?" prompted Dykeman, eager to press home his advantage.

James rubbed the back of a hand across his forehead. He was well aware that he needed to come up with some sort of an answer and he desperately thrashed around inside his head for something that would do; something that would fend off the policeman without making him look either ridiculous or guilty. But the stress of the situation seemed to have robbed him of his usual calm, clear mind and nothing suitable would present itself.

His inability to escape a tight corner with a display of effortless quick-thinking annoyed him, as it always did. In the course of his business life he often met men who possessed not only charm and a natural ease of conversation he struggled to match, but also a mind that could meet with grace and ease any challenge it was presented with. By comparison, he seemed to be a plodding, slow-witted dullard whose mind took an eternity to comprehend and address even an apparently straightforward matter.

He fixed his feet firmly in place, just in case he was still at risk of a wobble. From outside came the sharp-edged screeching of arguing crows. As it died away, Glass responded in the only way he felt he possibly could. "They were only words, spoken in the heat of the moment, Inspector. I really must insist you don't go getting the idea there was anything more to it than that. My wife was being most insistent about trying to find another firm of solicitors who could raise a successful challenge to Robert's will and I was finding her persistence rather stressful, hence the comment. I'm sure you can understand the situation," he added, as much in hope as expectation.

Dykeman had been expecting nothing other than a denial of lethal intent from James; he was hardly likely to own up to having ensured his wish came true. All the same, it had been interesting to see the obvious discomfort and struggle when presented with his own words. The sign of a guilty man? They were nowhere near being able to answer that question, not yet.

"I would take more care with what you say in future, Mr Glass. That sort of loose talk can get a man into a great deal of trouble."

"Yes, indeed. You're quite right, of course."

"Now then, I'm glad you mentioned your wife because we'd like another little talk with her. Don't suppose you happen to know where we can find her?"

"She was in the walled garden about twenty minutes ago, dead-heading and pruning some of the roses. If she's not there now, I would imagine she'll be somewhere else in the garden. Once she starts she normally goes on for ages. I'll walk you over there, if you like."

"No need for us to drag you away from your motorcycles, Mr Glass. We'll manage," replied Dykeman, before turning to his Sergeant. "Come on, Shapes. You might learn a thing or two about looking after your roses."

Shapes wasn't altogether sure he'd got any roses in his neglected garden, but he thought better of pointing that out, well aware that his boss liked few things better than a bit of gardening.

As the policemen departed, James tilted back his head, closed his eyes and let out a long, deep sigh. That conversation had not gone as well as he would have liked. The police were already far better informed than they had been on their previous visit and he felt he'd been pushed into saying considerably more than he would have liked. Just how his wife would respond to their questioning, he dreaded to think. Matters seemed to be slipping out of his control.

Chapter Nineteen

SUSAN GLASS MADE A small adjustment to her hat, so the wide cotton brim gave her eyes better protection from a sun that seemed to be growing brighter and warmer as it climbed steadily towards its noon summit. A confident and hungry robin had been hopping around and about her as she worked, ever hopeful she might unearth a worm or dislodge an insect. Every time the robin was about to move in close to her, it would twitter loudly to make sure she knew what to expect. If only she could speak the robin's language they would have been able to maintain a comprehensive and, no doubt, very entertaining conversation as she snipped away at the roses, removing the dead flower heads and any stems that looked diseased or were simply, to her mind, growing in the wrong place.

A huge, brown-furred feral cat that had long been a frequent visitor to the garden had slipped quietly in amongst the borders shortly after she had arrived. Now it was dozing on a nearby bench, stretched out in the sun, with one half-open eye on her and the robin. She would have liked to pick it up and fuss over it, but her lesson had been learned there; it was very definitely not a cat that either needed or tolerated close attention.

The morning had been so relaxing and enjoyable that the appearance of the two policemen, approaching along the wide gravel path from the house, did not at first cause Susan any concern or annoyance. She turned towards them as she locked her secateurs closed.

"Good morning, Inspector. Sergeant." Her voice was welcoming, if a little louder than she had intended. "I do hope you've come along to tell us you've already tracked down Emma's killer."

Dykeman stopped next to a tall, billowing rose bush, with a mass of soft pink flowers that had filled the air with a gentle, vanilla scent. He leaned towards it, the better to take in that wonderful smell.

"What a marvellous garden you have here, Mrs Glass. I'll not hide the fact I'm deeply envious. It's far larger than my own small patch. Although I'm more a fruit and veg man, myself."

"It's one of the things I've always liked best about living here and, at this time of the year, I can hardly wait to wake up each morning so I can spend another day out here. It's an utter joy," she added, smiling.

Dykeman abandoned the rose and re-focused on the matter at hand. "Sadly, to answer your question, no we haven't yet caught the killer, but we have made some excellent progress, which is what's brought us back here today."

Shapes extracted his notepad and pencil from their customary pocket in his jacket, in readiness for action.

"Tricky things, families, don't you think," said Dykeman, in an off-hand manner. His intention was to approach this particular interview cautiously, for he felt certain Susan would be an altogether trickier and more quick-witted opponent than her flustered husband.

"Families can be awfully difficult to manage, sometimes," she replied, after a moment's hesitation.

Dykeman nodded. "Especially when you're sharing the same roof. It's bad enough sharing the station with a couple of dozen other police officers, but at least they don't follow me home at the end of the day. Mind you, I can remember, as a fresh-faced constable, trying to get on with the old hands. I bought so many rounds of beer the first few months, I was surprised I ever had enough money left to pay the rent and feed myself." Dykeman chuckled and shook his head.

"You're well settled in now, I suppose," said Susan, now feeling rather disconcerted. What was the man going on about?

"Oh, yes. A regular part of the family now. But it must have been especially difficult for a part-timer like Emma to find a way of chiselling out a place for herself in a family as close-knit as this one. Some people are natural socialisers. My own mum could talk happily to anyone for hours on end. It didn't matter a jot if she'd never met them before in her life; once she got going there was no stopping her. Shapes, here, on the other hand, rarely says more than a dozen words at a time and likes things to stay just the way they are. I suppose it helps folks get along if they've got something in common, just like your daughter, Philippa, and Emma had with the horse-riding. They did both like riding horses, didn't they?"

"Yes, they did."

Susan sounded uncertain; she knew that. Where on earth was the man going with this long-winded excursion? There would inevitably be some purpose to it, or she hoped there would, but what that could be she was struggling to understand. She began to feel uneasy.

"Mind you," went on Dykeman, still deploying a conversational tone and a thin smile. "I suppose if you had some sort of leverage, something to strengthen your position, that would help make a difference, wouldn't you say?" He looked expectantly at Susan.

"Well... I'm not sure I understand what you mean. What sort of leverage did you have in mind?"

"Oh, how about some form of blackmail?" he said with enthusiasm.

The significance of that suggestion took a moment to register with Susan, but when it did she felt her cheeks flush and the secateurs slipped from her hand, landing on the path with a heavy thump. She looked away from Dykeman and breathed in deeply, as she attempted to regain her composure. So, he knew about the arrangement she had come to with Emma. Well, there was no changing that now. She would just have to make the most of a bad situation. Blasted man!

Susan bent down to pick up the secateurs, playing for all the time she could get. Once she was upright again she directed a raised eyebrow at Dykeman and asked, "Blackmail, Inspector? I'm not sure I understand your point."

"Oh, come off it, Mrs Glass, I'm sure you know damn well what I'm referring to," Dykeman snapped back. "Emma

Greene had you over a barrel. She'd been squeezing money and all sorts out of you for months. All in return for agreeing not to get any closer to your youngest son, Michael. Did you really think Emma would be able to keep something like that to herself?"

Susan stiffened, shocked the police knew about her difficulties with Emma. How on Earth had they been able to find out and so soon? But, damn the man, he had no right to talk to her like that.

"I don't think that has anything whatsoever to do with you, Inspector," she said, her voice filled with all the self-assurance and determination she could muster. "You really have no right to come to my home and talk to me like this." The nostrils in her small nose flared as she spoke.

"No right," snapped Dykeman, jabbing a finger in her direction. "This is a murder investigation we're talking about here and I'll ask whatever questions I bloody well like, especially when they have anything and everything to do with the case. Emma Greene was extorting money from you and now she's dead, stabbed in the heart, which, if you hadn't already worked it out for yourself, is something a woman is just as capable of doing as any man. So, if I was you, I'd stop throwing a strop and start co-operating, otherwise Shapes and I are likely to start wondering why you're so keen to avoid answering our questions."

Dykeman realised his heart had begun to race. Things were getting interesting; just how he liked it. The reaction from Susan was all the confirmation he needed and it was now his job to extract the whole truth from her. Blackmail was right up there when it came to motives for murder, he knew well.

Susan was seething with anger, her grip on the secateurs so tight it hurt her fingers. But she realised the difficult position she was in and tried hard to regain a semblance of composure, despite the overwhelming desire to let rip at the obnoxious man in front of her.

"Well?" demanded Dykeman, irritably, the fingers of his right hand rapping on the side of his leg.

Susan stared hard at him, lifting her chin to ensure she was looking along the ridge of her nose. She made a point of beginning her reply in a calm and measured tone, her grip on the secateurs relaxing sufficiently for the pain in her hands to abate.

"Michael has always been a quiet, some might say shy, young man. He's certainly never found it easy to mix with girls, despite sharing a house with three women. No mother would want to leave things to chance when she could see her son was going to struggle to find himself a suitable wife. So I have spent much of the last eighteen months doing my very best to encourage friends of ours in Daventry to see the benefit of their daughter, Alison, marrying Michael. They were only lukewarm towards the idea at first, but I chose my target carefully, Inspector. Alison is a plain-looking young woman and can hardly expect to have a long queue of eligible men calling at her home, something I could see she was only too aware of. Once she started to respond positively to the idea, her parents soon fell into line. Eighteen months, Inspector, and then that... harlot, Emma starts spending more time with Michael. I didn't realise at first what she was up to. She'd seemed happy enough stringing along that violent young man from the garage. But one day I saw the look in Michael's eyes as he gazed at her across the dinner table and I knew instantly what she was doing. I was livid. If I'd had my way she would never have set foot in this house again."

Susan paused for breath and looked away, her teeth gritted.

"But you weren't able to stop her coming to the house, I take it?"

"James wouldn't allow it. Said his brother would stop visiting as well if we did that and he didn't want to risk a falling out with him. They were very close."

"So, what happened next? Was it you or Emma that raised the subject of payment?"

"I suppose it was me, though I didn't offer her money, not outright. I started offering to pay for her and Philippa to go the cinema or on the occasional shopping trip. There were only small amounts involved and it seemed, at first, to be working, re-directing her attention elsewhere and away from Michael. But it must have occurred to her at some point that she could ask for more, so she did. It wasn't ever a great deal, a few shillings here and there to begin with, though it did gradually creep up. She never demanded money openly. She always made out that she needed something like a new dress or pair of shoes and that her mother couldn't afford such things. She was a far smarter young woman than most people gave her credit for."

"And how long had this been going on?"

"Six months, maybe seven, I suppose."

Dykeman rubbed the tip of a finger gently against the edge of an ear and looked again at the roses. If Susan was telling the truth about the amounts of money being so small, could that really have driven her to murder? It seemed unlikely, but not impossible. There was clearly no love lost between Susan and Emma. He brought his gaze back to the simmering woman standing opposite him.

"Did Emma keep her side of the bargain and stay away from Michael?"

"As far as I could tell. Of course, she couldn't avoid him entirely and I have my suspicions that Michael wanted things to go back to how they'd been before our arrangement, but I never saw her leading him on once I started paying her to leave him alone."

Dykeman made a mental note to see if it was possible to get another view or two on whether that had really been the case. When it came to a motive for murder, whilst small sums of money might not be enough, if Emma had continued her dalliance with Michael it might have been a different thing altogether. Mothers were frequently willing to go to any lengths to protect their children.

"It really would have been better, Mrs Glass, if you'd explained all this to us when we spoke to you yesterday. But at least we've got there now." He looked at Shapes. "Anything you want to add, Shapes?"

"You mentioned," said Shapes, addressing Susan, "the violent young man from the garage. Who would that be?"

"John Perch. He's always getting into fights at one or other of the village pubs. I understand he's banned from at least one of them."

"That's all, thank you, sir," said Shapes, scribbling once more in his notepad.

Dykeman wrinkled his nose. For now, there didn't seem to be anything else they needed to ask her.

"In that case, Mrs Glass, we'll let you get back to your dead-heading."

As soon as the policemen had left the walled garden, Susan collapsed on to the nearest bench, her head slumped forward on to her chest and her eyes shut. How on Earth had they found out about her arrangement with Emma and what was she going to do now? Events felt as if they were slipping out of her control.

Chapter Twenty

AS THEY FOLLOWED A narrow gravel path towards the rear of the house, leaving behind the splendours of the walled garden and a visibly shaken Susan Glass, Dykeman looked across his shoulder at Shapes.

"Don't reckon things could have gone any better there. What do you think?" he asked, well aware he sounded pleased with himself.

"She wasn't expecting us to know about the blackmail. Reckoned she was going to wet herself when you said about that. All the same, I'd like to know if she was telling the truth about the payments being only small ones. Make a right old difference if she was handing over big wodges of cash."

"Indeed it would, Shapes. I'm not sure how we'll be able to confirm the sums involved, but we ought to give it a go. Now then, we've yet to speak to the eldest son. Stephen, I think someone said his name was."

"That's right."

"We'll take a look in the house and if he's not there we'll have to track him down at work or wherever it is he's hiding. I'm already starting to wonder if he's another one who had some sort of grudge against Emma. Pretty much everyone else we've met seems to fall into that camp."

"There's someone looking out the French doors," said Shapes, nodding towards the house, which was now only about a hundred yards away. "Don't recognise him, so could be Stephen."

"Let's hope so. Would save us some time not having to make another trip up here specially to speak to him."

STEPHEN GLASS HAD HEARD from Beryl Bolant that the police were back at the house and it didn't take a genius to work out they would almost certainly want to interview him, as he was the only member of the family they'd not been able to speak to on their first visit. He'd already debated what he should and shouldn't tell them, deciding there was no need for them to know about aspects of his personal life that weren't, as far as he was concerned, relevant to the case. He wouldn't lie to them but he would be careful with his answers.

As he stood by the French doors, he saw them walk out of the walled garden. His mother was somewhere in there, tending her precious plants as usual. What, he wondered, had they been asking her? Something to do with Michael, in all likelihood. Everyone knew the fool had been madly in love with Emma. Good God, did the police think he might have killed her in some fit of jealousy? That would be ridiculous. Michael had always had enough trouble squashing the slugs their mother had frequently ordered them to pick off her plants after dark when they were children. The thought of him having the stomach to kill another human being was absurd.

The policemen were close now, less than a hundred yards from the house. He lifted the metal latch on the nearest door, turned the handle and pushed it open. A gentle breeze, warm on the skin, slipped in through the opening and caressed his face. He stepped out on to the terrace, hands in his pockets, his back towards the sun. Little and large, those two policemen. Or should that be Laurel and Hardy. The older, skinny one looked peculiar, like something from a Dickens novel, his clothes dishevelled, his hair matted and his face like that of a ferret. It was easy to think the police force might employ such people so they could use them to put the frighteners on timid suspects. Anyway, best to park those sorts of thoughts. Question time was almost upon him and he needed to remain calm and focused. Clear, simple answers and most definitely nothing to raise their suspicions. He took his hands out of his pockets, held them together behind his back and offered up a weak smile.

"I don't suppose you'd be Mr Stephen Glass by any chance?" asked Dykeman, as they stopped in front of the slim young man whose short black hair and brown eyes were accompanied by the sharp pointed nose that seemed to be possessed by all members of the Glass family.

"That's me," replied Stephen, amiably. "Stephen Thomas Glass, actually. Thomas being my paternal grandfather's first name. We're big on that sort of thing in this family."

"Inspector Dykeman. Banbury police," proffered the Inspector.

"I heard you were here. Thought I'd better make it easy for you to find me."

He shook hands with both men, although a little more reluctantly with the sergeant, whom Dykeman introduced as Shapes. Odd surname was that. Mind you, so was Dykeman, though he assumed that must be Dutch.

"Work, was it?" asked Dykeman.

"Pardon?"

"Yesterday. You weren't here when we called round. Were you at work?"

"Oh, I see. Yes. I'm training to become a land agent and property surveyor. Work for Hawk and Harris in Buckingham. Means I get out and about a good deal, which is better than being cooped up indoors all the time, I suppose."

Dykeman's mind was already beavering away, trying to weigh up this latest witness. Or was it potential suspect? It was hard to say so far. Handsome fella, no denying that. Spoke the way a lot of young people did, as if they weren't bothered by anything in the world. A sort of fake casualness. It was like they didn't want anyone to think they took anything too seriously.

"Yes, I suppose it is. Just like us, eh, Shapes?"

"Certainly is, sir."

"How about Monday? Were you at work on Monday morning?"

"Monday? What about Monday? Oh, of course. I see. No, no. I'd taken the day off."

"Went for a walk, did you? There seems to be a lot of that round here."

"Walk, Inspector? No, not me. Only when I have to."

"Where did you go, then?"

"For a drive, as it happens. Needed to get some space. I know it might seem daft when the house is so big and there's all this," he added, gesturing at the gardens. "But sometimes you just can't get away from the others. It can get a bit intense."

"A drive. And where would that have taken you?"

"Oh, nowhere particular. Just here and there," replied Stephen, rocking gently on the heels and soles of his shoes. "I like to drive. Helps take my mind off things."

"I'm afraid here and there won't do, Mr Glass. This is a murder investigation we're undertaking and you'll need to be more specific about your movements, if you want us to avoid getting the wrong idea and thinking you've got something to hide."

"Well, let me see." Stephen stopped rocking to and fro and, instead, levered himself up on to the tips of his shoes, before easing himself slowly down on to the soles. "I did stop for a while at Burton Dassett. You get the most remarkably good views from up there on the hill. Apparently you can see five different counties and the Malvern Hills on a good day."

"Was it a good day on Monday?"

"Sunny, yes. Bit of a breeze, though."

"And were you alone or perhaps there was someone who can confirm you were there?"

Stephen hesitated before answering. "I was on my own, the whole time, Inspector. No one to confirm my alibi, if that's what you mean."

"Shame," remarked Dykeman, scratching an ear. "What time did you get back?"

Glass rolled forward again on to the tips of his shoes and ran the fingers of one hand over his short hair. "I couldn't say for sure. Wasn't really paying much attention to the time. But, I suppose I would have been back around two-ish. Definitely after one and before three. Maybe one of the others noticed. Have you asked?"

"Not yet, but we will." Dykeman nodded at Shapes, as if to emphasise the point. "Which car is yours, the Austin?"

"The A35? Yes. Not really what I'd like to be driving round in, but all I can afford at the moment."

Going for a long drive all alone on the day of a murder didn't exactly place Stephen in the best of positions, mused Dykeman, but until they'd been able to prove him right or wrong there seemed nothing to be gained from asking more questions on that particular topic.

"How well did you get on with Emma Greene?"

"Alright, I suppose. We didn't really spend a great deal of time together. She seemed happier spending her time here with Philippa and Michael. Suspect I rather bored her. Little in common, you see."

"And how did you feel when you heard the terms of your uncle's will and that Emma was, in fact, your cousin?"

"The part about being our cousin, I wasn't all that bothered about. Surprised, yes, but bothered, no, not really. After all, once I've moved away from here there'd be no compunction for me to ever have anything to do with her again. But the will, that was a different kettle of fish. That was a bloody outrage. Her mother shows up one day at my Uncle Robert's claiming he has a daughter and, just like that, we're all supposed to believe her? Rubbish, if you ask me.

Fine way for the mother and daughter to get their hands on my uncle's money, which by rights ought to go to my father."

No hiding how he felt there, thought Dykeman. Some refreshing honesty. There was, though, something about the young man that didn't sit right. He couldn't put his finger on what it was, but his policeman's nose smelled a rat, of sorts. Maybe not a rat; a mouse, perhaps. Something smaller and less offensive.

"You've got plans to move away from the family home, then, have you?"

Stephen smiled. "Plans would be overstating it a bit. Ambitions, more like. I'd like to go somewhere there's more happening. Somewhere with more opportunities for an ambitious, hard-working chap like myself. It's not that I'm ungrateful, but Brayfield, Daventry, Banbury and their ilk aren't exactly thronging metropolises, bursting at the seams with exciting opportunities. Rather like the idea of making a trip to the USA. Been talking to a friend of mine about that recently. Who knows, maybe one day." He slipped his hands back into his pockets and his shoulders relaxed.

"I've got a friend in Canada. She moved out there recently." Dykeman tailed off, wondering why he'd mentioned Sheila Delph.

Shapes stepped in to the silence. "We'll need to get going soon, sir," he prompted. "If we're to get back to the station in time for your appointment with the Chief Inspector." It was a lie, but it was the best he could do at short notice.

"Chief Inspector?" asked Dykeman, his mind still somewhere over the Atlantic. What had he been asking Stephen? Damn it, he'd lost his thread completely. "Oh, yes.

You're quite right. So, do I take it you support your parents' efforts to get the will overturned?"

"Certainly do. Seem to be having trouble, though, finding legal people who can actually do their jobs properly. You'd think with the money they charge that sort of thing would be a walk in the park."

"Did you see Emma before you went out for your drive on Monday?"

"I did. At breakfast. Grandmother insists we all show up for breakfast at the same time. Bit of a traditionalist, she is."

"Nothing after that?"

Stephen shook his head. "No. I wanted to get out as soon as possible and, in any case, we usually all go our own ways after breakfast."

Dykeman felt the first stirrings of a stomach rumble. It had been a long and busy morning. The notion there was something more to Stephen Glass than appeared on the surface to be the case still nagged at him, but he couldn't develop that feeling into something more substantial and knew, from experience, it was the kind of thing that needed to be left to work itself out while he focused on other things, like finding some lunch.

"Well, Mr Glass, looks like we'll have to let you off the hook, as it were. Can't keep the Chief Inspector waiting. Thank you for your time."

"Glad to have helped, Inspector."

Stephen stood by the open French door, watching the policemen as they strolled off in the direction of the old stables. He breathed deeply, feeling the air being pulled through his nostrils. That seemed to have gone as well as could be expected, but, all the same, he prayed to God they didn't ever find out where he really went on the Monday morning.

Chapter Twenty-One

DYKEMAN'S PROPOSAL that he drive them back to the station produced such a look of childish disappointment on Shapes's face that, pathetic though he thought it was, the Inspector relented and with, a shake of the head, handed the keys to his Sergeant, whose face lit up in an instant. The satisfied look on Shapes's face left Dykeman with the feeling he'd just been played for a fool. There was, though, no way he was going to admit any such thing to Shapes, who scuttled round the car and climbed into the driver's seat with a decided spring in his step.

As they exited the stable block and turned on to the track that led away from Ashview Lodge in the direction of the main road, Shapes angled his head a little towards Dykeman. "What did the old woman want with you, sir? Tell you not to harass her innocent little children, did she?"

Before leaving Ashview Lodge, Shapes had needed to avail himself of the toilet and when he returned found the older Mrs Glass engaged in what appeared to be a rather one-sided conversation with his disgruntled-looking boss. When she saw Shapes approaching, the stony-faced woman turned on her heels and walked off towards the stable block, from which could be heard the fluctuating sounds of an engine being put through its paces. Shapes was keen to find out what she had said.

"She demanded to know what progress we'd made," replied Dykeman, re-buttoning the cuff on one of his shirt sleeves. "And when I told her things were coming along nicely she complained that was the sort of comment that normally meant someone hadn't made any progress at all."

"She's not completely wrong about that," observed a grinning Shapes, pushing the car into third gear with gusto.

Dykeman ignored the unhelpful comment. "Apparently, any fool can see it was John Perch who murdered Emma Greene. A man with a record of violence and an unrequited longing for the poor young woman, he must surely have killed her as a result of being overcome with fury at being turned down, yet again. Or words to that effect."

"Not a complete fool, then, is she? Thinking its Perch, I mean."

"It wasn't Perch who did it, Shapes," asserted Dykeman. "I'm prepared to put two bob on the line to back that up. Going to put your money where your mouth is?"

Shapes didn't hesitate. "Two bob it is, sir. Looking forward to spending my winnings already, I am."

As they reached the brow of the ridge, Dykeman looked out of the car, in the direction of the ditch in which the body of Emma had been found. It all looked so innocent in the bright midday sun, with the wind ruffling the leaves of the trees at the front of the nearby copse and a smattering of birds flitting low across the sky. It was likely, however, that for ever more people would steer clear of the spot, worried by the stories of the ghost of a vengeful young woman. They were the sort of stories that always started to circulate after such a terrible event.

"She did tell me something useful, though," said Dykeman, startled by the car lurching to one side as Shapes made a late move to avoid a deep pothole. "She confirmed Perch came up to the house on Monday, around lunchtime. She exchanged a few words with him, then sent him away, having lied that Emma was out riding with Philippa."

"Ah, there we go, then," declared Shapes, as he straightened up the car. "If he was up here then he had a damn good opportunity to kill Emma. Must have seen her walking along that path, lost his temper, stabbed her to death, shoved her in that ditch, then scuttled back to the garage. Wouldn't have taken him more than two or three minutes and it's so quiet round these parts it's no surprise no one saw him do it."

"Well, sounds like it's all sorted out. We can haul him off to the station, lock him up, then take the rest of the day off. Have a well earned break." Dykeman's voice was thick with sarcasm.

"Sounds good to me."

Shapes slowed the car at the junction with the main road, then pulled out on to the southbound side as a flat-backed lorry roared past in the other direction, hurtling down the hill towards the village.

"I think we'll hold off for a bit, if you don't mind, Shapes. Not least because Perch didn't do it."

"If you say so, sir."

Dykeman checked his watch. Thirteen minutes after twelve. The morning had slipped by so quickly and he'd need to make sure he left space in their day for his Sergeant to put away what would no doubt be a sizeable lunch. Probably best to stay on at the station so they could eat there. In any case, he still needed to get Dr Edwardes's full report, assuming he had completed his inspection of the deceased. The thought of going up to the hospital, to Sheila Delph's old place of work, made him feel depressed. Perhaps he'd phone the bloody man instead.

"So," said Shapes, having settled the car into a steady fifty miles per hour. "If it wasn't Perch who did it, then who do you reckon did?"

Dykeman rapped his fingers on the dashboard. "It would make a lot of sense if it was one of the Glass family. Several of them, with the likely exception of Philippa and possibly Michael, seem to have had some sort of reason for disliking her. And you can't get away from the fact that most of Robert Glass's money would have gone to his daughter rather than the family if she'd not very conveniently gone and got herself killed before her twenty-first birthday. But, I'm not counting my chickens, yet. That mother of hers is another one who interests me. I wonder if she might have been thinking she could get her hands on all that money."

"The mum?" said Shapes, in disbelief. "Can't see how that works. The daughter hadn't inherited yet. The family will get all the loot, won't they?"

"Maybe so, Shapes, but I don't trust that woman. I don't trust plenty of the others either, but that doesn't let her off the hook."

Shapes spent much of the rest of the drive back to Banbury mulling over his boss's suggestion, wondering if there was something Dykeman had noticed that he'd missed; something Jane Greene had said, maybe, or an odd look at a key moment. He couldn't see how she was a serious suspect, but he also couldn't stop himself feeling disconcerted at the prospect and worried he'd agreed to the bet on Perch too hastily.

BACK AT THE STATION, the two policemen bundled their way into the small office they shared to find it horribly stuffy; short of air and too hot. They'd forgotten to open a window before heading off to the solicitors. Shapes made a beeline for the nearest window and yanked it fully open, sticking his head out so he could fill his lungs with fresh, cool air.

Dykeman dropped his jacket over the back of his chair and picked up several notes that were laid out neatly on his desk. None of them caught his eye until he reached one that informed him Inspector Cranfield had phoned at ten-fifty. He read the note to himself then called over Shapes.

"Note from Cranfield. He's found a bus conductor who recognised Jane Greene when she got on his bus to Banbury on Monday morning."

"Blimey," replied Shapes, leaning in to get a closer look at the note. "Maybe your idea about her isn't so daft, after all."

"More than just a pretty face, Shapes. That's me."

Shapes said nothing, on the basis that he had nothing constructive to add.

Dykeman picked up the phone and dialled the number on the note. Cranfield wasn't there, so Dykeman left a message to say he and Shapes would drive up to Evesham after lunch, with the intention of interviewing Jane Greene.

It seemed their afternoon might well end up being as busy as their morning had already proved. And that thought in turn reminded Dykeman they had yet to speak to Edward Edwardes, and the sooner they did that the better, though the prospect seemed to have even less appeal now than it had on the drive back. Perhaps if he gave himself a bit more time to get used to the new pathologist and, more to the point, the loss of Sheila Delph then he wouldn't find the idea of calling in at the hospital such an unappealing one. Perhaps. But not yet. His mind was made up in a moment.

"Right then, Shapes," he announced, putting his jacket back on. "I'm going down to the canteen to get two cups of tea and, seeing how we've worked so hard this morning, I'm going to throw in a few biscuits as well. While I'm doing the important stuff, you can ring Dr Edwardes. See what he's got for us. I don't suppose there'll be anything new but, all the same, we need to cover all our bases."

With that, Dykeman strolled out of the office, not hanging around long enough to give his Sergeant chance to object or ask awkward questions. Shapes listened as his boss's footsteps echoed along the corridor away from their office. The significance of Dykeman's instruction wasn't lost on Shapes, who felt a little disappointed his boss had not felt up to facing his demons, or his most troublesome demon, to be precise. Dykeman had seemed to be doing so well now his attention was focused on their new case. It was a real shame. Opening the top drawer of his desk, Shapes pulled out an address book, leafed through it to the page he wanted and less than a minute later he was speaking to the new pathologist.

STANDING IN A SHORT queue in the canteen, waiting to pay for their tea and biscuits, Dykeman wondered if Shapes would guess at the real reason he hadn't phoned Edwardes himself. It seemed likely. His Sergeant was no mug and chances were he'd sussed it out straight away. The Inspector felt a tinge of awkwardness, even embarrassment, at the thought Shapes knew the truth of it.

He was staring at his tray, not really taking in the items parked on it, when he felt a firm tap on his shoulder.

"Hello, Dykeman. How's tricks?"

He looked up to see the annoyingly young and distinctly cheery face of Tom Gently looking back at him. The editor of the Banbury Globe was a not-infrequent visitor to the station, especially since many of his visits were at the behest of the Chief Inspector, who placed a great deal of importance on maintaining friendly relations with the press. Gently was also someone Dykeman spent a fair amount of time with himself, especially when it involved trips to race tracks, since both of them liked a flutter on the horses. His appearance in the canteen was a welcome one.

"Hello, Tom. I'm alright. The man upstairs dragged you in again, has he, or you here for some other reason?"

Gently chuckled. "Summoned. As a matter of fact, he wanted to speak to me about your latest case. Said I should go easy on you while it's still such early days. Might mess things up if I was to go putting my size eights in there too soon. All said in a friendly way, of course."

"Of course."

Dykeman paid for his provisions and waited next to a nearby table as Gently paid for his sausage roll and coffee.

"You had any breakthroughs, yet?" asked Gently, placing his tray next to Dykeman's.

"No, the boss is right, it is a bit too early just yet. Mind you, off the record, it's a nasty looking one. Seems like almost everyone the dead woman came into contact with had a good reason to have taken against her. The list of suspects is getting longer by the hour."

Gently raised an eyebrow and scratched the back of his neck. "That never helps. Anyone leading the pack at the moment?" he asked, more in hope than expectation.

"Me and Shapes disagree on that at present. We're off to Evesham in a bit to speak to the dead girl's mum. We've already spoken to her, but it seems she's not been altogether straight with us. Honestly, sometimes you get the impression people don't want us to catch the villains."

"True enough. Mind you, I suppose if you're the villain yourself then you'd not be keen on being too helpful," said Gently, light-heartedly.

"I suppose so, but they can't all have been in on it. At least, I hope not. God, what a case that would be."

"I don't know if it will help at all," began Gently, his tone all at once turned serious and his voice lowered. "But there's something about the eldest son, Stephen, you might want to know."

"Oh, yes. Been in one of your stories, has he?"

"Actually, no, but that was only because I intervened. I've known the Glass family in a minor way for some time. Or, rather, I've known the matriarch, Margaret Glass. Met her at several functions over the years."

"Bet that was fun."

"Ah, you've spoken to her already, have you?"

"We have. She gave me a right grilling not half-an-hour ago. Told me how to do my job."

"Sounds about right. Had similar comments myself, on occasion."

"You were saying, about the son."

"Yes. Last year – June, I think – one of the reporters put in a story concerning some complaints that had been made about the goings-on in a lay-by a couple of miles outside Stratford. Just outside our patch, but he thought it was of interest so did some digging and wrote it up. Very good writing, as it happens. I won't go into the details, but the gist of it was there were several men meeting in that lay-by to engage in the kind of sexual activity most of our readers wouldn't approve of. It would have generated quite a substantial postbag, of that I've little doubt."

"I expect it would," observed Dykeman, confident he knew where Gently was going with his little story. "I don't remember reading about that."

"That's because we didn't publish it. I had a friend at university who was that way inclined. He was set upon by a group of thugs one evening as he was leaving a pub with a male friend. The poor fella spent three days in hospital. I won't risk the Globe encouraging that sort of thing. Anyway, the point is, one of the men caught in that lay-by was Stephen Glass."

Dykeman nodded. "I had a feeling you were going to say that. Wouldn't have guessed it, though, from talking to him this morning. Seemed perfectly normal."

"I doubt he'd be going around advertising the fact. For one thing, that grandmother of his would probably have him kicked out of the family home."

"I think you're right," said Dykeman quietly, his mind having veered off elsewhere. Being a member of the Glass family and having something to hide was, in his experience so far, a combination best avoided. The obvious question to ask was, had Emma found out that?

"I take it that has some sort of bearing on the case," prodded Gently, having seen the reaction on the Inspector's face.

"Possibly." Dykeman tapped his fingers on the side of his legs, before bringing his attention fully back to the newspaper editor. "Let's just say, it raises some new possibilities."

"Well, in that case, I'm glad I mentioned it. Very nearly didn't."

"It will upset Shapes. His money's on a different horse. One I think the odds are about to lengthen on." Dykeman grinned.

"Running a book, are you?" asked Gently, his interest piqued.

"Just the two of us. We usually do on a case like this. Of course, Shapes hardly ever wins. He always backs one of the runners far too soon. Doesn't give himself time to properly assess the form of the whole field."

"Best not tell him you got your information from me, then," said Gently, smiling. "He still hasn't forgiven me for persuading him to back a different horse at last year's National after he'd said he was going to back the favourite."

"I remember. Cost him a fair few bob, that did. He was grumpy all the following week."

"Anyway, can't stand around here chatting all day. Work to be done. Let me know how you get on, won't you?"

"You'll be the first to know, as usual."

As Gently walked off with his rations in hand, Dykeman took a sip of tea from one of the cups on his tray, and returned to mulling over the possibilities that had arisen with this new piece of information. When all was said and done, it very much pointed to their having a new suspect to add to their growing list. Unfortunately, for the time being, things had just got more complicated, not less. There again, with a fair wind, he rather hoped by the time their trip to Evesham and return visit to Brayfield had been completed they would have started to narrow down the possibilities considerably. He sipped his tea again, then picked up the tray and set off back to his office.

JUST AS DYKEMAN HAD expected, Dr Edward Edwardes had found nothing even remotely helpful during the course of his inspection of Emma Greene's corpse. According to Shapes, Edwardes had seemed most interested in her hair, which he reckoned would be worth a few quid if her mum would give permission for it to be turned into a wig. Apparently it was an old custom that neither policeman found especially appealing. Dykeman, for one, hoped the practice had long since died out, as the thought of someone wearing a wig made from a dead person's hair gave him the colly-wobbles.

Lunch, which was taken as soon as Shapes had reported back, was a major operation on the part of the starving Sergeant, who made sure he was absolutely stuffed, just in case there was a long wait until his next meal. Dykeman could only wonder where the skinny fella put so much food, because it never seemed to show. Lucky sod.

As a result of Shapes's vast three-course lunch, it was Dykeman who drove them to Evesham, with his Sergeant spending most of the hour-long journey asleep. That suited the Inspector, who enjoyed the drive in peace and quiet. Even the occasional burst of mild snoring was largely muffled by the sound of the engine and the noise of the tyres on the road.

They arrived at Evesham police station without any mishaps and were quickly ensconced in an interview room, waiting with Cranfield while one of the station's WPCs escorted Jane Greene from the toilets.

"She wasn't happy when we brought her in," remarked Cranfield, who was leaning against a wall, his arms crossed in front of him. "Kicked up a right stink."

"She didn't come across as being the sort to fall into line tamely," responded Dykeman, leaning back in his chair while he tapped his fingers on the table in front of him.

"We would have left her in here if she'd been more co-operative, but she got so difficult to deal with I decided we'd better stick her in a cell. Gave her chance to cool down. Have to say, though, I'm not altogether hopeful it will have done the job."

Shapes was sitting next to his boss, busy picking wax out of one ear, then flicking it on the floor. He'd barely completed what had turned out to be a tricker task than he'd been expecting when the dramatic and echoing tones of a woman who was clearly upset could be heard approaching the room. All at once the two seated men sat up straight and Cranfield pushed himself away from the wall a fraction before the door opened and a barrage of vociferous complaints exploded into the room.

"It's disgusting. What have I done to be locked up in a cell like a common criminal," snapped Jane Greene, half-turned towards the following WPC, as she entered the room. As soon as she spotted Dykeman, her fire-filled eyes fixed him with a stare that made him flinch and his groin tighten; an unpleasant sensation that left him temporarily befuddled. "So, it's you, is it? You're the one responsible for all this?" The words landed with such a force they made Dykeman's head rattle like a Spanish maraca.

"We'll have less of that," commanded Cranfield, stepping forward. "You were brought in on my instructions and Inspector Dykeman and Sergeant Shapes were good enough to agree to my request for them to make the trip back to Evesham. Now then, Mrs Greene, please take a seat."

Jane looked at Cranfield, but decided she'd wouldn't say anything more to him, not yet. Instead, she turned her attentions back to Dykeman and sat down opposite him with a petulant shrug of the shoulders. The wooden base and back of the metal-framed chair was not comfortable; in fact, she told herself, it wasn't at all appropriate for someone who was in an emotionally delicate condition. With great effort, she managed to fill the bottom of her eyes with a well of small tears, which she then made a half-hearted effort to wipe away with her fingers. With any luck, the fat idiot opposite would start to feel sorry for her. That didn't feel like it was a big thing to ask, not after all she'd been through recently.

Dykeman did his best to hide the irritation that welled up inside him as soon as he saw the crocodile tears appear. Her performance left a lot to be desired and held out little prospect of winning her an Oscar. If he'd felt any sympathy at all when she walked into the room, that had now evaporated.

"Take your time, Mrs Greene," offered Dykeman. "We've no need to rush if you need a moment, have we now, Shapes?"

"No, sir. We've got all day." Shapes placed his pad and pencil on the table and folded his arms in front of him, well aware what game was being played and wondering why Jane Greene felt the need to muck around in such a way.

"No need to hold things up on my account," volunteered Jane, who found herself unable to maintain a slight wobble in her voice.

"Excellent," replied Dykeman, now free of the last vestiges of the intimidation he'd felt when Jane Greene had first stormed into the room, all guns blazing. "In that case, we'll get straight down to business and you can tell us all about the bus trip you made to Banbury on Monday morning."

He felt a moment's smugness at delivering his rapier like thrust with such skill and dexterity, not giving his opponent an opportunity to set herself to parry his attack.

Jane felt an uncomfortable quiver run up her spine and was unable to stop an involuntary twitch in her right eye, something that happened often during moments of stress. Thinking on her feet, she could she took a deep breath, looked threateningly at Shapes then back at Dykeman, who looked as though he reckoned he'd done the world's best job at catching her out. Horrible man.

"So what if I went to Banbury? I've got a right to. Just like anyone else. There ain't no law against it, last I heard." Jane's voice was strong and certain, but inside she was worried and wondering how the hell they'd found out about the bus trip. Who had seen her, when, to the best of her knowledge, there'd been no one on the bus who knew her? She had worried at the time it had been a mistake to make that journey and now she was angry with herself for giving in to the temptation that had teased her that morning. Why hadn't she just left things alone?

"Indeed, Mrs Greene, we're all free to catch a bus whenever we like; as and when they feel like turning up, that is. But you told us yesterday that you never went anywhere near Banbury on Monday morning." Dykeman paused a moment for effect. "Makes me wonder if you didn't take a second bus, this time to Brayfield. And, if you did, why you went there." Insinuation and suggestion was shot through Dykeman's words, or so he hoped.

Jane shifted on her chair and fiddled with the collar on her dark blue blouse. Idiot, she screamed at herself, silently. Idiot. Idiot. Idiot. She felt the sides of her neck warm as they flushed with blood. Well, there was no point in denying what they already knew to be true, but she had no intention of telling them the real reason for her trip. That would only complicate things.

"Well, seeing how you already seem to know so much - in which case I don't know why you're bothering to ask me – I did plan on going to Brayfield and, yes, to Ashview Lodge. I even got on the bus from Banbury. But I changed my mind and got off at Chiddington, then came straight back home. I suppose someone will have seen me do that too, just like they saw me do everything else."

Then it dawned on her, of course, the bus conductor or maybe the driver had seen her on the bus. Nosy bloody parkers. You'd think they had enough to do collecting their money without making a note of everyone who got on and off their damn bus. Still, at least she knew now what had happened and that made her feel a little less uncertain about herself.

"Chiddington, eh?" Dykeman glanced at Shapes, who was scribbling away in his notepad. "What made you decide to make the trip to Ashview Lodge? As far as we're aware, you hadn't been asked over for dinner."

"Fat chance of that, being asked to dinner by that lot. Too stuck up to ask the likes of me. You'd think they owned half the county the way they go on, especially Susan Glass."

Dykeman waited for an answer to his question and when it didn't come he pushed again, "I need to know why you were going to Ashview Lodge, Mrs Greene." He stared at her, hoping she would find it intimidating.

"Well, if you must know, I was going to bring Emma back home. I've never trusted those Glasses, not from the first moment I met them, and I know they used to give Emma a hard time. She used to tell me about it, how they made her feel little and unwelcome every time she went over there, especially when her father wasn't around. You'd think with all they'd got they wouldn't begrudge sharing a bit of it with someone in her position, but they made her feel so awkward and unwelcome she couldn't wait to come back home each time." She shifted forward to the edge of the chair, as her self-confidence returned. "I may not have had the education that lot got but I'm no idiot. I know they would have done everything they could to bully Emma into giving up her father's inheritance so they could get their greedy hands on it. That's why I wanted to bring her home. To get her away from that lot. I only wish I hadn't got off the bus at Chiddington, then she might still be with us now." Her voice trailed off and she sat there silent, starring at the table.

Dykeman couldn't decide what to make of things. Either Jane had just delivered as fine a performance as he'd seen in some time, or else she'd told them the truth. Given the circumstances and what they'd already heard about the Glass family, the latter option wasn't altogether out of the question. As he prodded and poked at Jane's reply, he found himself struggling to find a weakness in her defence. His rapier-like thrust, the one he'd been so confident had hit home, was starting to look more like a mistimed lunge. He rested his hands on this thighs, pushed them forward to his knees, then rapped his fingers on his knee-caps. What to do? Then a thought occurred to him; a welcome one, with some decent mileage in it.

"Do you think your daughter would have been so easily bullied? We've got the impression she was very capable of looking after herself."

Jane hesitated for a moment, before replying. "She had to learn how to look after herself when she was young. I couldn't be there for her all the time, not when I had to work all hours to put food on the table, and, of course, she had no father to turn to for help, not so far as she knew in those days. I was proud of the young woman she turned into. But even she couldn't have held out for long against that lot. Who could?"

As he listened to her speak now, Dykeman got the impression Jane was having to work harder than she ought to have needed to answer his question, almost as if she was making it up as she went along. There wasn't any hesitancy in her voice and she kept eye contact the whole time, but, all the same, there was something there that his inbuilt radar had cottoned on to. The problem was, he just couldn't work out what it was.

He glanced at Cranfield, who shook his head. Oh well, it seemed that was it for now. Shame, he'd been hoping for more. But she hadn't got herself off the hook entirely, not when she'd left him with that undeniable feeling something wasn't quite right. Maybe one last effort.

"If that's how you felt about things, then why did you let her go back to Ashview Lodge? Wouldn't it have been better to make her stay at home in the first place?"

"She knew her own mind, like she always did, and insisted she wanted to go. She was twenty years old, Inspector, not two. I could only do so much."

"Yes, I suppose you're right," observed Dykeman, scratching the back of his head. "Is that why you changed your mind and got off the bus in Chiddington?"

"Yes. I suppose I knew before I even got on the bus that I was wasting my time."

It occurred to Dykeman that someone didn't seem to make sense.

"There's one thing I'm confused about, which you might be able to help me with. If you're right about the way the Glass family treated your daughter, then why did she go back to Ashview Lodge? Wouldn't she have been better off coming back here, to Evesham?"

"I reckon she wanted to rub their noses in it. The money, I mean. She didn't say so, but that's what I think. Would serve them right, too."

Plausible, decided Dykeman. Certainly would be in keeping with what they'd found out about the young woman already. In fact, the more he considered things, the less convinced he was that Emma would allow herself to be bullied by the Glass family. So far, all the evidence pointed in the opposite direction.

"Well, thank you for your time, Mrs Greene. It's much appreciated."

"You going to take much longer catching my daughter's killer? Wasting all this time harassing me when you ought to be chasing whoever did it. It ain't right."

"We're doing all we can, Mrs Greene, I can assure you of that."

Dykeman watched Jane as she climbed to her feet and turned to walk out of the room, which was by now feeling warm and stuffy. Was that a hint of a smile on her face? He couldn't be sure, but she certainly didn't look disappointed, which only strengthened the notion there had been something more there for him to unearth, if only he'd been able to tease it out of her.

"What do you reckon?" asked Cranfield, as the door of the interview room shut behind Jane Greene and her accompanying WPC. "I got the impression she was keeping something back."

"I agree," replied Dykeman, glad of the opportunity to stand up and stretch his arms out in front of him. "But I couldn't put my finger on what it was that didn't quite seem right, sad to say. What about you, Shapes, got any ideas?"

Shapes was leaning back on his chair, arms on the back of his head, yawning so wide it looked painful to the other two men. He sat up abruptly and rubbed the corner of one eye, stifling another yawn as he did so.

"Keeping you awake, are we, Shapes?" asked Dykeman, his voice heavy with sarcasm.

"Sorry, sir. It's got a bit stuffy in here." He rubbed the corner of his other eye, before adding, "She's a lying git, is what I reckon. The only reason she wanted to get her daughter away from the Glasses was so she could get her own mits on the money. Or as much of it as she could grab. And I bet Emma knew what she was up."

Cranfield nodded thoughtfully. "Sounds entirely plausible. Jane Greene doesn't strike me as a woman who'd want to miss out on an opportunity like that."

"I agree," chipped in Dykeman, popping his hands into his trouser pockets. "But on the other hand, I don't see how bumping off her own daughter would help her get hold of the estate, since it looks like it will go the Glass family now."

"She might not have known that or had the wit to think it possible," suggested Cranfield.

"True enough," came Dykeman's response. "But is she really the sort of woman who would kill her own daughter in the hope of getting rich? Isn't that a bit of a leap, given what we've seen and heard so far?" Dykeman's voice was heavy with scepticism, though, truth be told, he wasn't entirely convinced either way himself and, if not for the woman's obvious deceit, he would have crossed Jane Greene off his list of suspects altogether.

"That is the big question," replied Cranfield. "and if I'd not known that sort of thing done before I'd say it was a daft idea. Unfortunately, where money is concerned, some people will do the very worst of things."

"I suppose you're sticking with Perch?" Dykeman asked his Sergeant, firing a raised eyebrow in his direction.

"Certainly am. Not heard anything here to change me mind on that one."

"Perch?" asked Cranfield.

"The young mechanic at the garage in Brayfield. Had a bit of crush on Emma, who seemed to have had a whale of a time stringing him along," replied Dykeman.

"He's a possible then, is he?"

Dykeman looked again at Shapes, who grinned.

"To be fair to Shapes," replied Dykeman. "Perch is in the running. Motive, opportunity, both there. But I don't think he's got what it takes to murder someone, not even when he's in a bad mood."

"Motive and opportunity, That's a pretty strong combination," suggested Cranfield, before spotting the unsettling grin that had appeared on Shapes's face. "Any other likely suspects?"

Dykeman puffed himself up a tad. "Indeed there is. We got some new information not long before we left to drive up here and we'll be heading back to Brayfield next to have another word with Stephen Glass. Seems he's another one who's caught this disease of not being entirely honest with us. Looking forward to hearing what he has to say for himself."

Shapes screwed up his nose but kept quiet. Dykeman could hope all he wanted, but Perch was their man, no doubt about it.

Cranfield looked at his watch. "Well, I ought to let you get on your way. I suppose it will take you a good hour to get over there?"

"That's alright, I'm going to let Shapes do the driving, while I have a nap. That alright with you, Shapes?"

"Certainly is, sir. Always happy to do a bit of driving and we'll get there in half the time it would take us if you were at the wheel."

Chapter Twenty-Two

THE FRESH BRUISE ON Dykeman's knee was still throbbing, badly, as the two policemen stepped into the study. Shapes had sworn it was a deer running across the highway that had caused him to swerve so violently on the Daventry Road and not the result of reckless high speed driving on his part. Dykeman hadn't been convinced the first time Shapes made his excuse and it hadn't sounded any more believable when he'd repeated it as they pulled up outside Ashview Lodge.

Whatever it was that had really caused the violent lurch, Dykeman had woken with a start, just in time to feel his knee smack against the glovebox of the car. He'd sworn, copiously, and suggested Shapes's driving was a load of old rubbish, or words to that effect. Had he got any sympathy in return? Fat chance. All Shapes did was suggest they turn round and double-back so Dykeman could collar the deer and charge it with behaviour likely to endanger the safety of a police officer. Shapes's subsequent laughing hadn't matter matters any less annoying.

The knee had throbbed considerably as they made their way from the car to the rear entrance of the house. So much so that Dykeman suspected the pain might put him right off his mark when it came to interviewing Stephen Glass. What good was that going to do their investigation? He simmered gently, relishing the bubbling feelings of self-pity.

Michael Glass had let them into the house before showing them through to the study, barely saying a word, despite a solid effort on Dykeman's part to engage him in conversation. The youngest of the two Glass boys could hardly get away quickly enough once he'd pushed open the study door and told his brother he had visitors.

"Inspector. Sergeant. Must say I wasn't expecting to see you back so soon," said Stephen, as the policemen entered the study. "Do you have news?"

"Not exactly," replied Dykeman, looking around the room. It was a modest size, the two walls either side of him lined with shelves packed with books; the one opposite dominated by a large window that looked out on to the front garden. It had that formal, old-fashioned feel to it such rooms had in houses of this sort and it left Dykeman feeling a little inadequate, which annoyed him. He made an effort to let such feelings slip away; it wasn't successful. Stephen was sitting behind a large oak desk, an assortment of newspaper and magazine pages spread across the surface and a pair of long, sharp-nosed scissors in his right hand. "Scrap book?" asked the Inspector.

Stephen stared at the mess on the desk, the look on his face seeming to suggest he'd forgotten why it was all there. After a moment he replied. "Oh, the articles. Yes, I like to collect useful bits and pieces about land management and that sort of thing. Find they come in handy at work. Helps to give people the impression I'm up to speed with all the latest developments. Bit of a chore, actually, so I tend to save things up for a once a fortnight effort."

"Very commendable," offered Dykeman.

"Please, take a seat," said Stephen, gesturing towards a pair of ornately-carved wooden chairs.

"We're fine as we are," replied Dykeman, keen to retain the position of dominance he had in being on his feet, towering above the seated suspect. "I suspect we won't be here very long."

"I see," said Stephen, not at all sure what the policeman was implying. "So, how can I help you?" He placed the scissors on top of a little pile of articles and folded the fingers of his hands together, resting them on the edge of the desk.

"Was Emma Greene blackmailing you, Mr Glass?"

The question hit Stephen with such force it took his breath away and, for a brief while, he sat there, starring into the space between him and Dykeman, his eyes wide and unblinking. It was in the end the lack of oxygen reaching his lungs that brought him back to the room, gasping for air. He began to fumble with the scissors, then dropped them back on to the desk, before trying to straighten himself up, only to find the effort beyond him. As his shoulders sagged, he felt sunk lower into his chair.

"I... I don't know what you mean..." he stuttered, his gaze now fixed on the desk.

"I think you know exactly what I mean." Dykeman paused briefly. "You see, we came into possession of some new information this morning. Information about you and your romantic preferences."

Stephen would have collapsed on the spot had he not already been sitting down. He closed his eyes and his head dropped forward, his chin resting on his chest. How had they found out about the one thing he had been so desperate for them not to discover? He had always made such great efforts to ensure the secret he shared with a very few close friends never became more widely known. They all took such terrible care, scared witless at the consequences if others found out. Unless... He felt his heart thumping in his chest and his breath shortened. What was he supposed to do? What could he say?

"Did she find out?" prompted Dykeman.

Stephen was confused by the unexpected change of tone in Dykeman's voice. Gone was the demanding sound of officialdom, replaced with a softer note of understanding. It was only four words, but he could hardly miss the alteration. The notion that the man standing opposite him might have some consideration and compassion, rather than the contempt and disgust he had been expecting, threw him; perhaps he ought to make the most of a horrible situation and take the apparent olive branch that had been extended to him.

He closed his eyes and nodded, barely enough for the other two men to notice, then looked up and past Dykeman, into empty space beyond.

"Yes. She knew." The words were only just audible.

Dykeman brought his hands together behind his back. "How did she find out? I assume you were discrete."

Stephen tried to look the Inspector in the eye, but the best he could do was to fix a weak gaze on his blue-striped tie. The knot wasn't pulled properly tight and stood half an inch away from the buttoned collar. It was the sort of little failing his grandmother would jump on in an instant. To her, such minor drops in standards were the sure sign of worse things to come and it was essential they were stamped out at once. He could hear her voice ringing in his ears from the many occasions he'd been called out for falling short. Lord only knew how she would react if she were to find out he preferred the company of men over women.

"She caught me and... my friend in the back of my car. It was parked in the garage, here, as we'd done a few times before. I thought we were safe, but I forgot to lock the garage doors and she had gone looking for Philippa, thinking she might be somewhere around the stables. It was just... bad luck, I suppose, that she poked her head round the corner of the garage door..."

"You were, er, in the act, so to speak?" asked Dykeman, rocking awkwardly on his feet.

"Close enough. She didn't have to use her imagination to know what was going on."

"And how did she respond?"

Stephen felt a surge of anger ripple through his body, leaving him more than capable now of meeting Dykeman's gaze. "She was an absolute bitch. It took her a moment to realise what she had stumbled upon, but as soon as she did, she saw what an opportunity it gave her. I suppose I didn't help things very much. I rather feel to pieces. Started pleading with her not to say a thing to anyone. But the look on her face ought to have told me I was wasting my time looking for some sort of understanding. She didn't make any demands straight away. Told me we would speak later and agree how best to keep things quiet. I imagine all she was really doing was giving herself time to decide what she was going to demand in return for keeping her mouth shut."

"Money, was it?" asked Dykeman, coming to rest once more on the flats of his feet.

"Yes," replied Stephen. "Small amounts, at first. What she called little treats, as a sign of my thanks for her understanding. She also had me give lifts to her and some girlfriend from Evesham. The cinema, a couple of shopping trips to Leamington, for which I also had to provide both of them with spending money. Then the amounts involved started getting larger. I objected one time but she got very angry and told me in no uncertain terms what would happen if I refused." He stopped, apparently done, then added in a voice riddled with helplessness, "I'd never before felt that things were so hopeless."

The anger had subsided, noticed Dykeman, gone almost as soon as it had emerged, and he stood there now looking at a dejected and fearful young man. If he was, indeed, feeling fearful, he had good reason to. Had they heard a better motive yet for killing Emma? But why own up to what had happened if he had, indeed, murdered his tormentor? Bluff and double-bluff were all part of the game they were playing. He knew that well from prior experience. Take nothing on face value, but question and probe until each and every claim has either been proven or disproven. But motive counted for a lot. It nagged at Dykeman, a bit like Shapes pleading for food whenever he was hungry. Perhaps the direct approach he'd already used successfully might unearth some more gems.

"Sounds to me, Mr Glass, as if you had a damn good reason for wanting Emma dead. What do you say to that?"

Stephen buried his face in his hands and shook his head without saying a word.

"So you're denying you killed her, I take it?"

"I didn't kill her," came the softly spoken reply, as Stephen dropped his hands limply into his lap and sat forlornly, his eyes downcast and the colour drained from his face.

Dykeman was tempted to haul their suspect down to the station in the hope that another grilling, this time in a less familiar and comfortable environment, might extract a confession, but he knew their hand wasn't yet a strong one. There was no actual evidence to place Glass at the scene of the crime, and, betting man that he was, he preferred to stack the odds more generously in his favour before making such a call. Was he going soft, he wondered to himself? Would he have done things differently in the past? Damn it, why couldn't he make his mind up? He glanced at Shapes, who stood there silently, pencil and notepad in hand, his face a picture of concentration. No help to be had there.

"Convenient for you, though, isn't it? Her being dead."

"Yes, I suppose it is."

Then a new thought occurred to the senior policeman. "Did your friend know she was blackmailing you?"

Glass shook his head. "No. I didn't see any point worrying him about it."

Ah, well, considered Dykeman, it had been worth a try. He looked again at the cuttings on the desk. Well, they'd got a nice clean confession, which had been the main objective of this particular visit. But it wasn't a confession to murder and, if they were to pin that on him, they'd have to place him at the scene of the crime at the right time. As things stood, they had no chance of being able to do that, more's the pity.

"If you have any travel plans for the next few days, Mr Glass, you'll be needing to cancel them. I'm certain we'll be wanting to speak to you again. Soon, I should imagine. It won't look any too good for you if we find you've cleared off. Is that understood?"

"Yes, Inspector, I understand."

The policemen left Stephen slumped in his chair, his eyes shut and his chin once again resting on his chest. He looked for all the world like a man who'd just been told he hadn't long to live, thought Dykeman.

As he closed the study door behind them, Shapes wasted no time in asking Dykeman for his thoughts. "What did you make of that, then, sir? You caught him out good and proper there."

Dykeman looked up, his eyes panning the wide hallway. "Not here, Shapes. Too much chance of being overheard. We'll have a chat in the car."

They had barely taken a first step towards the front door when they heard a familiar voice call out to them from behind. They turned to see Margaret Glass standing just outside the kitchen door. She was, considered Dykeman, an odd mixture of enfeebled old age and unflinching determination. Her ancient Edwardian ankle-length black dress may have been unable to hide the fact she was slightly awkward in the way she stood, as if it required more effort than she could easily give, but there was no missing the steely look in her eyes. It pointed to a still fully functioning and clear mind. He found it hard to imagine that anyone would fail to do anything other than jump at her command.

"Mrs Glass, how can we help you?" asked Dykeman, noticing the sharp-nosed pair of scissors she was clutching.

Margaret Glass looked down at the scissors, having noticed how they'd caught his eye. "I prefer a pair of scissors to secateurs whenever I'm dead-heading. Odd, the ones I normally use can't be found anywhere. Now then, how are your enquiries coming along, Inspector? I suppose you must have identified some suspects after all this time."

Dykeman wasn't entirely sure if she had asked a question or made an accusation. Perhaps she had managed to do both at the same time.

"Our enquiries have been going very well indeed, thank you, Mrs Glass, and there are several suspects we are currently investigating. Though, you'll appreciate, we can't say anything about them."

A raised eyebrow, thought Dykeman, can rarely have said so much as the one Margaret now deployed with such effectiveness. "I'm not a complete invalid, Inspector. My body may not be what it once was but my brain continues to function perfectly well. Of course I know you can't go around telling all and sundry who your suspects are. What do you take me for?"

Dykeman suspected that, if he looked, he would find Shapes had taken several steps backwards, towards the front door, leaving him all alone to face the full onslaught from Margaret Glass. But he resisted the temptation to look and focused on bolstering his own defences. What he wanted to say in reply was that he took her for an old battleaxe, but thought better of it. She seemed more than capable of standing up for herself. Then he thought about trying a bit of flattery, but wasn't sure he was up to it. Oh, sod it, why not give it a go.

"Sad to say, Mrs Glass, not everyone is as sensible or aware of protocol as you are. It's best to assume the worst, just in case."

"Never mind all that," the old woman replied, dismissively. "Do you have a proper suspect? Or perhaps you've found a witness whose been able to point you in the right direction?"

Her piercing blue eyes glared at Dykeman, seeming to dare him to reply with a load of waffle and old flannel. It was a distinctly unnerving sensation, especially as that was exactly the sort of answer he wanted to give. He swallowed, then eased himself up on to his toes and back down again, all the while fumbling for some sort of reply that wouldn't spill any beans yet also satisfy the demand for a proper response.

"Serious suspects we most certainly do have, Mrs Glass. The problem is that we currently have too many suspects. Witnesses, on the other hand, are in short supply, there being no one who saw anything on Monday that points us to incontrovertible evidence. But I've no doubts Shapes and I will get there, in the end. We almost always do, eh, Shapes?"

An odd, breathless noise came from the direction of his Sergeant, who, Dykeman found, had made it almost as far as the front door. The gutless little worm. The man was always complaining he didn't get enough attention from women and now, as soon as one fixes her beady eyes on him, he falls to pieces and clears off as quick as his feet will carry him. Quite what was going to happen when Ivy Davey got him alone was anybody's guess. Dykeman considered a heart attack a distinct possibility.

"Well perhaps you and that odd looking man of yours would like to get a move on. It's a murder we're talking about here, not sheep rustling or the theft of someone's stamp collection. In my day, this sort of thing was sorted out promptly, not drawn out over days and days, though I suppose the police have to observe all manner of silly little rules and regulations these days. Lord knows, if the abolitionists get their way, there'll even be an end to the death penalty and then where will we be?"

"Er, quite. Yes, well, like you say, we'd best be getting on. Lots to do and the day's more than half done."

Dykeman was sure he could feel Margaret's eyes boring into his back as he and Shapes bundled out of the front door. If he thought she was physically up to it, he'd not put it past her to have stabbed Emma to death, though he imagined she was the sort of person who was more likely to accost their victim in the night and suck out all their blood.

DYKEMAN'S INITIAL INSTRUCTION to Shapes was to drive them straight back to the station, but even before they reached the main road he had changed his mind. As they got to a spot on the track more or less opposite the ditch in which the body of Emma had been found, he told his Sergeant to pull over. They sat there in silence for a moment, as Shapes waited for his boss to speak.

"What do you think about that?" Dykeman eventually asked.

Shapes scratched at a damp armpit. "I reckon Stephen Glass has a bloody good reason to have topped Emma. Not in a million years would he have wanted word to get out that he was... well, you know."

"I agree. Motive and, most likely, opportunity, he had them both." Dykeman tapped a couple of fingers on the dashboard and looked across the field in the direction of the deep ditch into which he had insisted Shapes clambered to inspect the corpse. It was so close to the house it made him wonder if it wasn't too close. Would a member of the Glass family really commit murder there when they might have plenty of opportunities to do the deed further afield? Wouldn't that make more sense? Did sense have anything to do with it? "Would you have killed her there if you were one of the Glass clan?"

Shapes shrugged his shoulders. "Don't see why not. You'd be able to sneak back home pretty sharpish with hardly any chance of being caught. And you'd know what's what, where the tracks go and who regularly walks through when. You'd be taking a bigger chance, I reckon, if you did it somewhere else, especially if you didn't know the place."

"Mm."

"Anyway, I still say it don't matter. We've not heard anything today that changes my mind about Perch."

Dykeman gave his Sergeant a look of disapproval. Then, as if he wasn't already befuddled enough, this talk about dead people brought Sheila Delph back into Dykeman's thoughts. He did his best to push them aside, but they refused to go away, leaving him unable to focus properly.

"One thing I would like to know is was it a planned, cold-blooded killing or a spur of the moment thing where our killer simply lost control?" asked Dykeman, as he attempted to shake off memories of the former pathologist.

"Mercy killing?"

"Do what?" asked Dykeman, looking askance at his Sergeant.

"Just checking. You sounded like your mind was on other things."

There was an implication in those words that Dykeman couldn't miss, but he chose to ignore it all the same, embarrassed that it was so clear what his mind had been lingering on.

"I'll make a mercy killing of my own pretty soon, you carry on like that."

The heat of the sun had already begun to warm the inside of the car, a little more than was comfortable. Dykeman wound his window down a couple of inches and sucked at the cooler air that tumbled in.

"My money's on a revenge killing," chirped Shapes as he wound his own window all the way down, then rested an arm on the bottom of the frame.

"As in the revenge of an abandoned lover, would that be?"

"Yep. Your trouble is, sometimes you like to over-complicate things, when the obvious answer is the right one," answered Shapes, brimming with confidence. Indeed, he felt more confident about this case than he'd done with any other for, oh, at least a couple of years.

"Let's put that one aside for now. You know, Emma seems to have upset so many people you have to wonder if they didn't all get together to do the deed."

"Committee killing?"

Dykeman nodded.

"No, there'd have been more stab wounds," said Shapes, brushing aside his boss's speculation. "Mind you, they could have done it like some sort of fox hunt. They might have got out their horses and chased her across the fields. The one who caught her got to stick the knife in while the others cheered them on."

"I'm surprised we've not encountered that sort of thing for real by now. So many of the people we meet in these rural locations seem to be as mad as spoons and I wouldn't put it past them. We're not doing too well, are we? I mean, here we are talking total rubbish because we don't have enough to go on yet to pin the murder on someone."

"Early days."

"And everyone seems to have been lying to us, too."

"There's a lot of suspects."

Dykeman yawned, checked his watch, then scratched an ear. "Later than I realised. Let's get back to the station so we can have another look through all the statements. See if there's something we missed."

Shapes hesitated. "Not thinking of a late one, are you, sir?"

"Not if we don't have to. I don't see any point stretching things out for the sake of it. Why's that? Afraid of walking home on your own after dark?"

Shapes took to inspecting the steering wheel, as he muttered, "Remember, I've got an engagement."

Dykeman grinned. "Oh yes. I'd forgotten about that. How silly of me. He slapped his Sergeant on the shoulder and laughed. "Didn't your mum warn you about women like that?"

Shapes was tempted to remind Dykeman about his own women-related issues, but thought that would be going too far, even if it wasn't meant to be anything more than a put down. He wiggled his nose and sniffed, before replying, "My mum was a woman like that. She used to keep reminding my dad all the time that if he didn't look after her proper, she'd always got a long line of admirers waiting to spoil her something rotten. He used to tell her she was imaging things, but I reckon he knew she wasn't. Poor old sod would hardly say a word for ages afterwards."

"I wasn't sure you had parents, Shapes. You hardly ever mention them. Anyway, make sure you put on some clean underwear before you go out tonight. You never know what might happen."

Dykeman started laughing so much he was still chuckling, tears, running down his cheeks, as Shapes turned the car on to the main road and slammed his foot hard on the accelerator pedal. Sometimes, he felt like he could commit a murder himself.

Chapter Twenty-Three

THURSDAY MORNING WAS overcast and damp. Rain had fallen heavily in the small hours and there were still little puddles of water dotted along the sides of roads and pavements. The leaves on the trees outside the police station glistened as if they'd been polished and the occasional drop of water slipped from them to land on the ground with a faint plop.

Dykeman found his walk into work a most refreshing experience and one that left him with an inexplicable feeling the day ahead was going to be a rewarding and enjoyable one. Might it, he contemplated, even see a key turning-point in the investigation?

It was an odd thing, the mind. For starters, why was it that the less effort you made to get to grips with a problem the quicker you often got to an outcome? And how come you could often find yourself grabbing an answer to some tricky issue out of thin air when you were wrapped up doing something else altogether?

He had been dead-heading his sweet peas in the back garden the previous evening, while his lamb chops cooked in the oven, when the thought came to him that perhaps they had been going about things the wrong way round.

Instead of trying to work out who had both a motive for, and an opportunity to, kill Emma, why not establish who had neither motive nor opportunity? It was such a simple change to make, but it seemed now such an obvious one he wondered why he hadn't thought of it sooner.

As he'd half-expected, Shapes was no where to be seen when he reached the station. If Ivy Davey hadn't locked him in a bedroom cupboard then she'd probably left him such a nervous wreck he'd been too tired to wake up at his usual hour. He tried to picture Shapes locked in one of Ivy Davey's wardrobes, but found it too unsettling and brushed the thought away.

Having hung his coat on the rack in their office, Dykeman rubbed his hands together with glee at the prospect of giving his Sergeant a damn good grilling when he eventually made it into work. He'd be expecting, no, he'd be demanding a full and detailed report, juicy bits and all.

But, just as he seemed to be enjoying himself, a sudden and unwelcome feeling of jealousy began to well up inside him. He knew at once what that was all about. Sheila Delph. When would he be free to move on? It wasn't fair. With great effort he pushed the feeling aside, determined not to let such thoughts cloud his day, and strode out of the office, in search of a cup of tea and a rich tea biscuit from the canteen.

DYKEMAN SPENT LONGER than he had intended in the canteen, the result of giving in to the temptation to pick up a copy of that morning's Daily Express so he could peruse the runners and riders in the day's race card. There had been one or two tempting bets he'd have liked to place, but the bookies didn't open for another two hours. There was also the small matter of their investigation to focus on.

By the time he did eventually push open the door to the office once more that morning, he found not only Shapes but also Sergeant Stanley Blunt standing around the former's desk, deep in conversation, Shapes holding a small ream of papers in one hand.

"Morning Shapes. Blunt." Dykeman announced his arrival cheerily.

The two sergeants broke off their conversation and replied in kind. Both, noticed Dykeman, wore expressions that indicated they were well satisfied about something or other.

"What you got there?"

Shapes grinned. "I think we've got our man, sir." He took the top paper from the bundle he held and leaned across the desk so he could hand it to Dykeman. "Stan brought these along just now. The boys have pulled together a really decent picture of the Glass family finances, especially those for James Glass. That one covers his financial affairs."

Dykeman scanned the single page quickly, then took a second, careful, read through one particular section. "Well, well, would you look at that." He jabbed a finger at the sheet of paper. "Doesn't that just give the man a motive for murder?"

"That's what we thought," answered Shapes, with something of a sparkle in his eye.

"Fifteen thousand pounds down the plughole at Lloyds of London last year and now his firm is so hard up none of the partners got a payout this year. What about the bank?"

"There's a few quid in accounts there, but not the sort of money you'd need to keep a house like Ashview Lodge on the go," replied Blunt. "They must be feeling the pinch."

"And, off the record," added Shapes, "we had it on good authority that firm he works at is having such a hard time it could go belly up by the end of the year if they don't get some serious new business in soon."

"Still think we should be hauling Perch in for questioning, eh, Shapes?"

Shapes sniffed and scratched the back of his head before replying. "We've got new information now." That was his excuse and he was sticking to it.

Dykeman chuckled. "If James Glass isn't our man, then someone else in the house must have been doing the dirty work for him, because it looks pretty bloody obvious the family couldn't let all that money end up in the hands of Emma Greene. But it doesn't do us much good if we can't come up with some evidence that links him to the murder. I know it can be an annoying inconvenience at times, but courts have a habit of liking to see hard proof before they're prepared to convict."

Shapes looked at Blunt as he pushed one of the papers on the desk towards him. "Go on, your men found it so you ought to tell him."

"Thank you, Stanley." Blunt, in turn, pushed the sheet of paper towards Dykeman, adding, "If it's evidence you want sir, then how about this? Do you think it might do the trick?"

Dykeman looked at the second sheet of paper, almost afraid to read what was written on it for fear it might all be an elaborate wind-up by Shapes. Praying it wasn't anything of the sort, he glanced at his Sergeant, whose face showed not a hint of mischief. Dykeman picked up the single sheet and read through what turned out to be a statement taken by Constable Dartington from a Mr Roger Anderson, a resident of Brayfield. It took only a short while to read, but by the time he'd finished Dykeman was aglow with the overwhelming anticipation of success.

"I don't believe it," he said, delighted at the turn of events. "You haven't made this up, have you, Shapes? Not roped Blunt here into some mischievous scheme of yours."

Shapes hook his head, still grinning happily.

Dykeman read the statement a second time, just to be sure. But there it was, all they needed to move to an arrest. Roger Anderson had reported seeing a man in the vicinity of the murder scene while he was out walking his dog after his lunch on Monday. He'd heard the church bells strike two a little before, so was certain about his timing. Dartington had originally thought it was Perch that Anderson must have seen, but when Blunt had read it he'd noticed it couldn't be Perch. For one thing, they'd been told by the garage owner that Perch was back at work by then and, for another, the description was of a man less well built than Perch and there was no mention of red hair, which was hardly the sort of thing a witness was likely to miss.

"Good work, Blunt. Excellent job. I'll have to get you a pint or two for this."

"Thank you, sir. Do you think it could be James Glass that Anderson saw?"

"Well, it certainly wasn't Perch and there's nothing there to say it couldn't have been James." Dykeman breathed in deeply and rubbed a hand over his belly.

"Don't you think we've got enough for an arrest?" asked Shapes.

"Oh, I think we've enough to bring him in for more questioning, but I'm just not too sure about an arrest just yet. He might cave in under questioning, of course, especially if his nerves are already shot. But what would really give us what we need is finding the murder weapon."

"We took a good look all over that hillside, sir," observed Blunt. "Could he have dumped it somewhere away from the village or maybe hidden it in the house?"

"We ought to have another look. Let's get everyone we can up there this morning. We'll go over the whole hillside with a fine-tooth comb, then see about the house. You'd better try and get us a warrant, Shapes. Give the judge the old hurry up and tell him there's a chance the killer could put the murder weapon beyond our reach if we can't get in there straight away."

"Will do, sir," replied Shapes, smartly. Excitement was afoot and he was already looking forward to a most enjoyable day. Could even be an arrest to be made. Always the most enjoyable part of an investigation, was that.

"I'll see who we can get our hands on for the search party," added Blunt, also bristling with enthusiasm and energy. "It's been a quiet morning so there ought to be a good few people available."

"We're close now," said Dykeman, placing the sheet of paper back on the desk. "Let's see if we can't make an arrest before the end of the day."

SHAPES TURNED THE KEY in the ignition and satisfied himself the engine in the Ford Anglia was turning over nicely before he pushed the gear stick into first and let out the clutch with a smooth, practised ease. He was looking forward to taking on the damp, possibly slippery, roads as they raced up the B4036 to Brayfield, all too aware that he had more than good enough reason to put his foot down. Always the best way to drive a car, as far as he was concerned. As he arced the vehicle towards the car park exit, his fingers caressed the steering wheel much as they had done Ivy Davey's firm buttocks the night before. Been a bit of a shame, it had, that she'd not allowed him to do anything more than have a quick fondle; if he didn't know better, he'd say she'd been stringing him along, making sure she got a second date. Well, if that had been her game, it had worked; they were going out together again the following Saturday, to watch whatever film was on at the town's cinema. One thing was for sure, he'd be looking to get them tickets for a pair of seats as far away from any of the other cinema-goers as possible; he didn't plan on spending all his time watching the film.

"Look out, Shapes," hollered Dykeman, slapping a hand on the dashboard.

Shapes left Ivy Davey behind at the cinema just in time. Another second and he wouldn't have been able to hit the brakes quickly enough to stop them ploughing into Constable Dartington.

"What the bloody hell is that idiot doing?" growled Shapes, knocking the car out of gear and easing his right foot partially up off the brake pedal.

The constable had shot out into the open right in front of them as he rounded the corner of the main station building. So close had they come to running him down that, as both he and they lurched to a halt, Dartington found his legs pressed hard up against the front of the Anglia. He stepped back gingerly, looking down at the gleaming metal bumper.

Even before he'd managed to wind the window down more than a couple of inches, Dykeman was barking his annoyance through the opening at the startled constable. "What the hell are you playing at, Dartington? You could have got yourself seriously hurt there. What do you want?"

Breaking the spell that the car's bumper had temporarily held over him, Dartington looked up. When he spoke there was a nervous wobble in his voice. "It's Mrs Glass, sir. She's been run down by a car in Brayfield. On her way to the hospital now, so they say."

"Mrs Glass," repeated Dykeman, irritated at getting only a partial update. "Which one?"

"Which what?" asked Dartington, swallowing as he noticed his hands had started to shake.

"What's wrong with the man?" Dykeman asked Shapes, who simply shook his head and pursed his lips. "Which Mrs Glass, Susan or Margaret?"

"Er, the younger one," answered Dartington, squeezing his hands into tight fists. "Mrs Susan Glass. An ambulance reached the house about five minutes ago. Her daughter phoned just now. Said she thought you'd want to know."

"Well, that puts a cat amongst the pigeons," observed Dykeman, solely for the benefit of his Sergeant, before leaning his head out of the now fully open window. "Did the driver stop?"

"No, sir. Seems to have been a hit and run. There was a witness who saw the car head off up the B4036 towards Daventry, but they didn't get a look at the driver. Too far away for them to see."

"Anything else?"

Dartington let his hands open slowly, then began to stretch out his fingers. "No, sir. That's all the daughter could tell us. Upset she was."

"Alright. Tell Sergeant Blunt to go ahead with the search as planned. Shapes and I are going up to the hospital to see if we can speak to Susan Glass, then we'll join up with the search party as soon as we can. Got that?"

"Yes, sir."

As Dartington marched off, Dykeman pulled his head back into the car and turned towards Shapes. "Well, let's not go jumping to conclusions. It might be just a... "he hesitated, aware he was about to suggest it was nothing more than a coincidence, and coincidences were something he always insisted to be nothing short of nonsense. Simply to suggest the possibility would have Shapes laughing all the way to the hospital. "It might have nothing to do with the murder."

Shapes held off commenting, at first, savouring the sweet, sweet taste of opportunity. It was one of his favourites delights. "You were going to say, it's just a coincidence, weren't you?" It was more an accusation than a question.

Dykeman bridled, realising attempting to deny the charge was futile. He'd have to fall back on the one card he could always rely on: pulling rank. "Get us up to the hospital, Shapes. Pronto. There's work to be done."

Shapes couldn't help grinning as he eased the Anglia out of the car park and on to the road. Not only was that one point to him, it was also another sign that his boss was on the way to recovery, edging ever further away from the dark days he'd recently spent so much time enveloped in.

SUSAN GLASS LOOKED as though she'd gone half-a-dozen rounds with Rocky Marciano, with both her arms tied behind her back and a blindfold fitted for good measure. As he stared at her from the end of the hospital bed, if he'd not been told otherwise by the doctor, Dykeman wouldn't have believed it possible she didn't have a single broken bone nor, indeed, anything worse than an impressive collection of cuts, scrapes and bruises. Mind you, her left eye was not only blackened, it had swelled to the size of an orange, causing her to look like something out of a Hammer Horror movie; Revenge of the One Eyed Woman, or some such thing, mused Dykeman.

"Well, I have to say I'm impressed you managed to get away without any serious injuries, Mrs Glass," said the Inspector, cheerily. "Must have the constitution of a horse."

Susan Glass would have objected to the suggestion she bore any kind of resemblance whatsoever to a horse, but her head throbbed appalling and her jaw ached, which made speech an unwelcome and painful effort, so she let things pass. In any case, under the circumstances, the comment seemed of little significance. She was far more keen to know what progress had been made in arresting the driver who had mown her down. Her mind had already given thought to the prospect of suing them; the money would be a welcome addition to the family funds, especially as things had been rather tight of late.

"Dr Ronson's amazed," continued Dykeman. "Said he would have expected several broken bones from such an impact. Shapes was hit by a car once, weren't you, Shapes? Got very upset he did. If it hadn't been one of our young constables behind the wheel, he would have charged him with dangerous driving, wouldn't you, Shapes?"

"Sir," came the non-committal reply. Shapes had wanted to charge Constable Nevin, despite his being one of the boys, but Dykeman had insisted he be let off with a firm word to take more care in future. It still rankled.

"I understand you didn't manage to see the driver, is that right?"

"Yes, that's correct," came the quiet, tired reply.

"But we seem to have a witness, which is handy. Got the licence plate as well, sensible person. It's a shame they escaped north up the B4036 rather than heading our way, as that means it will be up to the Northamptonshire force to track them down and make an arrest, but they're a decent bunch, so we shouldn't have to wait long before we get some news."

Dykeman was forced to wait a moment as a nurse with chubby fingers took Susan's temperature, recorded it on the clipboard that hung on the end of her bed, then cast a disapproving eye over Shapes, before marching off to her next patient.

"She didn't like the look of you, Shapes."

"Don't care. Her loss, not mine."

Shapes hadn't even given the woman a second glance, noticed Dykeman. There could only be one reason for that: Ivy Davey. He turned back to Susan.

"I appreciate it might be hard to tell, Mrs Glass, but did you get the impression it was just an accident or might it perhaps have been deliberate, you being hit by that car?"

"I couldn't say," came the weak reply. "It happened so quickly." Susan winced at the effort required to deliver every word.

"Shame, it would be helpful to get an idea whether or not it was deliberate. Could have a bearing on our case."

"Inspector." It was only the one word but it was wrapped up in a volatile mixture of seething anger and burning frustration and James Glass fired it into Dykeman's left ear from an uncomfortably close distance.

Dykeman leaned away at once, caught unawares. "What the..."

"My wife has been mown down by some madman and is visibly in no condition to be subjected to an interrogation. You will desist immediately and leave her alone."

Dykeman looked, with some surprise, at the wide-eyed, tight-skinned face of a man on the point of losing his self-control. What did he expect? They were bound to want to speak to his wife, given they were in the middle of a murder investigation centred on the Glass family. Some people could be far too touchy. It wasn't like they'd hauled her off to the station.

"Mr Glass, you're here already," replied Dykeman, breezily.

"Of course, I'm here. What did you expect me to do, take a trip to the coast, perhaps?" His voice was thick with a mixture of sarcasm and annoyance.

"Your wife's been very fortunate. Something I'm sure we're all pleased about, wouldn't you say, Shapes?"

"Quite so, sir. Very pleased." Shapes nodded his agreement.

"Are you done?" It wasn't so much a question from James as a demand. His nostrils were flared and, noticed Dykeman, his breathing was more shallow and rapid than normal. The poor man was naturally concerned, but he really needed to avoid getting so worked up; it wouldn't do him any good at all.

"We are, indeed, Mr Glass," answered Dykeman. "That is, we're finished with your wife, but we do have some more questions for you."

Dykeman's demeanour changed in an instant, his light-heartedness replaced with a much more serious attitude. It had been his intention to speak again to James at Ashview Lodge, ideally after the planned search had been completed, but things had changed. Now was the time for their questions. And they wanted answers, not excuses and evasion.

"Me?" James looked at Dykeman, as if he was expecting some sort of explanation. When none was forthcoming his irritation was clear to hear. "What do you want to speak to me again for? Can't you see I have more important things on my mind right now?"

"Your wife won't be running off anywhere soon," started Dykeman, holding up a hand to silence James, who was clearly intent on speaking again. "And, whilst I acknowledge she's had a very nasty experience, she's been fortunate enough not to suffer any life-threatening injuries. On the other hand, we've unearthed some interesting facts concerning yourself, Mr Glass, and we most definitely do need to speak to you now. If you'd rather not talk to us here we can always take a trip down the road to the station, if that's what you would prefer."

Dykeman was not in the slightest bit interested in hearing anything more from James. The man had already lied to and misled them and now they'd dug up information that gave him a good reason to ensure Emma Greene didn't live long enough to get her hands on her father's money. If he didn't stop complaining, they'd haul James off to the station without any more warning, in handcuffs if needs be.

From the far end of the ward came a short, sharp cry of pain. It broke the emerging tension between the two men in an instant and, when he brought his attention back to

Dykeman, James found himself without the will to object further.

"I won't be long, darling," he said softly to his wife, reaching out to rest his fingers on the back of her hand. "You get some more rest and I'll be back as soon as I can."

Susan smiled weakly at her husband and closed her eyes as her head tilted a little to one side.

IT TOOK NOT A LITTLE of his natural charm and engaging manner, but Dykeman nonetheless managed to persuade the ward sister, a short, thin, rather stern woman called Ethel Inkling, to give them access to a temporarily vacant side room. She had been very clear about the temporary nature of the vacancy, as well as a the measures she was entirely willing to take in order to evict the three of them should the need arise. Dykeman had smiled broadly and thanked her profusely before closing the door on her with a sigh that he instantly hoped she hadn't heard. The grin on Shapes's face said it all. It disappeared as soon as Dykeman noticed it.

James stood with his back to the room's solitary, small window, his arms folded and face stern. "So, what is it that's so desperately important we have to discuss it now, Inspector." There was an edge to his words that suggested he'd better get a damned good reason for the intrusion or else there's be trouble, though if you had asked him what action he might take he wouldn't have been able to tell you, since he had no idea what his options were.

Dykeman noticed how flawlessly clean and tidy the small room was. Even the pillows and sheets on the bed displayed barely a crease or wrinkle and a just detectable hint of polish tickled his nostrils. The rigorous attention to detail of the nursing profession never ceased to amaze him and, on occasion, he even went so far as to wonder if such mental discipline might make the average nurse suitable material for the police force. They could do with one or two more WPCs on the force, for those occasions when it was inappropriate or downright embarrassing for a man to carry out a task. But, he was allowing his mind to wander when he had a potentially very rewarding job to do. He looked hard into the eyes of James Glass before he spoke.

"You're a man in trouble, Mr Glass. If we're not mistaken, and I don't believe we are, you are, in fact, a man in a great deal of trouble. Financial trouble, that is."

He let the words sink in, watching James closely. There was a brief flicker of uncertainty in the man's eyes before he responded.

"I'm not sure I understand you. My finances are quite alright."

"Pull the other one, it's got bells on it," snapped Dykeman, keen to press his attack. "You're broke. That firm you're a partner at is in trouble and last year you lost a packet at Lloyds of London. You must be down to your last few quid by now."

James felt his cheeks begin to grow warmer and the harder he tried to stop it happening the worse it made things. Maintaining eye contact with the bloody Inspector was almost as difficult to do, though he was determined not to betray his concern over Dykeman's accusation. Damn the man, how had he found out so much and in such a short space of time? The firm's troubles were supposed to be a secret, for fear it might drive away new business or cause existing clients to go elsewhere and that was the last thing they needed. The problem was, there were employees who knew the truth and people in the trade were always talking to one another. It was inevitable, he supposed gloomily, that sooner or later someone would let slip their predicament.

And as for those bloody losses at Lloyds, they could hardly have come at a worse time. No one had ever told him how exposed he really was when he committed such a sizeable amount of the family's reserves to what he had expected to be a reliable and steady source of income. It had cleaned out most of their remaining savings, something he still hadn't fully admitted to Susan and his mother. His stomach turned at the prospect of having to tell them the whole truth.

"Well?" growled Dykeman, his patience already wafer thin.

"You seem to have some well-informed sources, Inspector." Glass struggled to keep his voice calm and balanced.

"Fancy that, us, a couple of policemen, having well-informed sources." He laid the sarcasm on thickly, pressing his advantage at every opportunity. He could smell blood.

"It's true, I lost a lot of money at Lloyds last year. Some unusually bad storms in the United States. It was quite a shock, as it happens. No one informed me the losses could be so heavy."

"And your firm? Up the proverbial creek without a paddle, is it?"

Shapes smiled to himself, delighted to see the old Dykeman back in the room, swooping in for the kill. Relentless, he was, when he knew he was on to something, and the less cooperative the suspect was, the harder he went at them. It was working already with James. The poor sod looked like he might fall in a heap any second. No point in him trying to fob them off with a load of old flannel; he might as well come clean and be done with it. Shapes's pencil flicked over his notepad in keen anticipation of the next response from Glass.

"I wouldn't go that far, no. We're having a hard time of it, that much I'll admit, but we've still got our heads above water and enough money coming in to pay the bills. One or two sizeable new customers will make a considerable difference, I'm sure." He coughed into the back of his hand and finally gave up on the attempt to maintain eye contact with the fearsome policeman standing in front of him.

"You don't sound too convinced about that. But never mind, the fact is you and the other partners didn't get a big fat bonus this year, did you?"

James shook his head, looking over Dykeman's shoulder at the door, wondering now how much longer he could keep all this from his wife. "No, there was no bonus."

"So, I'm right in saying you're hard up, struggling to keep your head above water?"

James seemed to deflate, his body sagging. "I suppose so."

Excellent, thought Dykeman, not that there was really ever any real chance of James convincing him otherwise, unless he had a habit of keeping a suitcase stuffed full of cash hidden in the cellar. Now, the trickier part of the operation.

"In fact," he went on, puffing himself up so as to further intimidate James, "you are so hard up I'd say there's every chance you could lose the family home and that wouldn't go down too well, would it now? Especially not with your mother, I'd hazard a guess."

James shook his head and his hands dropped down by his sides, a change in demeanour not lost on Shapes, who felt a swell of pride at his boss's impressive performance. It was just like the old days; the ones before Sheila Delph had cleared off overseas with some wally in a flash suit. He scribbled happily on his notepad as Dykeman continued his interrogation.

"The thing is, if I was to cast around for some idea as to how you might drag yourself up out of the bloody big hole you've dug yourself into," Dykeman paused briefly, keen to let the reference to a hole in the ground register with Glass. "I'd say the most likely course of action would have been for you to ask your brother for a loan, maybe even a straightforward handout. After all, you seem a tight-knit family, do you Glasses. I imagine that even when he went and died you might have been thinking there would be a silver-lining in the shape of his estate passing to you. So it must have come as a serious shock to find he'd gone and left a note saying that Emma was his daughter and she would be getting all his money." There was a flicker in James's eyes, noticed Dykeman, but he remained silent, seemingly aware the Inspector hadn't finished his piece. "What were you to do? Who else could you turn to? And, no doubt, every passing day just made things that little bit worse. Another bill here, more things to buy there. Always money going out and not enough coming in. You must have started to get desperate, especially when your mother and your wife began berating you for not being able to find a bunch of solicitors who reckoned they could successfully challenge that will. Must have become intolerable somewhere along the way. What was it that finally pushed you over the edge? Another accusation that you weren't up to the job of being head of the family? One bill too many? Is that why you stabbed your niece?"

James brought his eyes to bear on Dykeman. A silence fell over the room as he took a slow, deep breath, before giving his reply in a tone which, though it started out steady and even, had, from the start, a surging undercurrent of great anger.

"You know, Inspector, I can appreciate you have a tricky job to do and I'm extremely keen that you find who it was that murdered Emma, but, in the course of the last few months, I have lost my only brother, seen my niece murdered and now my wife mown down in the street, lucky to come through with just cuts and bruises. All of that after I'd been nearly bankrupted by my Lloyds losses and the lack of partners' profits at our business. Then what happens?" His voice rose in increments and his frame stiffened as he spoke. "You show up at my wife's hospital bed, drag me off to this room and accuse me of murdering my niece and all because you've got no bloody idea who really did it. Well, you either charge me or get out of my way because I'm bloody well going back to my wife."

James's eyes had become little pits of fire, his cheeks flushed with anger and his hands were rolled into fists, all of which Dykeman had taken careful note of. A rather impressive theatrical performance or a genuine display of anger and frustration from an innocent man? One thing was certain, they didn't have enough to make a charge stick. Suspicion alone wouldn't impress even the most sympathetic of judges. Dykeman's face remained impassive, unlike that of James, who seemed on the point of self-combustion. Ah, well, it was a shame, when things had seemed to be moving along very nicely indeed, but there was clearly not going to be any admission of guilt forthcoming here. Still, best to keep him on his toes. Just in case.

"I hope for your sake, Mr Glass, that what you have said is true. We've not done digging into your background yet and right now I have half the station out on that hillside where your house is covering every square inch of ground. When we find the murder weapon we'll soon enough be able to put our finger on the guilty party."

He stepped to one side, so that he was no longer barring James's way to the door. Needing no more encouragement and starring daggers at Dykeman, James walked across the room, yanked the door open, then stormed out into the corridor, slamming the door shut behind him with such violence the glass panels in the window almost shook loose.

"Stroppy git," observed Shapes, tucking his notepad and pencil into his jacket pocket.

"Yes, but is he a stripy guilty git or an innocent one?" asked Dykeman, scratching the back of his head.

"I thought you had him for a moment there, especially when he realised we'd found out what a mess he's in with his money," commented Shapes, as he moved across the room and took a cursory look at the window to make sure the glass panels were not in any danger of actually falling out.

"Thought the same thing myself. Shame." Dykeman looked up at the large clock fixed high up on the wall.

"Do you think he did it?"

"I don't rightly know. I reckon he could have done it, no doubt about that. He certainly had a bloody good motive and plenty of opportunity too. But this business with his wife... you know I don't have much truck with coincidences, but it's odd, I have to admit, that she happens to get hit by a car now of all times." Dykeman rolled his bottom lip over the top one and tapped his fingers against the side of his legs.

"Can't see how anyone benefits from killing Susan Glass," commented Shapes, stifling a yawn.

"I know and that's the problem. It might be a genuine coincidence and that thought's upsetting me." He shook his head. "Sod it. Come on, we might as well get off to Brayfield. See how they're getting on with the search."

Their plans were, however, temporarily interrupted. As soon as Dykeman stepped into the wide, bright corridor he was confronted by the ward sister, standing with her hands on her hips and her face such a picture of disapproval it ran the risk of giving a person nightmares.

"There's a call for you on my phone. It's a Sergeant Blunt. He insists it's urgent." Her voice was so sharp-edged she could have cut stone with it, mused Dykeman, wishing he was a little further back, out of her reach.

"Ah, thank you. I didn't know he had your number."

"He didn't," she grumbled. "The switchboard put him through. You'd think they'd know better. We've enough to be getting on with here without having to chase around after the likes of you. Anyway, what's done is done. You'd better hear what the man has to say, then I can get on with things."

DYKEMAN REPLACED THE receiver with considerably more care than he normally did, scared stiff that to do otherwise would offend the ward sister, who lingered outside the room clearly impatient to regain access.

"Well, that tidies up that loose end," announced Dykeman, with a satisfied air. "The driver of the car that ran down Susan Glass handed herself in at Daventry nick about fifteen minutes ago and they called it straight through. Seems she had no idea who Susan Glass is and wasn't out to bump her off. She simply lost control of her car on the bend where Susan happened to waiting to cross the road."

"Coincidence then," remarked Shapes, barely able to conceal a smile.

"Just this once," replied Dykeman as he gestured to the ward sister to let her know they were finished. "We'll let the Glasses know then head off to Brayfield. Not sure if it makes it any more or less likely James Glass killed Emma Greene," he added, reaching for the door handle. "So, for now at least, we'll put it to the back of our minds and keep our fingers crossed something turns up on that hill."

A LEGACY OF DEATH

"Just so long as it's not another body," said Shapes, as he followed his boss out the door.

Chapter Twenty-Four

THE MOMENT DYKEMAN stepped out of the Ford Anglia, the wind did its best to whip away the hat he'd taken along specially for the occasion. He wasn't often given to wearing one of the things, but the unpredictability of the weather and the likelihood they would be outside for a good part of the day persuaded him it would be a sensible precaution. Now he was wondering how he'd manage to keep the damn thing on his head.

"Winds picked up," observed Shapes, as he set about buttoning up his knee-length woollen coat.

"Very observant of you, Shapes. Now then, who we got on our little search party?" asked Dykeman, as much to himself as to his Sergeant. He looked along the line of uniformed figures walking, heads down, across the field to their left, making their way from the main road towards where he and Shapes stood.

"Bloody Nora," exclaimed Shapes, jabbing a finger in the general direction of the approaching figures. "There's Heffalump. He'll have a heart attack getting this much exercise."

"Can't remember when I last saw him walk more than twenty feet in one go," said Dykeman, taking a second look, just to be sure it really was Inspector Harry Heffalump Houghton stumbling across the stubble-filled field. "He'll be needing a rest in a bit. Hope someone's brought a good supply of tea and plenty of grub."

A pair of seagulls, as far in land as they could get on the island of Britain, arced high overhead, their piercing cries suggesting to Dykeman they too couldn't believe it was really Heffalump they could see below.

The two new arrivals remained by the side of their car as the search party advanced towards them, step by careful step. Occasionally, one of their number would stop, bend down to inspect something lying on the soil, quickly discard whatever it was, then recommence their onward journey. A solid quarter of an hour later, Dykeman, who had been leaning lazily against the side of the Anglia, took half a dozen steps towards Constable Rob Dartington, who, having completed his traverse of the first field, was now gratefully stretching his arms above his head and arching his back in an effort to loosen the many and various muscles that were by then aching uncomfortably.

"No joy, then?" asked Dykeman.

"No, Sir. Just some old nails, bits of glass and a rusty toy car. Lanky's got that," he added, turning his head towards PC George 'Lanky' Bunch, who had almost reached the growing cluster of policemen. "Got that car, Lanky?"

"Bedford van," replied Lanky, holding out a small, battered and heavily rusted toy vehicle. "One for the scrap heap, I'd say."

Dykeman prodded a toe at a clump of stubble. "Which field you plan on doing next?"

"Sarg wants us to move on to the field behind you, then work our way through the rest of 'em as they carry on round the back of Ashview Lodge. Says we'll have a break then, before going over the ground where the body was found and, after that, it'll be the path down to the village and the woodland either side of that."

Sergeant Stanley Blunt had been a policeman all his working life and, as he approached the little group of his colleagues, Dykeman knew the look on his face was one of professional satisfaction and enjoyment of their exertions on the open hillside. It was the sort of down to earth, methodical policing the old man liked.

"Stan," offered Dykeman by way of a welcome. "Enjoying yourself out there?"

"Certainly am, sir. Bit of fresh air and exercise does a fella a power of good. Nothing in this field, sad to say, but if there's something out here we'll find it, there's no doubting that." He looked furtively over his left shoulder at a large, plodding figure still struggling across the uneven ground towards the Ford Anglia. "Poor old Heffalump's done in already," he said, in a low voice. "Reckon he'll need a rest and a cup of tea before he can carry on."

Dykeman laughed. "I bet he will. Probably hasn't had this much exercise in one day since he was at school. Well, we'll leave him to sort himself out while we get on to the next field. Where do you want me and Shapes?"

"If you don't mind joining the end of the line, sir, where Heffalump was, that would be very helpful."

A LEGACY OF DEATH

IT TOOK THE SMALL PARTY of policemen another hour and a half to reach the end of the last field behind the Glass family home. More than once Dykeman had looked up, towards the rear windows, to check whether they were being watched. Though he never managed to spot anyone, he didn't doubt that members of the family would be keeping an eye on them; it was only human, after all, to be curious.

He wondered if Emma's killer was amongst them and, if they were, how they were feeling. Scared witless at the sight of a search party combing the land around their home, when they knew somewhere out there lay the murder weapon? Or perhaps they weren't the least bit concerned because they had disposed of said weapon somewhere else. He tried hard to convince himself it was the former; that gave him added encouragement to carry on with hope in his heart.

Eventually, Blunt called them to a halt and they retired to the cars, where stocks of biscuits and flasks of tea lay in wait, as reward for their labours. In fact, the reward was greater than expected. The Heffalump, who had retired to the safety of his car after spraining an ankle, had driven into the village with one of the constables and bought what appeared to the assembled officers to be every pastry and cake the bakers could possibly have had on the premises. He had laid out this enormous feast on a rug in the open boot of his car and even went so far as to wait for all of the others to help themselves before he tucked in; an occasion so rare and barely believable that it would soon go down in station folklore.

Some twenty minutes later, Blunt had the group back on their feet, fanning out in a loose arc, working their way across the open ground that led up to the cavernous ditch where the body of Emma Greene had been found.

"Going back in, are you, Shapes?" teased Dykeman as the two men looked down into the abyss, at the bottom of which now lay a scattering of tiny puddles.

"Not unless you pay me, sir. And bring a ladder. It was bloody hard work getting out of there," sniffed Shapes, kicking a stone into the void.

"You know, had our murderer chucked a few branches or shovels of dirt over her body, I reckon no one would have seen it, unless they happened to fall in and land on top of it. Makes you wonder why they didn't bother," mused Dykeman.

Shapes looked into the ditch again. "That's a good point, is that. Must have been in a hurry, I suppose."

"Possible. But why? What would make them think they didn't have the time to grab a few broken branches from the edge of the woods there? Wouldn't take more than a few minutes to do that."

"Maybe they saw someone coming. You've got the path up from the village, plus the one here that runs from the main road off towards Little Ashford. And then there's the chance of someone driving up the track from the road."

"Mm. But wouldn't you think about coming back later and covering the body? Or am I over-doing things and thinking too logically?"

"No, I reckon you're right, sir, it would be the sensible thing to do, but we know people don't always think straight when they've just committed a murder. Tend to go a bit funny in the head, they do. Bet they thought about it after the body was found, though."

"We didn't find any blood anywhere else, away from this ditch, did we?"

"Nope. But that don't mean she wasn't stabbed somewhere else. They could have wrapped her up in a blanket and tipped her in here later."

"But why here, when, like you say, there was always a chance they could get interrupted? Why not dump the body in the middle of some out-of-the-way wood or an old quarry? Seems like an odd thing to do, bringing the body here. No, I reckon Emma was killed here, almost certainly close to this ditch."

Shapes had been going to suggest the killer might have driven a vehicle up to the edge of the ditch, so as to dump the body with the minimum of fuss, when a shout went up from the middle of the search cordon, which had reached the edge of the nearby woodland. It was an area of land where clumps of coarse grass grew amongst a scattering of scrawny elder and thorn trees on ground that was pock-marked with rabbit holes in various stages of completion.

"Who was that?" asked Dykeman, looking up.

"Johnston," replied Shapes, spotting the waving arms of the hatless constable. "Looks like he's found something."

DYKEMAN AND SHAPES stood side by side in silence next to their car, waiting for the rest of their party to spruce themselves up and tidy away the remains of the food and drink they had left on car seats and in footwells in anticipation of returning to consume it later. That now seemed an unlikely occurrence.

Standing on top of a small hillock a short distance from the others, Stanley Blunt cast a thoughtful eye over the land they had spent so many hours picking over with such care. He felt a warm, professional pleasure at the way he'd managed the whole affair. Opportunities of this sort were few and far between and he was glad it had not turned out to be one of his days off.

"Stan," called Dykeman, putting an end to Blunt's happy contemplation. "Over here please." He looked across his shoulder at Shapes as Sergeant Blunt stepped off the hillock. "Seeing how we've got this lot here we might as well make the most of them. Should help us avoid any mishaps."

"Sir," said Blunt, as he came to a halt in front of the senior officer.

"I can't imagine anyone in Ashview Lodge is going to try legging it across the fields when we going knocking on the door, but if they do I'd rather it was the likes of Bunch and Johnston chasing after them than me and Shapes. Poor old Shapes ain't the man he used to be."

Blunt grinned. Shapes mumbled.

"If you take one constable, Blunt, and loiter outside the front of the house," went on Dykeman. "Then the others can spread themselves out along the length of the back garden, discreetly, if you don't mind. And don't forget to have someone stationed by the stables. That's where they keep their motors."

"Will do, sir. Don't you worry, if anyone tries to make a run for it, they won't get far."

"They'd best not, Stan. We'd never hear the last of it if they got away when half the station's here. Right then, me and Shapes will drive on up. That way we should have everyone's attention while the rest of you get into position. I don't want to go drawing attention to what we're up to."

"Do you think we should ask Heffalump to take a car down to the main road, so he can block off the entrance to this place, just in case?" asked Shapes, looking over Dykeman's shoulder at said Inspector, who was sitting in the driver's seat of his car and looking as though he'd just completed a week-long trek across the Gobi Desert. "I don't think he'll be much use chasing after villains on foot."

"Good idea, Shapes. Should help the old sod feel like he's doing something useful. See to it, will you, Blunt."

"Sir."

"Right, then. Let's get cracking. We've got a killer to apprehend."

"INSPECTOR. I WOULD say it's a surprise to see you, but I imagine you would quite correctly doubt my sincerity. Are you coming in?"

"Thank you, Mrs Glass, we are."

Margaret Glass stepped aside to allow the two policemen to enter the hallway. She had been watching them, on and off, from first one then another of the bedrooms, right from the moment they had arrived in their little convoy of unattractive police cars. Police officers weren't at all the same sort of men they had been before the last war, when you could rely on their possessing at least moderately good manners and showing some sort of respect to the public, on whose behalf they worked. Now they seemed to make a special effort to be brusque, even rude, as if they were under the mistaken belief that such behaviour helped to extract information from suspects and witnesses. No one liked to be treated in such a way, so why should anyone help as well as they might? The world had changed in so many ways and not all of them were for the better.

"Are all the family members here, in the house, Mrs Glass?" asked Dykeman, glancing towards the lounge.

"They are. We had been expecting you would call by, so decided to gather in the lounge." She gestured towards the room in the manner a school teacher does when she wants her class to move on.

"Very considerate of you all." Dykeman gave Shapes a look that made it clear he didn't think anything of the sort.

The two policemen walked into a room heavy with the sound of silence. As Margaret made her way to an armchair on the other side of the room, Dykeman paused, taking in the scene, almost at once feeling a tingle of excitement run up his spine. Ah, here he was, walking on to the set of a major production from stage left, the smell of sweaty bodies in the air, drifting in from the expectant audience, lost in the glare of the spotlights. He was the leading man, arriving with perfect timing to deliver his big scene, filled, with powerful, moving dialogue, exuberant gestures of hand and face, and the subtle, tension-building use of faultlessly deployed moments of silence. Bloody hell, he hadn't felt such exhilaration since... he couldn't think when. Indeed, he had to take a moment to remind himself why he was, in fact, there; a young woman had been brutally killed, just as she was about to enter the central part of her life, equipped with enough money to ensure she had every opportunity to make it a very enjoyable time.

The faces looking back at him wore an odd mixture of expressions. This was, in his experience, a common occurrence in these situations, but he still found it odd and a little unsettling. You would have thought every face in the room would be filled with an expectant desire to learn that he had identified the killer and was there to let them all know they could now sleep safely in their beds. But the assembled family members each looked to have their own concerns and expectations.

Philippa Glass, was who wearing a long, shimmering red dress that he thought more appropriate to a cocktail party, was sitting nearest to him, at one end of a settee. She looked to be on the verge of tears which surprised him, since she had seemed a pretty level-headed young woman.

Next to her sat Michael Glass, whose tight little face and restless, shifting body suggested he would rather be anywhere else than where he was now. Dykeman suspected that if he told the boy he was free to go, he'd leg it out of the room faster than Shapes moving to nab the last offerings from a plate of biscuits, and that was going some.

Squeezed on to the far end of the same settee was Stephen Glass. He too looked restless, his eyes shifting constantly from one thing to another, seemingly doing his best to avoid making eye contact with anyone else in the room, including the Inspector, himself. Dykeman suspected that, of all the people in the room, Stephen felt he had most to lose should his motive be brought out into the open.

Margaret sat alone and aloof, her back so straight it wouldn't have surprised Dykeman in the least if she'd managed to stick a broom handle up the back of her dress while he was looking elsewhere. How the hell anyone was ever comfortable sitting like that he didn't know. Her gaze was focused on him and it was piercing, to put it mildly. He began to instinctively shrink away from her. It was an unsettling experience and took some of the shine off his sense of being the centre of attention and the one in control. Quite how she was going to respond when he instructed Shapes to make an arrest was something worth waiting to see. Shapes might not survive the experience.

Finally, his eyes found James and Susan Glass sitting together on another settee, the husband's eyes still lit with the fires of frustration and anger. A thin shimmer of sweat lined his forehead and his hair was not as neat and tidy as on previous occasions.

As for Susan, it was hard to know how she was feeling. What with the swollen eye and recent near-death experience, he wondered if she even had it about her to realise what was going on. He didn't doubt that, had she been her normal self, Susan would have been steadying herself for a full-frontal assault on him and Shapes if he should so much as hint that one of her family had done some wrong, let alone committed murder. But she'd had all the stuffing almost literally knocked out of her and she sat there quietly, her eyes dull and barely focused, holding her husband's hand.

The gathering might, in fact, have been larger, had Shapes got his way. Following the discovery on the hillside of what he felt sure was the implement used to murder Emma, Dykeman had set out his plan to entice the killer into an admission of guilt. It had come as no surprise when Shapes had tried to insist they sweep up John Perch and have him join them at the house. For some reason the Inspector found impossible to fathom, Shapes was persisting in his belief that the garage mechanic was the man who had done the horrible deed. But Dykeman had no time for such mucking about; he was sure he knew where to find their killer and it didn't need Perch to be present for that to happen, so he told his Sergeant to forget about it.

Yes, everyone he wanted there was present and correct and one of them, he was certain, would be feeling very nervous indeed. It was time for his performance to begin and he needed to make sure it was a good one if his plan was to succeed.. He slipped his hands into his trouser pockets and strolled towards the centre of the room. If a tad nervous, he was, he realised, really rather looking forward to it.

"Well, then, here we all are." He paused, momentarily. "Though, of course, we're not all here, are we? There's one person missing. Emma Greene." He walked on a little further, until he was able to turn and look back at all the members of the Glass family. "Terrible, it was, looking down on her in that ditch. A pretty young woman, with the bulk of her life ahead of her, attacked and killed in cold blood, then dumped in a deep, damp ditch." He let his gaze glide past the family members and on to the lone figure of his Sergeant. "Poor old Shapes there, it was, who had to get down into that ditch so he could take a look at the body. See if there were any clues that might help us out. Not a pleasant job, was it, Shapes?"

"No, Sir. Not pleasant at all. Made me wonder if Emma was still alive when she was dumped there. Would have been bloody terrible if she was, left there all alone, her life blood seeping out of her."

Impressive, thought Dykeman, surprised at his Sergeant's creativity.

"Of course, when we started looking for suspects it seemed natural to think it could have been a spur-of-the-moment thing. After all, these things do happen, more's the pity. Perhaps it was someone she knew well, but it could just as easily have been someone she'd never met before. Either way, it was possible to imagine some minor disagreement getting out of hand and, well, we know what happened in the end."

Michael had stopped fidgeting, noticed Dykeman, and now had all his attention fixed on the senior policeman. Stephen, on the other hand, seemed to find his brown brogues, or perhaps it was the floral patterned carpet, of more interest. A genuine lack of interest or maybe a conscious attempt at pretending disinterest when, in reality, he was worried sick?

"But our view of things soon began to change," continued Dykeman, with a mild up-tick in the strength and depth of his voice. "You see, it became clear that Emma wasn't the well-behaved, innocent little thing that some people, your local vicar included, took her to be. In fact, she was far from being anything of the sort."

His hands were out of his pockets now, his fingers playing on the sides of his legs as he built momentum, working steadily towards his planned reveal. But not too fast, he told himself. Let the guilty party stew a bit. Who knows, they might even own up before he got as far as unmasking them; they might find the tension more than they could bear. That would certainly save some time and make things easier for the judge and jury.

"It began to seem like every time we interviewed someone new we unearthed another person who had good reason to hate the mere sight of Miss Greene. In fact, it got to a point where we realised we needed to shift the focus of our investigations. It became clear we ought to be looking a lot closer to home."

That last sentence was an important one; deliberately aimed at ratcheting up the tension. He hoped it left the guilty party in doubt where he expected to find the killer. It had an instant impact on Philippa, whose eyes widen and her thin lips parted.

"I know some of you thought the young garage mechanic, John Perch, ought to be our prime suspect and it's true, he does have a reputation for having a nasty temper and occasionally turning to violence. It wouldn't be the first time a lover spurned had decided if it wasn't to be them that got the prize then no one would." He cast another glance in the direction of his Sergeant, busy scribbling away in his notepad. "Shapes is something of a ladies man and, for a while there, his instinct was to think Perch was the most likely suspect we had. After all, he had motive, of a sorts, and opportunity. But it never did fit right with me. Suppose it's that instinct you build up over so many years in this job. No, Perch was upset at being dumped. Had his pride knocked about a bit. But he's too sure of himself to feel the need to resort to murder. He knows he'll find someone else soon enough."

There was a movement to his left and he waited as James climbed to his feet and puffed himself up before throwing in his two pennies worth, in a voice bristling with frustration. "Inspector, I appreciate the trouble you are taking to explain the course of your enquiries to us, but, really, can't we just cut straight to the point. Susan needs to rest, not be kept here half the day listening to every little detail of your investigation."

Whilst Dykeman's face remained impassive, inside he was rather pleased to have triggered such a show of emotion. There was sure to be more of the same before they were done.

"I won't be much longer, Mr Glass. Please sit back down."

James hesitated, his whole body beginning to surge with an explosive cocktail of anxiety and anger. It took a considerable effort to bottle it up and sit back down, which he did with a clear display of annoyance. His wife took his hand and squeezed it gently.

"I'll be honest with you, we even considered the possibility Emma's mother might have killed her in the mistaken hope she would then get her hands on the estate left by Mr Robert Glass. But that one was pretty quickly crossed off the list." Not entirely true, he admitted to himself, but it would do for now. "And that left us with one other possibility, one that soon began to look more and more promising. Could it have been a member of this family who murdered Emma?"

It took a moment for the words to fully sink in, but when they did there was a flurry of movement and an exchange of disbelieving looks and barely audible comments, all of which Shapes found mildly amusing. Things were going just as expected. It was as if he and Dykeman had scripted the whole thing. Now then, which one of them was going to kick off?

James scrambled to get back on his feet, spluttering with indignation, his face turning an unpleasant beetroot red. But before he managed to get very far, he was intercepted by an outstretched hand which, weak though it was, had the intended impact. As he looked to his right, his wife shook her head ever so gently and whispered for him to stay where he was. He looked back at Dykeman with rage in his belly then, reluctantly, slumped back on to the settee.

It was, in the end, Philippa who spoke next, her voice surprisingly calm thought Dykeman as he swivelled his head in her direction.

"You can't really mean that, Inspector. Why would one of us want to kill Emma? She was our own flesh and blood." Her brow was a little furrowed and the lines deepened as she spoke.

"I'm afraid I do indeed believe that someone in this room murdered your cousin, Miss Glass, and it would hardly be the first time something of the sort has happened."

He looked from face to face as he spoke, searching for a tell-tale sign of discomfort or, perhaps, outright panic. When none was forthcoming he considered it a blessing of sorts, since it meant he could carry on with his performance, which he was very much enjoying. In any case, he was absolutely confident they wouldn't be leaving the place without someone wearing Shapes's handcuffs.

He was about to speak again when he found himself interrupted by an odd thought, not at all sure why it had popped into his head. They didn't have a dog, did the Glass clan. Didn't every family living in a big country house have at least one dog? He'd thought they always came with such a house; bit like the doors and windows. Perhaps he should have seen that as a suspicious sign when they'd first rolled up. Unclear where that thought had come from, Dykeman pushed it aside and got back to the business at hand.

"You see, the thing is, we've discovered that most of you in this room," his right hand carved an arc through the air in front of him, "had a damn good reason to wish ill of Miss Greene. I would even go so far as to say that more than one of you has benefited considerably from her death."

"Now you've gone too bloody far..." James roared with indignation as he pulled himself forward to the edge of the settee, an accusing finger thrust in Dykeman's direction.

"Darling, please, no..." Susan placed a hand on her husband's arm and for a moment he was torn between continuing his tirade and obeying his wife's wishes. The hesitation provided enough of a gap for Margaret to seize her opportunity.

"I don't imagine any of our secrets are entirely unknown to the other members of the family, Inspector," she began, her stare pinning Dykeman to the spot. "Such things rarely are. What might seem to you a terrible and embarrassing secret is, in fact, of no real consequence to this household. I suppose you've discovered that Michael, the poor boy, had a terrible crush on the horrible girl and that she strung him along for all it was worth? And that Susan had fallen into the habit of paying her to leave him alone, in the mistaken belief it would bring an end to her selfish behaviour?"

Well, well, it seemed there wasn't a thing the old bird missed, thought Shapes as he looked on, glad it was his boss on the receiving end of what sounded very much like a ticking off. Perhaps she'd grab hold of him by the ear next and take him into the hallway to give him a sound spanking. That would be a sight to behold.

"We are, indeed, aware of both those things, Mrs Glass. Not exactly commendable behaviour from Miss Greene..."

"And far from being the right way to deal with it," snapped Margaret, her gaze briefly flitting across the room to Susan or, thought Dykeman, perhaps it was her son. He couldn't be entirely sure.

"Perhaps not," continued Dykeman, before licking his drying lips. "From what we've been told, Emma thought it was a bottomless well she could come back to as often as she liked and, by all accounts, her demands grew over time. Wasn't that so, Mrs Glass?" he looked directly at Susan.

At first, the younger Mrs Glass did nothing more than look down at her lap, apparently embarrassed at what had happened. The room waited in silence. When she did speak, all she said, in the same quiet voice as before, was, "That's correct."

Looking then to his right, Dykeman found the two youngest members of the family open-mouthed at the news. Apparently, he mused, whilst secrets might not remain hidden from all the family members, some hadn't been party to this particular one.

"And then there was you, Mr Glass." Dykeman cleared his throat, allowing a little time for the rest of the family to shift their attention to James. "Seems you've had a run of bad luck this last year or so when it comes to money, wouldn't you say?"

James glared at Dykeman, but managed to keep his response brief, if rather barbed. "We've already spoken about that."

"Indeed we have. But I'm not so sure, despite what your mother says, that the rest of the family are aware just how hard up you really are." He cast a glance at Susan, but it seemed to him she likely knew the truth for there wasn't so much as a flicker of interest on her face. "Substantial losses at Lloyds of London and now there's to be no payout for the partners at your firm. Not much land left to sell off here and I've not noticed any Picassos hanging on the walls. Your brother's death would have been a shock, I'm sure, but I bet, once you'd had time to grieve, you saw a silver lining in that particular dark cloud, in the form of his pretty impressive estate."

"Please get to the point, Inspector," demanded Margaret, resting her hands on the arms of the chair. "This is taking an eternity."

Dykeman glanced at her but chose to ignore the interruption. The old dear could wait; he was pleased with the way things were going and keen to maintain the momentum.

"The prospect of all that money from your brother's estate must have seemed like manna from Heaven after such a prolonged period of stress. Any debts paid off, then plenty of money left in the bank to tide you over until things picked up elsewhere." He pushed himself up on to his toes, then eased himself back down. "And then what happens, it turns out Emma is Robert's daughter and it's her that's going to get all the money. It must have been one almighty shock, must that. Just when you thought your luck had turned, fate steps in and slaps you round the chops. As far as we can make out, you had nowhere else to go for help, least ways not without leaving yourself up to the neck in debt, you might never be able to pay off."

James's face twitched, noticed Shapes, as he grabbed a look in between scribbling notes. Just a little bit more and the man was going to explode. But would that include an admission of guilt? It was hard to say.

"I can imagine the sleepless nights," continued Dykeman, now rocking gently on his heels. "Wondering what the hell was going to become of this place. A pretty heavy responsibility. And desperate times can often call for desperate measures, as Shapes and I have seen many a time, eh, Shapes?"

"Certainly have, sir. Some very desperate measures, at that."

"I imagine you'll be expecting your brother's estate to come to you now, won't you?" Dykeman asked the simmering James, trying to weigh up just how much harder he needed to push. The answer appeared to be, not very.

But James didn't get chance to answer, at least not before his wife spoke, her voice a tad more solid than before. "My husband didn't murder Emma, Inspector, and yes, of course, Robert's money will go to him now. Those are the terms in the will."

The interruption appeared to take the edge off James's growing frustration and anger. Dykeman noticed, with a good deal of disappointment, that some of the fire went out of his eyes and his shoulders softened. Damn the woman, she may be in a bit of a state but she'd just done a fine job of undermining his skilful effort at winding her husband up to the point of exploding. Could he now salvage something from the wreckage?

"Is that true, Mr Glass? You really didn't murder your niece?"

Susan promptly stepped in again, "Don't let him get to you, darling. Just tell him the truth." She brushed the back of a hand softly against her husband's cheek.

He took a deep breath before answering in a controlled, if cold, voice, "I did not murder my niece, no, and I would do no such thing, no matter how bad things got with our finances."

Sod it, the woman had completely pulled the rug from under him, groaned Dykeman inwardly, taking care not to let his disenchantment show. Still, his performance wasn't done yet. There was one more scene to be played out before they reached the end. He looked down at his shoes, taking no particular interest in them, just allowing himself a moment before launching into this final scene.

He looked up at James. "In that case, we'll need to move on to the one remaining suspect. The one person left here who might have felt they had a good reason, a need even, to end the life of Emma." His eyes moved on from James to his wife, resting briefly on her thin, pale lips, before shifting a second time, on to Stephen. "And that would be you, Mr Glass."

Dykeman looked on, waiting for a reaction, though uncertain what that might turn out to be. In the event, Stephen seemed to freeze, his eyes no longer blinking and his breathing, apparently, temporarily stopped. As he waited, Dykeman became aware of a murmured remark from Philippa but he didn't properly pick it up, since his concentration was fully on the eldest son. Stephen seemed to make an effort at moving his lips, but it was as if they had been glued together and almost at once he gave up on the effort. Ah well, decided the Inspector, he'd have to chivvy things along himself.

"You see, Stephen has a secret. Not one he would want to have bandied around the place. And with good reason. The trouble was, that pesky, nosy, nasty little cousin of his found out, didn't she, Stephen? She caught you and your boyfriend in the act?"

This time Dykeman could hardly fail to hear the gasps of astonishment. Interestingly, they didn't come from any of the women in the room, only the father and younger son. The women, perhaps, had worked things out for themselves before. Well, that wasn't entirely a surprise; in Dykeman's experience, women usually had a better sense for this sort of thing than men.

Stephen let out an involuntary gasp as his lungs finally insisted on a fresh intake of oxygen. As he closed his eyes, his head slumped forward, his face coming to rest in the palms of his hands, his elbows pressed into the arms of the chair.

"It turns out, Mrs Glass, you weren't the only one handing out cash to Emma. Stephen was being taken to the proverbial cleaners and, by all accounts, she was still threatening to tell the world what she knew. It seems it wouldn't be going too far to say that she was rather enjoying herself. Not a pleasant thing to do, I'm sure we'd all agree, would we not?"

No one answered, which was the response Dykeman had been expecting. All the same, he could feel their eyes on him, waiting, wondering.

"This isn't a world that looks kindly on your sort, is it, Mr Glass? I can imagine that would be the end for you; round here, at least. You'd have to move away, start all over again, but always knowing Emma could show up any time and start her little game all over again."

Stephen, his eyes still closed, lifted his face just far enough away from his hands to be able to shake his head slowly.

"The problem for us had not been identifying a lack of motive and even opportunity," continued Dykeman. "It was both a decent witness and the murder weapon we lacked. Or, at least we did, until this morning, when we found these, a short distance from where Emma's body had been dumped."

He pulled a small, clear plastic bag out of his pocket, unfolded it with exaggerated care, then held it up in front of him, so everyone in the room could see what was inside: a pair of sharp-nosed, blood-stained steel scissors.

"Good God," exclaimed James, staring wide-eyed at the little plastic bag. "You mean, those were used to murder Emma?"

"They were indeed. Probably about as good a set of scissors as you could hope to have to hand for a job like that, what with them being so sharp-nosed. I doubt it took a great deal of effort to stab through clothes and flesh."

Dykeman moved the bag in a slow arc so as to make sure everyone got a clear view of the contents. In truth, he couldn't be sure they were the murder weapon, since they hadn't yet been passed on to forensics for them to check for a blood match. He was, all the same, as confident as he could be they had found the murder weapon. He also had high hopes there would be fingerprints to be found on the scissors. But none of that mattered right now, because he was just as certain he knew who the killer was and having the murder weapon to hand was a key part of his plan to unmask them.

Happy that everyone present had been given a clear opportunity to see the contents of the plastic bag, Dykeman folded it in half then slipped it into a jacket pocket before turning his attention to the stunned figure of Stephen Glass. The young man, it appeared to the Inspector, still either had nothing to say or else found himself unable to put his thoughts into words. Dykeman had no such trouble.

"But happy find though this is," he went on, patting the pocket which now contained the scissors, "it's not the only bit of good fortune we had this morning. You see, we met a chap out walking his dog. Not a local man, mind. He drives over here from Bowlington once or twice a week with his dog, a spaniel, which he walks from the village to Little Ashford and back, before having his lunch at the Red Lion. One of his favourite walks, he told us. And you can probably imagine how surprised he was to find us lot out scouring the land on his way back today. What was his name, Shapes, I forget?"

"Spencer, sir. Reginald Spencer."

"Ah, that was it. Pleasant man. Retired now, but healthy looking. Probably all that walking he does. Anyway, it turns out he was here walking his dog the day Emma was murdered and, what's more, he remembers seeing someone using the track near that deep ditch around the time we believe Emma was killed." He paused and licked his lips, eking out this part of his performance for maximum effect in the hope the added tension would help tip the killer over the edge. "It was quite a decent description he gave us. Wouldn't you agree, Shapes?"

Shapes rubbed the top end of his pencil against the side of his face, making out he had an itch that needed scratching. Well, if his boss could do a bit of play-acting then so could he. "Not sure we could have hoped for a better one, sir. Very helpful, he was."

The tension in the room was palpable, not a word of interruption from any of the family members, all of whom sat entranced, hanging on Dykeman's every word, which was precisely where he wanted them. And now it was time to bring his theatrical performance to a swift and, he hoped, successful end. He just hoped he'd done as good a job as he believed he had, because he had no alternative plan to fall back on.

"In fact, it sounded remarkably like someone in this room," he continued, his voice hardening as he spoke. "Someone we had seen holding just such a pair of scissors in this very house. Someone who sounded just like you, Mr Glass." He delivered the sentence with some force and it was a clear accusation that he aimed squarely at Stephen Glass.

Almost at once there were raised voices trying to drown him out, a plethora of objections as to why it could not possibly be the eldest of the two Glass boys who had murdered Emma. But Dykeman remained deaf to them all, simply allowing a wash of mingled, indeterminate sounds to sweep over him as he maintained his focus solely on the young man sitting a short distance away.

Stephen remained silent, his head tilted forward a little, his whole body slumped, looking as if it might even have started to sink into the settee. His gaze was lost somewhere in the space between himself and the carpeted floor. It seemed to Dykeman as if Glass felt relieved, a huge burden that had been slowly but surely crushing the life out of him now lifted. He waited, wondering if a confession was going to be forthcoming, but it was hard to read Glass's face; he looked a little sad, perhaps, as well as relieved, but if there was anything else there, Dykeman couldn't yet see it. Perhaps he needed a little nudge; something by way of encouragement.

But at the very moment Dykeman thought to open his mouth, he was cut off at the pass by a strong, clear voice that emanated from the other end of the room. He turned towards the voice, and was, in truth, a little surprised at what he heard.

"You do disappoint me, Inspector. Are you really such a fool as to think Stephen murdered Emma?" Margaret was on her feet, resting one hand on the arm of the chair she had vacated and the stony look on her face was that of a matriarch out to protect her own at any cost. Old she might be, thought Dykeman, but she still had a ferocity he could easily imagine her having in her younger days and the commanding tone in her voice would have done any school teacher or hospital matron proud. Shapes took half a step away from her in response.

"You think otherwise, do you, Mrs Glass?"

"I don't think otherwise, I know," she snapped, her hand tightening into a small, bony fist on which the skin was almost translucent. "He couldn't possibly have killed Emma. He doesn't have what it takes to do anything of the sort, even if that little harlot was blackmailing him. In any case, he couldn't have done it because I did."

A brief moment of silence followed, broken by gasps from the two other women. But Dykeman didn't want interruptions. Timing was everything.

"And what makes you think we should believe you, Mrs Glass? After all, you are a rather old and frail woman. You don't look like the kind of person who'd be able to overwhelm a fit, young thing like Emma Greene."

She starred at him, her nose twitching just enough to be noticeable. When she finally decided to reply it was with such certainty and confidence that it left very little room for further challenge. "I believe you found those scissors hidden in a rabbit hole on the edge of Turner's Copse, precisely where I stuffed them before returning to the house. They were unwrapped, sharp end pointing in."

Dykeman was truly taken aback, though he did his best not to let it show. He knew, indeed, that Stephen wasn't their killer, but he had expected his accusation to provoke an intervention not from the eldest Mrs Glass but from Susan. Indeed, were it not for the small matter that Margaret had quite correctly identified where the murder weapon had been found, he would have suspected her of attempting to take the blame in order that her much-loved grandson might escape the noose. He looked towards Shapes, who did nothing more than shrug his shoulders.

"Well," demanded Margaret. "Are you going to arrest me or just stand there for the rest of the afternoon looking bemused and befuddled?"

"Mother, you can't possibly..."

"Be quiet, James. If you had sorted out this ridiculous mess yourself then I wouldn't have needed to act. You've only yourself to blame if I've caused you any embarrassment."

Despite the confession that had been offered, Dykeman found it a little difficult to bring himself to believe the small, elderly woman standing before him like some modern day Boudicea was their killer. Did she really have the strength to do something of the sort? And how had she done it, simply walked up to her victim, whipped out the scissors and stabbed away? He also wanted to know if the attack had been planned or was an opportunistic assault. His head fair rattled with questions.

He adjusted his tie, then fiddled with a cuff before going in search of answers. "Why would you have murdered Emma, Mrs Glass? As far as we are aware, you are one member of this family she hadn't abused or blackmailed."

"Well, let's get one thing clear before we go any further," started Margaret, addressing the whole room, not just Dykeman. "That awful individual was no daughter of Robert's. I've no doubt whatsoever that her mother set out from the beginning to trick Robert into believing Emma was his. I imagine she was, in fact, the result of some dreadful..." she struggled for a moment to come up with the right word, "liaison with a man her mother barely knew. It was unfortunate for Robert that he happened to come along at a convenient time for Emma's mother. Of course, once she had seduced Robert into a misguided affair, it was a simple matter of pretending he had brought about a pregnancy and, as he always was the sort to accept his responsibilities, he duly did what he felt was the right and proper thing by accepting what he was told and making appropriate arrangements. But have do doubt about it, Emma was not his daughter."

"But..."

"Please don't interrupt, Inspector. Once we were told the contents of Robert's will, I simply couldn't allow things to stand. The effrontery of the woman in accepting the news with barely a murmur of surprise and her insistence that she would not turn down the terms of the will was barely credible. I had no intention of allowing her to enjoy the fruits of her mother's lies and deceit. I had imagined that James would be up to the job of finding a suitable solicitor to overturn the will, but his feeble efforts got us nowhere and time, you will appreciate, was not with us."

Margaret began to cough. It persisted, to her obvious annoyance, and Philippa rose to her feet to fetch her grandmother a glass of water from a jug on the cabinet by the doorway.

"Thank you, dear," responded the matriarch as she handed the partially emptied glass back to her grand-daughter. "Once it became clear James was incapable of dealing with the matter, I knew I would have to take action myself. I can't say that I had murder in mind from the start, because I did not. I rather hoped the obnoxious girl and her squalid mother would accept a generous payment to settle the matter, but Emma wouldn't even listen to my offer. Indeed, she was obscenely rude whenever I tried to broach the matter with her. Well, I wasn't going to just sit there and watch our family be ruined as our so-called granddaughter absconded with Robert's wealth and stained our family's reputation forever by insisting on being known as a Glass, so when I bumped into her on the path by Turner's Copse, and I happened to feel the scissors in my coat pocket, I took action. I only stabbed her the three times, in the heart I believe." She paused to take a deep breath, before adding, "The look of shock on her face was quite pleasing, in its own way."

Dykeman was rather shocked by the last sentence. Its cold-hearted, callous nature left him feeling more certain that Margaret did indeed have the strength of character to murder her granddaughter; a realisation that made him shiver.

"No doubt the mother will try to steal Robert's money now, but as the girl didn't legally inherit until she was twenty-one there will be no possibility of a claim being successful, which means the money will stay where it should have done all along, within the real Glass family."

In a move that Dykeman found both unexpected and, in its own way, coldly dismissive, Michael, who had barely twitched a muscle while his grandmother spoke, stood up and, without a word or a final glance in the direction of Margaret, walked directly out of the room. It attracted no comment from the other family members, apart from Margaret herself.

"The poor boy will get over it. I suppose he never knew until now quite how devious and greedy Emma could be."

"Mother," stammered James, leaning forward, his forearms on his thighs. "Robert never had any issue with accepting Emma was his daughter. He admitted to having had an affair with Jane Greene..."

"Oh be quiet, James," she retorted with a look of contempt. "If you'd acted like a man in the first place it wouldn't have been necessary for me to do anything. Perhaps you will learn something from this horrible affair." She turned back to Dykeman. "I really do think it is time you took me away now, Inspector. Handcuffs, I suppose?"

Dykeman hesitated before deciding there was no point in prolonging things. He couldn't come up with any obvious holes in the matriarch's statement. "That won't be necessary,

Mrs Glass. I think Shapes will be able to keep you from absconding without the use of cuffs." He waited for his Sergeant to complete his final few notes before issuing him with instructions. "Take Mrs Glass outside and read her her rights, Shapes. I'll be with you in a moment."

The astonished looks on the faces of the other family members made it plain they were as surprised as Dykeman at Margaret's admission. He was at a loss what to say to them and decided to keep things brief and practical. He turned towards James.

"You'll be needing to make arrangements for a solicitor, Mr Glass. Perhaps Rich and Cueillettes can help you. We'll take your mother back to the station, where she'll be formally charged and due process kicked off."

James nodded, before asking in a flat voice, "Will my mother hang, Inspector?"

"It's not for me to say, but if a jury finds her guilty, it's hard to see how the judge won't hand down the death sentence, Mr Glass. Murder is murder, however old the guilty party should happen to be."

Chapter Twenty-Five

DYKEMAN DIDN'T VERY often visit Shapes at his home, a small two-up two-down terraced house on the western fringes of Banbury. There rarely seemed to be any reason to do so. Mind you, now that he was standing there in the living room, waiting for Shapes, he did wonder, as he looked around, if that might have something to do with how odd the house appeared. Odd? Was that the right word, he asked himself? It was true to say things were a little messy here and there, and you wouldn't exactly call it homely, but it was far from being a hovel. Then he realised it was the décor that had swayed him into thinking odd was the one word that best summed up the place.

For starters, it seemed like almost everything in the house was brown. Brown carpet. Brown curtains. Stripey wallpaper in various shades of brown. The light shade was brown and the settee and two matching armchairs were very definitely brown; so dark, in fact, they weren't far off black. He knew, as well, that the same colour scheme continued into the kitchen, where the floor tiles, cupboards, table, chairs and worktops were all brown too. And, come to think of it, there was a largely brown runner on the hallway floor.

Mind you, he did have to acknowledge that he hadn't ever actually asked Shapes if he'd inherited all this brown when he moved in. For all he knew, his Sergeant might have simply decided he was happy enough with things as they were or just couldn't be bothered to change anything. How long had he lived in the place? Dykeman wasn't sure, though he knew Shapes had been there since before the two of them started working together. Maybe he could buy Shapes something for the house next Christmas. Something that was any colour other than brown. A new light shade, perhaps, or tablecloth. Then he could make up some excuse to call round and see if it had been installed in place of its predecessor.

Footsteps on the stairs stirred Dykeman from his musing and he lifted the keys for the Ford Anglia out of his pocket, rolling them round the palm of his hand. It was Wednesday, the seventeenth of August, ten in the morning, and they had a funeral to attend. Jane Greene had been granted permission to bury her daughter, something about which she had agitated unrelentingly ever since Margaret had been arrested. In Jane's mind, there had been no justifiable reason to delay proceedings so long and her complaints had been frequent and abusive.

Shapes strolled into the room, whistling both loudly and badly, noted Dykeman.

"What's that you're murdering?"

"Apache."

"Apache?"

"It's the new one from The Shadows," he added, cheerily, slipping his black jacket on. "We off then?"

"We are indeed, but we'll have less of that in the car. I'll have a headache by the time we get there if you carry on."

Shapes was still whistling as he locked the front door behind them.

ONCE UPON A TIME, DYKEMAN had felt nothing but awkward and out of place at such funerals. The police were never really wanted there, not least because it reminded everyone how their nearest and dearest came to be enclosed in a wooden box heading towards a large hole in the ground. And, in his experience, there was hardly ever anything to be gained from his presence. He thought it possible that, should he ever find himself attending a gangland funeral, there might be a chance of spotting and collaring some on-the-run villain, but they weren't the sort of funerals that took place in a relatively quiet little place like Banbury, thank God. However, he knew their presence at this funeral was expected, not least of all by the Chief Inspector, who seemed to think not attending risked giving a gross insult of truly Titanic proportions to the relatives of the deceased.

So, here they were, him and Shapes, standing alone a little way off from the grave and the main gathering of mourners, in the lee of a large oak tree which sheltered them from the already warm rays of the sun, which had risen into a clear blue sky at day break and not been bothered by a single cloud since.

The mourners were few in number, causing Dykeman to wonder if there were plenty of other people, aside from those they knew about, that Emma Greene had upset or offended during the course of her short life. Her best friend, Vicky Hemmings, was there, wearing a calf-length black dress that looked too big for her and a wide-brimmed hat in deep green that was angled too far back on her head. Tears streamed down her make-up streaked face, despite her attempts to mop them up with a large white hanky. Big wet sobs that battled attention alongside the chattering of birds.

"Looks like she's the only friend here," observed Shapes, with just a hint of sadness in his voice.

"It does. I suppose it's a wonder Emma had any at all."

"Poor cow."

Dykeman wasn't sure if Shapes was referring to Emma or Vicky, but he decided there was no need to ask since the comment could be applied to either woman equally well.

Denise Bergen, the clothes shop owner from Evesham, was also there, dressed just as Dykeman would have expected, immaculately, in a knee-length black dress that somehow managed to look both suitably conservative for the occasion and at the same time stylish and modern. How that was possible was beyond Dykeman; the ins and outs of dress design were way out of his sphere of understanding. Her small, round, flat-topped black hat reminded him of the sort of thing Audrey Hepburn would wear and it suited her to a tee. Even the little handbag she clutched in front of her belly with both hands had style. But the thing he noticed most of all were her lips, coated, as they were, in what appeared to be a dark purple shade of lipstick that glistened softly in the sun; appropriate for a funeral it may have been, but it somehow still managed to send a tingle of desire running through his bones.

Jane Greene cut an altogether different figure. As was to be expected, she was clad from top to toe in black, but her hair looked as though a two-year-old had been let loose on it with an assortment of toys and Dykeman suspected her wide-brimmed hat hadn't been pinned in place properly because it looked as though anything stronger than the faintest of breezes would whisk it away. However, all of this was as nothing compared to the look she wore on her face, which was as dark and menacing as a stormy winter's day. He suspected that no one, not even the vicar, would be getting a civil word out of her all day.

It didn't much bother Dykeman if she chose not to speak to him or Shapes. It felt like she'd been doing her level best to avoid having anything to do with them ever since they'd arrested Margaret Glass. Straight after the arrest, Dykeman, feeling as pleased as punch at having brought the killer to book, had considered driving up to Evesham to inform the bereaved mother himself, but, in the end, decided he really ought to remain at Banbury nick while Margaret went through the routine of being charged and giving a formal a statement. Instead, he'd phoned Henry Cranfield, who'd got back to him an hour or so later to inform him that Jane had listened quietly to the news, then, without making any comment, had asked him to leave the house. Probably the relief of all that stress, he'd suggested. Dykeman hadn't seen any reason to disagree with this view.

But when he'd approached Jane, first at the coroner's inquest then when they had arrived for the funeral, she had looked him in the eye, said not a word in return and walked away. It left him with the distinct impression she would have preferred it if they'd stayed away from the funeral. He was miffed she hadn't thanked him in some way or other for collaring her daughter's killer, but then he remembered the questions they'd asked her, with the obvious implication they considered her a suspect. Perhaps she had some justification for giving them the cold-shoulder after all.

Standing with Jane at the graveside were a couple the vicar had told him were her cousin and his wife, an ugly woman with a big, round belly, which had elicited a less than generous comment from Shapes when they had first seen her. The cousin had provided an arm for Jane to lean on as they walked the hundred and fifty yards to where a six foot deep hole in the ground awaited her daughter. He wondered if the mother had recognised the irony of her daughter's body having been found in the bottom of another very deep hole.

As the vicar said his final words and sprinkled a handful of soil on the lowered coffin, Vicky Hemmings started sobbing again and then a robin, looking lively and bright-eyed, landed on a branch of the oak tree next to the two policemen, warbled something in a noisy tone that neither man could understand, then was gone in a flash.

"Looks like it's time to leave," said Dykeman. "Come on, let's head back to the car."

"If we're quick we can get away before the others reach the car park," remarked Shapes, sounding hopeful.

AS IT TURNED OUT, SHAPES was the cause of their failure to depart the cemetery before some of the other mourners showed up to do likewise. Distracted, he insisted, by the sight of a heron skimming across the tops of the trees that bordered one side of the cemetery, he'd managed to step off the gravel path and knock over a potted rose that someone had placed at the head of a particularly well-tended grave. Dykeman had insisted he tidy it up before they move on.

As a result, they arrived at the car park at the same time as Denise Bergen. Things could have been worse, thought Dykeman, trying hard not to stare at that damn lipstick.

"Hello, Inspector. Sergeant."

"Mrs Bergen," replied Dykeman.

"Are policemen not allowed at the graveside?" she asked, her flawlessly sculpted eyebrows lifting just a little.

"We're not always welcome, I'm afraid. But the Chief Inspector is a stickler for having an official representative at such funerals. We've all noticed, though, that he always manages to make sure he has something else to do that means he can't make it personally. Funny that, eh?"

"I suppose the relatives aren't particularly keen on being reminded just why it is they are burying their recently departed loved one," she offered.

"I suppose not. Funerals aren't the nicest of places to be, as it is. Who wants Shapes showing up knocking over the flowers and scaring away the children?"

Shapes refused to rise to the bait and remained silent.

"I imagine you got a rather better welcome than the Glass family. I hear they were told to stay well away today," continued Denise.

"Yes, we heard that too. I'd guess most members of the family were happy enough with that, with the exception of the daughter, Philippa. Apparently she and Emma got along well, despite everything."

Denise looked back in the direction of the new grave. "These kind of occasions always remind me of my grandmother's funeral. It was the first time I can remember ever really being aware of the presence of death. I felt sick at the graveside, then cried silently all the way home. Part of growing up, I suppose."

"It was my first pet rabbit that did it for me," chirped Shapes, before his boss could comment. "When it popped its clogs, my dad buried it in the back garden. Gave it a proper little ceremony, he did. Then every time I went out back again, there it was. I stopped going in the back garden for a while. It upset me too much."

Dykeman looked at Shapes, wondering if he'd had that little speech bottled up inside him ever since the rabbit's funeral.

"I didn't know you were so sentimental, Shapes."

"Hard on the outside, soft on the inside, sir."

"If you say so."

"Will the court hearing be in Oxford?" asked Denise.

"It will," replied Dykeman.

"I imagine that will be another horrid experience for Jane. Poor woman."

"Luckily for her, as Margaret has admitted her guilt it means a trial isn't necessary and the hearing shouldn't last more than one session, just so long as she doesn't change her mind between now and then. It will just be up to the judge to decide whether she'll swing for what she's done. I can't see why she wouldn't."

"I have to say, I'm not all that happy with the death penalty, even for those who admit their guilt," observed Denise. "But then again, I suppose I'm not a bereaved relative desperate to obtain justice for my loved one."

"I suppose not," was all Dykeman felt inclined to say by way of a reply.

They said their farewells after that, before heading for their respective cars and escape from the gloom and doom of the cemetery.

"Nice lipstick," observed Shapes, in a casual tone, as he slipped the Anglia into first gear.

"Eh, what?" asked Dykeman, caught totally off guard.

Shapes grinned as he let in the clutch and the car lurched forward.

Dykeman felt the colour rising in his cheeks and tried to mask the fact by pulling his hanky out of a pocket and blowing his nose, loudly.

"I've heard Stephen Glass is clearing off to Essex," said Shapes, still smiling. "Apparently he reckons its best not to hang around these parts, now his secret is out."

Dykeman wrinkled his nose. "Can't say I blame him. Probably head for the Scottish Highlands myself. Get as far away as possible."

They stopped at the exit of the car park and waited for a small lorry to pass before they joined the main road, heading for the police station.

"Thought I might make a bid for Uncle Robert's money myself," commented Shapes, already closing on the back of the slow-moving lorry. "Claim I'm his illegitimate son from some seedy wartime romance with a factory worker in

Coventry, now trying to claim what is my rightful inheritance."

"The sad thing is, Shapes, it wouldn't surprise me if you did do that. I suppose you'd settle for being paid off, so long as they made it worth your while?"

"A nice round hundred would be enough to have me drop my claim. Could use it to spoil Ivy. Take her somewhere foreign. The Channel Islands, maybe."

Dykeman looked sideways at his Sergeant, wondering if he really thought the Channel Islands were somewhere 'foreign'. Shapes probably thought Cardiff was foreign and there wasn't even any sea between Cardiff and Banbury.

"About time you took Ivy out again, isn't it?" prompted Dykeman in an attempt to unsettle his notoriously tight-fisted Sergeant.

"I'm taking her to see a West End show, I'll have you know. Oliver! It's a musical. A new one. All the rage, says Ivy." Shapes sounded chuffed and patted the steering while as he drove along, uncharacteristically slowly, behind the lorry.

"You what?" exclaimed Dykeman, turning his head to face Shapes. "You, going to a musical? You can't be serious."

"What do you mean?" asked Shapes, making out he was deeply offended. "I'm a man of culture, I'll have you know. I've been to see a pantomime. Twice."

"Thirty years ago, or more, I'll bet. And that's nothing like a proper musical. You won't last. You'll either be asleep or in the bar before it's halfway done."

"Ivy promised me a fondle afterwards, if I'm good." Shapes was grinning again, even more than before.

Dykeman flinched at the thought of his dirty-minded Sergeant getting frisky with a woman who looked like she ate a whole box of porridge for breakfast every morning, then had a few slices of toast, just to be sure she made it through to lunchtime. As for what she was capable of doing with a man, he didn't like to think.

"Anyway, won't that cost you an arm and a leg? You'll have to cough up for a hotel and the train fares as well, you know."

"Got me savings. Don't go out much as a rule, so plenty of my pay ends up in the building society."

Dykeman had no response to that. Bloody Nora, who'd have thought that one day Shapes would be taking a woman down to London to see a West End musical? It must be this great new world they were supposed to be entering now they had reached the 1960s.

He sat there in silence for the rest of the short journey to the station, his mind turning to thoughts of his own situation where women were concerned. That dark, purple lipstick of Denise Bergen flitted through his mind again.

It occurred to him that he hadn't thought about Sheila Delph at all for three whole days. Perhaps he was finally coming to terms with the notion that she was gone from his life forever, lost to another man and another land. Sad, yes, but there was no point in brooding on it forever. There were other women out there, after all. He just needed to be patient and keep his eyes and ears open. Time was all that was needed.

Maybe Ivy Davey had a friend in need of some company? There again, perhaps not. That sort of woman might be alright for Shapes, but not for him. He needed someone with a more gentle touch. Someone who'd blend in as much with his life as he was expected to blend in with hers. He suspected Ivy would be making a good many changes to Shapes's life, once she'd got him signed up for good. He chuckled quietly to himself, wondering if Shapes had given any thought at all to the idea that Ivy might be looking for a good deal more than the occasional weekend away. He settled on a bet with himself. Six months, that was how long he'd give it. Six months until Shapes crept meekly into the office one morning and announced awkwardly that he had some news to share.

The End

A LEGACY OF DEATH

The Golf Club Murder

If you've enjoyed reading *A Legacy of Death* then why not take a look at the fifth story in the series *The Golf Club Murder*.
https://benwesterham.com/books/book-details-the-club-of-death/

Free Book

IF YOU ENJOYED MEETING Dykeman and Shapes then why not find out how it all began as they investigate their very first murder case together. Download your free copy of *Murder at Stockton Farm*, sit back, relax and enjoy yourself as bruised egos and repeated misunderstandings ensure that solving the case isn't the only challenge the two policemen will need to overcome before the day is done.

https://benwesterham.com/bookoffer/

A LEGACY OF DEATH

If you enjoyed this book then please consider leaving a review on the site where you bought it.
Many thanks,
Ben Westerham

BEN WESTERHAM

From the David Good private investigator series

From 'Good Investigations'
"Mr Good," she purred like a hungry cat meeting a blind mouse, "and I do hope you will be." She slid beautifully, effortlessly in to the knackered old punter's chair, and I swear the thing wrapped itself lovingly around her sexy, lithe frame. Then she tempted me with those dark bewitching eyes, calling me closer, closer, closer

A LEGACY OF DEATH

From 'Good Girl Gone Bad'

If you ask me, good girls can be the baddest there are, if the fancy takes them. Maybe it's because they save it all up for one big splurge, then go mad bad. I don't know, but what I do know is that anyone who tries telling you some little darling of theirs' wouldn't say boo to a goose is either stupid, misinformed or both. Any goody two shoes type should carry a health warning, 'Danger, Good Girl. May go bad at any moment'.

From the Alexander Templeman espionage series

From 'The House of Spies'

MY FINGERS WERE TINGLING from the force of the blow and my head pounding as my heart beat madly. I was exhilarated. There is no other way to put it, such was my sense of excitement at what I had just done. But there was also an edge of fear now over what I had started and the knowledge that there was no going back, no means of trying to explain away my assault as some sort of unfortunate accident. I was committed to a course of action, with no guarantee of success and no real idea of the consequences of failure, other than they would not be good.

A LEGACY OF DEATH

You can find out more about Ben Westerham here www.[1]benwesterham[2].com[3].

---

1. http://www.benwesterham.com/

2. http://www.benwesterham.com/

3. http://www.benwesterham.com/